POINT BLANK

A MASON SHARPE THRILLER

LOGAN RYLES

INKUBATOR
BOOKS

To Cap Daniels -
For all the guidance, friendship, and inspiration.
I can never thank you enough.

Published by Inkubator Books
www.inkubatorbooks.com

ISBN (eBook): 978-1-83756-006-6
ISBN (Paperback): 978-1-83756-007-3
ISBN (Hardback): 978-1-83756-008-0

1

I drove with the sun at my back, gray clouds covering the eastern sky. Eight or ten hours had passed, and the only sounds to break the silence had been the hum of tires on the road.

My left arm, still sore from the healing gunshot wound to my shoulder, lay in my lap. Each breath stung. After nearly a thousand miles on the open road, my mind filtered out the passing signs and chugging trucks, so that all I saw was the dashed white line guiding me east.

Toward those storm clouds.

I hadn't packed any bags. I hadn't needed any. I just took my keys, my wallet, and the Smith & Wesson .357 magnum lying in the passenger seat next to me.

It rested next to Mia's Bible—clean, and ready.

Loaded with five rounds.

But I only needed one.

2

TEN WEEKS EARLIER

Y ou never forget the day you stare death in the face. I was parked off Camelback Road in the Phoenix Police Department's Mountain View Precinct, chowing down on a cheeseburger while my partner ranted about the Phoenix Suns' inevitable demise in the playoffs. Jacquie was from Arkansas, but she moved to Arizona sometime in middle school, and had been a basketball fan her entire life.

I was born in Phoenix and had learned years ago to spare myself the heartbreak of being a Suns' fan, but I didn't stop Jacquie from ranting. It was how she passed the time.

"Team ain't been straight since Shaq left," Jacquie grumbled. "I say clean house. Gut everything. Fire the coaches, the GM. Fire the water boy. Am I crazy?"

I just grunted and surveyed Camelback, subconsciously praying for something to happen. My meteoric rise from patrolman to homicide detective, compliments of the Sundevil Killer investigation last summer, had been thrilling in the extreme. Until it wasn't. I thought life would be an endless stream of cold bodies and cryptic clues in the homicide division.

Turns out it was a lot of sitting. A lot of cheeseburgers. A lot of listening to Jacquie fuss.

"Hey!" Jacquie snapped her fingers inches in front of my nose. "You awake?"

"What?" I blinked out of my stupor. Jacquie's dark eyes blazed.

"I asked you about the honeymoon."

"What about it?"

"Do you want the time share?"

I scratched my jaw, taking a moment to reset. Then I remembered.

"No. I'm taking her to North Carolina. This little island off the coast...nice spot."

Jacquie grimaced like I had just kicked a puppy. "I've got the deal of a lifetime on a resort in Cancun, and you wanna go to *North Carolina*?"

I waved her off, wadding up my burger wrapper. "It's not like that. Mia grew up vacationing there. It's special to her."

Jacquie still looked incredulous. I rolled my eyes.

"What would you know? You've got the romantic instincts of a tumbleweed."

Jacquie snorted. "If by that you mean I've got the good sense to stay single and let hot guys buy me drinks, you may have a point."

My phone dinged and I grabbed it before Jacquie could pontificate further on the virtues of evergreen adolescence. It was an email from the Professional Standards Bureau, the PPD's internal investigations division.

The subject line read:

Complaint Review—Excessive Force Violation.

I tossed the phone into the console and looked out the window, slurping Coke. Jacquie sat quiet for a moment, then spoke softly.

"PSB?"

"Yeah."

"That thing from last week?"

"Probably."

Again, she was quiet. I knew what was coming and wasn't in the mood for it, but Jacquie was a lot like her beloved Suns —she never adjusted her game plan.

"You gotta ease up, man. The celebrity shine is fading. You can't ride the Sundevil case forever."

"I'm not riding it," I snapped. "I'm doing my job. They say investigate, I investigate."

"Yeah, okay, but in case you hadn't noticed, this ain't Iraq. You aren't a Ranger anymore, roughing up insurgents to find IEDs. This is a civilized city. You can't knock people around."

I didn't answer. Someplace deep inside, I knew she was probably right. I knew hunting killers would be different from hunting terrorists, but I didn't really think it should be. They both took lives. A few bruises on the path to justice seemed a small price to pay.

Jacquie reclined her seat with a long sigh, the prelude to her post-lunch nap. "Just don't worry about it, dude. They'll chew your ass for a while, then put you on some kind of performance improvement plan, and that'll be that. Three weeks from now you'll be sipping margaritas pool side in Cancun."

I turned, an expletive ready to fly. Then I saw her churlish grin, and I flushed a little.

"You're impossible," I muttered.

Jacquie leaned back and, for the first time all day, the cruiser was quiet. I watched cars rushing by along Camelback, and thought about Mia. Thought about the little house on Saint Ellen Island I had rented for the week, and quiet nights by the fireplace. It would be cold in North Carolina in early December. Jacquie was right—Mexico sounded great.

But I knew Mia better than that. Sentimental always won out over fancy. Heartwarming over opulent. She was the second-grade teacher who actually kept the finger paintings her kids drew for her, and would take cheap wine and a Hallmark movie over a four-star dinner any night of the week. A little house with flower beds over a penthouse balcony.

A washed-up Army Ranger on a public service salary over a power-tie businessman.

And that was why I loved her.

I closed my eyes and thought about North Carolina. Thought about sleeping in, and staying up late. Thought about uninterrupted days, just her and me.

It was enough to make me forget the email. I was halfway asleep when the dash-mounted radio screamed to life with a digital alarm loud enough to wake the dead.

"All units in the area of Mountain View Precinct, we are receiving reports of possible active shooter at Harris Morrison Elementary school."

My heart leapt into my throat, and for a split second the world stopped turning. I heard the words, but I didn't really believe them. Passing traffic on Camelback ground to slow motion as the dispatcher barked through the radio.

"Repeat: possible active shooter, Harris Morrison Elementary. Suspect armed with shotgun and or handgun. Multiple shots fired. All units respond code three."

I blinked once, and the fog simply vanished. I shoved the car into drive and hit the emergency light switch before stomping the gas, not even waiting to check for oncoming traffic. A horn blared and tires screamed as my unmarked cruiser pivoted left on Camelback, then roared amid the cars.

Jacquie remained calm, lifting the radio and reporting

that we were three minutes out. She may have taken questions or asked for details. I heard nothing save the thunder of the motor. My heart pounded, and I thought of Harris Morrison—a forty-thousand-square-foot brick building resting amid a blue-collar suburb.

A defenseless elementary school.

Mia's school.

I'd been there only forty-five minutes earlier, swinging in to drop off Mia's lunch and slip into a janitorial closet for an uninterrupted kiss. I could still smell her perfume on my hands and feel her lips against mine, but as I screamed through a turn toward the school, those memories faded, and new images replaced them.

Pictures of bodies lying on the floor, from active shooter training videos used in both the Army and the Phoenix Police Department.

Fields of carnage.

"Sharpe!" Jacquie screamed, breaking through my tunnel vision. "*Stay calm.* We should wait for backup."

The school appeared at the end of the street, the playground surrounded by a chain-link fence and lying empty. The drab brick walls dark with dirt and neglect, Mia's Toyota Corolla parked in a line of cheap cars.

I heard Jacquie's words, but didn't really register them. I was already tearing my seat belt off, reaching for the department-issued Glock 23 holstered on my hip.

And feeling woefully under-armed.

When I was a beat cop I kept a shotgun next to my seat, and an AR-15 in the trunk. But as a homicide detective I was meant to arrive after the shooting ended. They only gave us a compact pistol.

And, like a fool, I had settled for it.

I slammed on the brake and spun to a stop in front of the

main entrance, slinging the door open. Jacquie shouted for me to wait.

"Stay here!" I shouted. "Secure the exit!"

Then I was gone. Rushing across the sidewalk and up to the glass door, shoulders low, pistol held at eye level. My heart thumped, but my breathing was calm. Measured.

Years of combat experience saturated my steps as I slipped through the wall and stepped into a wash of air conditioning and the stench of cheap detergents.

The security guard was dead. So was the receptionist. I recognized the spray-pattern of buckshot across their chests and noted multiple 12-gauge shells scattered across the floor. The shooter had stepped through the blood and left footprints leading down a hallway to the left.

Toward Mia.

I broke into a run, sweeping around each corner and clearing the first classroom.

Third grade. Three students, one teacher. DOA, 9mm casings on the floor.

The horror of the scene hit me like a fist, but I didn't allow myself to register. I moved immediately to the next door and found it locked. Then I heard a scream, and the blast of a shotgun from down the hall.

I skidded around the corner, sliding through bloody footprints.

And my world just stopped.

Mia stood in front of her classroom door, blocking the shooter's path. Both arms spread against the wall, her petite frame standing rigid. Her face blaring fearless defiance at the man in front of her.

He was tall, and skinny. Dressed in all black with a black ski mask and Mossberg Shockwave pointed at her gut. The school's special needs teaching assistant lay on the ground next to him, already dead from the last blast.

I saw it all in a fraction of a second, my finger already dropping to the trigger. Already screaming for the shooter to turn.

I fired, and he fired. Mia's face washed in pain and she slumped forward. My bullet took him in the side of the head and knocked him sideways, dead before he hit the ground.

Then I heard the harsh snap of a 9mm as the second shooter opened fire.

The first bullet took me in the back, near my left shoulder. The second scraped my neck.

I pivoted automatically, spraying bullets toward his position just around the corner. I saw muzzle flash and tasted gunpowder. A third round scraped off my arm, and my pistol locked out over an empty magazine just as the shooter flopped over, his face and chest a mess of forty caliber holes.

I hit the floor in a puddle of blood, the Glock slipping from my fingers. My head smacked the concrete and the ceiling overhead spun. Suddenly, everything felt very quiet. Very still.

I clawed my way onto my stomach, my hands slick with my own blood. I could hear every heartbeat. Feel every breath leaving my body like the last one.

My vision blurred, tunneling to black as blood gushed from my shoulder. I heard voices shouting, and doors slamming.

And I fought toward Mia. The lake of crimson spreading from her body reached my fingers and I slipped, slamming chin-first into the floor.

The world spun again, and a hand closed around my arm. I heard Jacquie shouting—screaming for a medic. Pleading for me to hold on.

But all I saw was Mia's face. Staring vacantly at the wall. Eyes wide. Soul empty.

And then the tunnel closed in, and I saw death.

3

PRESENT DAY

I pulled the Corolla off the highway someplace in Oklahoma to fill the tank. I swiped my credit card and huddled in the chill of a stormy wind. I could smell rain on the air, and the gas station's radio broadcasted warnings of incoming severe weather.

I didn't care.

The fuel nozzle clicked off over a full tank, and I started the car again, returning to the highway. The rhythmic hum of the tires across endless miles of perfectly flat highway had become monotonous now, and I felt my eyelids droop a little. But I didn't pull over. I popped caffeine pills and drained a bottle of water, then locked the cruise and kept driving.

East. Toward North Carolina.

Thirty minutes after leaving the station, my phone rang. It had rung twice since leaving Phoenix, and I had ignored both calls. Checking the screen now, I was unsurprised to see Jacquie calling. She glared at me with a middle finger raised, a beer in one hand.

Her trademark look.

I stared at the screen, blinking hard as sleepiness overtook my worn mind. The phone rang twice more.

Then I rolled down the window and flung it into the passing ditch, enjoying the bite of the wind on my face.

I swept fast-food trash off the passenger seat and wrapped my fingers around the familiar grip of the Smith & Wesson, transferring it to my lap.

I didn't roll up the window.

I just drove.

4

NINE WEEKS EARLIER

The rhythmic beep of a hospital machine was the next sound I heard. Blurry lights and fog greeted my eyes, but I couldn't move.

All I felt was pain. In my back, exploding from my core, and radiating out to my extremities. My arms were numb and a harsh plastic hose was jammed down my throat.

I was conscious of all of it, but didn't really register anything. I just hurt.

And I thought of Mia.

I saw the school in fragmented memories. Like a DVD disc that was scratched and skipped without pattern or reason from one distorted scene to the next. Just momentary flashes of things happening, people screaming.

Guns firing.

Then I faded to black again.

"MASON?"

The voice warbled, as though the speaker were underwater. But I recognized the Arkansas twang, suppressed by years of the speaker trying to pretend she was from anywhere but.

My eyes fluttered, and again I felt pain. But not from my core this time. Now my head split with a dynamite headache. I gasped for breath and noticed the feeding tube was gone, leaving my mouth hollow and dry.

"Mason? Can you hear me?"

I didn't move. A shuffling sound shifted next to the table, and the sharp edge of something plastic touched my tongue.

A straw, I thought. I sucked greedily on the water and again tried to open my eyes. It was so bright in the room it hurt to look at anything, but I managed to keep them open. The water ran dry, and the straw vacated my mouth.

I slouched against the pillow and just lay there. Motionless.

Where am I? What happened?

I screened through my memories, searching for the last thing I could recall. I was driving—I remembered that. Driving quickly. Aggressively, like I used to drive overseas, in an Army Humvee.

Were we chasing somebody?

"Mason?"

I rotated right, just a little. Jacquie's ebony face came into view—blurry, but familiar. Framed by kinky black hair, strain in her eyes.

A wave of relief washed over me, and I felt her hand slide into mine. She squeezed my fingers and spoke a little louder.

"Dear God, Sharpe. Say something."

"What happened?" I rasped.

Jacquie blinked hard, then looked across me toward somebody else in the room I hadn't yet seen. She ducked her head and wiped her eyes with her free hand.

"You don't remember?"

I thought again. Remembered the car...driving fast. Slamming on my brakes. Getting out at...

The school.

I closed my eyes and shook. My throat went dry and my chest felt like somebody had pressed a boot against it—forcing down. Crushing me slowly.

I saw Mia on the floor. The blood on my hands.

It all came rushing back.

"Mason."

The next voice was deeper, and a little gruff. Despite the fog in my brain I recognized the speaker and fought to open my eyes again.

Captain McGrath stood at the foot of my bed, dressed in a black suit with his hands crossed over his belt. His bald head shone beneath the fluorescents, and he just leered there like a buzzard on a power line.

Waiting to swoop down.

"We need to talk about what happened," McGrath said.

Jacquie's voice snapped. "*Good grief*, Captain. He just woke up!"

McGrath held up a hand. "Calm down, Jacquie. I'm on his side."

On my side?

McGrath laid both hands on the foot of my bed and lowered his head.

"Mason...the doctor will talk to you. I just want you to know you're all right. And...you're a hero. Okay?"

He made eye contact and pursed his lips, as though it had pained him to speak the words. I didn't doubt it had. McGrath was the son of a cop. The grandson of a police commissioner. He graduated high school and shipped straight to the police academy.

He was the definition of a career man, and he didn't like

ex-military cops. He thought we were trained in all the wrong ways. Trained to be soldiers, not guardians.

I never understood the difference, but McGrath ruthlessly investigated any complaint leveled against me, no matter how petty or contrived, and he never had my back. Not once.

I said nothing. I just stared as he made a show of nodding a few times, then mumbled some sort of sympathy for my loss, and left the room.

I rotated my head toward Jacquie, searing pain shooting down my spine. She avoided my gaze, still clutching my hand. I spoke through dry and busted lips.

"M...Mia?"

Jacquie cried. Tears slipped down her round cheeks, and she squeezed until my fingers cramped. At last she looked up, her large brown eyes traced with red, and shook her head.

"I'm so sorry, Mason. I should have been there."

I closed my eyes, and this time, the memories flooded in like a storm. I saw it all in replay, just as it happened. Remembered screaming as I fired. Remembered Mia standing at the door, blocking the path to her students. Defiantly glaring down at the gunman.

"She saved their lives." Jacquie's whisper was so dry I barely heard it, but I tilted to face her again. She cupped my hand in both of hers and licked her lips. I saw a tremor in her cheeks.

"The kids, Mason. Mia saved her kids. She died a hero."

I stared at the wall, my face blank. The words registered in my battered mind, but they didn't mean anything.

All I saw was the blood on the floor.

Mia lying lifeless in the midst of it.

5

They discharged me from the hospital two weeks later. A series of doctors and surgeons called me the luckiest man in Arizona, and spent a lot of time breaking down the nature of my wounds, and how if the bullets had struck just a little to either side, I would have died. Or been paralyzed.

I didn't care. I listened dumbly while they discussed treatment and physical therapy plans for my left shoulder, which was the most damaged by the gunfire. Apparently the shoulder joint was dislocated, and I'd lost a lot of blood. It would take weeks for mobility to be restored, and months more for a full recovery. The mass of muscles I had built up across my back, arms, and chest over the last decade served as a sort of armor that spared me more devastating damage.

That, paired with an under-pressured target round of 9mm. I remembered the 9mm casings strewn across the first classroom, and cursed myself for not expecting a second shooter.

It was the obvious conclusion. One man might carry both a shotgun and a pistol, but he wouldn't alternate between the two unless he ran out of ammo for his primary. The presence of 9mm casings in the context of a booming shotgun just around the corner were a clear giveaway of two shooters.

But I rushed in anyway. Because I wasn't thinking about shooters. I was thinking about Mia.

McGrath visited me in the hospital. He told me in detail about the ongoing investigation into the two men who assaulted the school—a couple of psychotic eighteen- and nineteen-year-olds from across town, who apparently had been stalking and harassing two of the teachers for months. Shortly before the shooting a neighbor reported a stolen pistol and shotgun from the back seat of his truck.

The Phoenix PD would be launching a new gun security program throughout the city to promote responsible gun ownership and raise awareness about the dangers of stolen guns.

Again, I didn't care.

"Sign here, Mr. Sharpe."

A nurse held discharge papers toward me, and I signed dumbly. They had already disconnected all the monitors and machines from my body, and had handed me a sack full of medication to consume over the next couple of months.

Painkillers and antibiotics, mostly.

Jacquie bustled into the room pushing a wheelchair just as the nurse left. She wore civilian clothes, and I wondered how long it had been since she'd been to work. She visited me every day while I was in the ICU, and on several occasions I woke in the middle of the night to find her slumped over in a chair next to me, sleeping sitting up.

Now she bore a wide smile, and smacked the back of the wheelchair with enthusiasm.

"Come on, big boy. It's freedom day!"

I dropped my feet off the bed and endured the throbbing

pain in my back without comment, brushing Jacquie's hand off when she leaned in to help me up.

"I've got it," I muttered.

I staggered to my feet, leaning against a lunch cart to steady myself, then shuffled past the wheelchair and headed for the door.

"Hey!" Jacquie snapped. "Where are you going? Get your butt in this chair!"

I ignored her, stumbling into the hallway and turning for the elevator. My head spun and my feet ached, but it wasn't hard to remain standing. My left arm rode in a sling, giving me an odd sense of stability as I shuffled into the elevator.

Jacquie followed with the wheelchair. I ignored her and hit the ground floor button. She put a foot in front of the door as it started to close.

"Seriously?"

"I'm not riding in a chair."

She pursed her lips, and for a moment I thought she might punch me. Then she muttered a curse and left the chair outside.

We rode in silence to the ground floor, then she held my free arm and helped me across the lobby to the exit where her Dodge Charger waited under the awning.

I rode shotgun, folding into the car and slouching against the seat. My hands shook a little, and I couldn't tell if my nerves were fried or if my body was craving morphine.

I made a mental note to flush the pain pills, and buckled my belt with my good arm.

Jacquie settled in behind the wheel and hit the push start. Then she reached behind my chair and lifted a grocery sack into my lap.

"I got your stuff," she said. I looked down at my lap to see my car keys, wallet, cell phone, and favored Victorinox pocketknife lying in the bag. Familiar things that I hadn't even thought of in weeks.

"Where's my gun?" I whispered.

Jacquie looked sideways at me, both hands resting on the wheel. For a long moment she didn't answer.

"Come on, Jacquie."

She tilted her head toward the glovebox. I hit the switch and found my Smith & Wesson Model 340PD wrapped in a suede leather holster lying within.

The Glock 23 was a department-issued piece, and would have been confiscated after the shooting as part of standard procedure. But the J-frame Smith—my backup weapon, usually kept on my right ankle—was personal property, and I hadn't even fired it, anyway.

I slid the revolver out of the holster and clicked the cylinder open, noting five empty chambers where five rounds of .357 magnum usually lay.

I looked to Jacquie. She shrugged.

"You don't need bullets right now."

I clicked the cylinder shut and replaced the gun in the holster, then deposited it into the grocery bag without comment. It wasn't worth arguing about.

"Are you hungry?" Jacquie asked. "Want some Raising Cane's?"

The thought of my favorite chicken finger restaurant turned my stomach, and I shook my head.

"Just take me home."

Jacquie gave me the side-eye again, but she navigated the Charger toward south Phoenix anyway.

The little home Mia and I had combined our meager salaries to afford was situated in a developing portion of town. As thousands of Californians departed SoCal in search of more affordable living and lower taxes, the Phoenix housing market had exploded to the point of pricing out the working class, leaving us little choice but to buy small and buy on a less safe side of town.

The eight-hundred-square-foot, two-bedroom home was humble by any American standard, but Mia loved it. She planted tulips out front, put rocking chairs on the porch, and made a friend of every resident on our street. On week nights we remodeled and painted, and Saturdays we drove to South Mountain Park, the largest city park in America, and hiked the beautiful ridges there.

It was simple. Perfect.

Exactly the sort of life I dreamed of sharing with Mia.

Jacquie stopped the Charger at the end of the driveway and reached for the door. I put a hand on her arm, just staring at the two rocking chairs resting on the porch.

A couple packages lay next to them, and Mia's Toyota Corolla sat in the driveway. I guessed somebody had it towed for me.

Probably Jacquie.

My shoulders slumped, but I gave her arm a little squeeze.

"Thank you. For everything."

Jacquie made a dismissive motion with one hand. "Let's get you inside. You need a shower, *and food*. You know what? I think I'll cook some fajitas."

"Jacquie." I faced her. "I just...need to be alone now."

She looked confused. Then frustrated. But she didn't say anything. I slid my arm through the grocery sack handles and reached for my door.

"If I call, you better answer," Jacquie warned.

I gave her a weak smile and gritted my teeth as I left the car. My body had already assumed the position of the Charger's seat, and it didn't want to move.

I shut the door and stumbled to the front porch, conscious of Jacquie watching me from the driveway. I fumbled with the keys and dropped them once before unlocking the deadbolt, then I drew a deep breath, and stepped inside.

The house was cold, and silent. Dust hung in the air, and the smell of dishes I failed to wash the morning of the shooting stunk from the kitchen.

I dropped the grocery sack and stumbled to a cabinet, blindly filling a glass with two inches of bourbon before I stood next to the sink and surveyed the room.

Mia's clothes lay piled on the table next to a mess of brushes and oil paints. Two years previously, just before we met, she took up painting as a stress reliever, and was wonderful at it. Her work—mostly oil paintings of water landscapes—covered the walls of our little home, and filled the spare bedroom.

I stepped to the table and fingered the canvas, tracing the penciled outlines of a new piece she was designing. It was a lighthouse rising out of the trees, with a quiet bay surrounding it. Dark storm clouds boiled overhead, but breaking between them were streaks of sunshine, gleaming across the water. Mia had scribbled a little note in the top corner, just a few words in her elegant handwriting.

It's the sunrays in the storm clouds.

I swallowed hard and moved into the living room, where more paintings adorned the walls, and books littered shelves. My violin hung from a peg next to the TV, joined by framed prints of our engagement photos.

I turned away from the living room and stumbled to the bedroom.

Our quiet sanctuary was still, and empty. Dry flowers rested on the nightstand next to Mia's worn leather Bible, dust gathering on the cover. I walked to her side of the bed and sat down, the bourbon in one hand, the Bible in the other.

Tracing the cover. Remembering how she used to curl up in bed and read each morning.

I didn't understand her faith. I didn't understand her God. But, as I stared at her name scrawled in elegant gold script across smooth leather, I couldn't hold it back anymore.

I crumpled over, and the floodgates opened. The bourbon hit the floor and exploded in a dark stain over clean carpet, but I didn't notice. I just shook, clutching the Bible with both hands, and embracing the darkness.

I thought again of the face of death I'd seen as I lay bleeding out in that school.

And I cursed myself for not allowing it to swallow me.

6

PRESENT DAY

I awoke to a sharp tapping and sat up abruptly in the Corolla. A commanding voice called to me from outside the car, and I blinked away the sleep to see a sheriff's deputy tapping the glass with the butt of his flashlight.

It took a moment to remember where I was. The sky to the east crested with orange, and the parking lot of the grocery store I had stopped in was slowly filling with early morning shoppers.

Someplace in Alabama, I thought. I couldn't remember.

"Sir? Can you step out of the car, please?"

I squinted up at him, and saw the young face of a rural county cop. One hand holding the flashlight, the other resting on his department-issued Glock. He looked tired, and I figured he was probably finishing his shift, not starting it.

Then I remembered the Smith resting in my lap, still clutched in my hand. I looked down and was relieved to see the tail of my shirt covered both—probably the only reason the cop hadn't drawn on me.

"Sir, I need to see some ID."

I left the Smith beneath my shirt and withdrew my hand, starting the car. The cop repeated his request, but I simply shifted into drive and navigated back to the highway.

He watched me go, standing next to his cruiser, one hand still resting on the Glock. Too tired to pursue.

North Alabama was rolling and green, and North Georgia looked much the same. I crossed through Atlanta and leaned back into the seat, glancing down to the picture of Mia pinned to the dash.

She smiled up at me with glowing cheeks framed by raven hair, a reference to her distant Cherokee heritage. There were a lot of Cherokee in North Carolina, I heard. Mia grew up south of Raleigh, the only child of two orphans—a banker and a dental hygienist.

They were good parents. Adoring, doting parents, who understood the value of family. They spent late nights with Mia playing board games and watching Disney movies, and when she was older they loaded up every summer for a two-week vacation to her favorite place in the world—Saint Ellen Island.

It was an idyllic life. Perfect, right up until the moment a drunken fool in an F-150 plowed through a red light and sent the family sedan spinning into a ditch.

Mia had scars across her stomach from shattered glass and twisted metal.

Her parents died on the scene.

She was seventeen at the time. Shopping, colleges and dreaming about being a movie star. The life insurance money was enough to make her comfortable, but she couldn't stay in North Carolina. Not anymore.

The closest she ever made it to Hollywood was Phoenix, where film school morphed into educator school, and the movie star dream faded into a passion for taking care of children. The first time I met Mia she was in a bar, surrounded by a half-dozen of her teacher friends.

It wasn't love at first sight. But six drinks later, slow dancing on a desert patio under flickering tiki torches, I knew it was special.

Six months later, I knew it was forever.

A horn blared and I jerked the Corolla back into my lane as an irate trucker rushed by. I set the cruise control at seventy and slouched back, glancing at the picture again.

My hand falling to the gun under my shirt.

I reached Eastport, North Carolina, midafternoon, my mind so numb that I barely noticed the fading trees succumbing to residential outskirts.

Mia had never mentioned Eastport during her frequent reminiscing of beachside vacations on Saint Ellen. The island lay just off the coast, accessible only by ferry. Or, at least, that's what I read online while booking the little cottage that was to be our honeymoon suite.

I hadn't really cared about details, then. I didn't care about them now.

The blacktop rolling into town was straight and flat. I passed colorful cottages on both sides, along with a wooden sign decorated with a pelican, welcoming me to the historic town. The ground was wet and the sky roiled with clouds, but it wasn't raining.

The thermometer on my dash read forty degrees. Brutal weather on the coast. January in North Carolina.

Beyond the homes I saw a little diner on the left, and a two-story mint green building labeled as the police station on my right. A couple Ford Explorers painted in department blues and grays sat out front, but I didn't see any cops.

I didn't see any people at all. The town was dead quiet and still, as if everybody were on vacation.

Beyond the police station, twin rows of little shops faced Main Street—typical tourist trap places, peddling gifts, knickknacks, and antiques. They were all closed, and I kept driving until a sign directed me to turn left for the ferry.

The terminal consisted of a large multistory structure built on a harbor packed with little sailboats and small yachts. I parked the Corolla and surveyed the bleak sky as I slipped the revolver into my pocket. I looked to Mia's Bible, still resting in the seat next to me, and almost picked it up.

Instead, I left it there, exiting the car and not bothering to lock the doors. I didn't want it with me. It felt wrong somehow, with what I was about to do.

I walked through icy puddles to the ticket counter and found a single cashier waiting behind glass, watching a movie on her phone. She looked up, almost as though she was surprised to see me, then asked what I wanted.

"One, please," I said.

"Round trip?"

I looked down the concourse to the shaded ferry landing, now empty. Not a soul in sight.

"One way."

I paid, then returned my hand to my pocket, my fingers closing around the cold frame of the Smith.

It felt comforting, somehow. Familiar.

Inviting.

The ferry was named *Ranger*, and it glided against the pier with a diesel grinding and a wash of wake. A few people got off, and I passed the officer my ticket before being ushered aboard.

It was warm inside, and the motor throbbed as we churned out to sea. Seagulls swooped down around the ferry, and the glass fogged with salt spray. I watched desolate coastline slowly fade on both sides as the boat churned toward the island. The gulls gave way to misting sea spray, and *Ranger* lurched with each passing wave.

I saw the lighthouse first. It was tall and brown, built of concrete or brick, with the light pod on top offset to one side. I recognized it immediately from Mia's painting, and my stomach twisted.

Ranger parked against another soggy pier, and I made my way through the terminal and onto the island. It was colder off the mainland. I shivered and huddled into my jacket, mist gathering on my face. The chill made my left shoulder ache and burn, almost as though the bullet from ten weeks previously was tearing through again, blasting away muscle and flesh.

I ignored it and walked down the middle of the road. It was three miles from the ferry, through the heart of the island, to Cape Ellen on the southeast tip. I passed the lighthouse on my left, but didn't bother to tilt my head back to admire the aged structure. Trees leaned in on both sides, creating a canopy over winding asphalt, and, as wind stirred their limbs, a perpetual mist sprayed over my bare head.

Jacquie was right. January in North Carolina was no time for a vacation. But Mia wouldn't have cared. She wanted a winter wedding because her parents had one, and she would have loved the island for the memories alone.

We might have never left our rental.

My throat burned as I reached the end of the road, three long miles later. Sandy dunes, two and three stories high, blocked my view of the coast, but I could hear waves on the other side, joined by the squawk of more gulls. I followed a footpath between the dunes and over a long wooden boardwalk before finally breaking out onto the beach, and staring out over the open Atlantic.

I was alone. White sand spilled out on either side, falling

gently to gray water that rushed over the beach in a steady, crashing rhythm. A hundred or so seagulls swooped in and out of the water and danced along the wet sand, pecking for small fish and sea life to make an early dinner. Gray clouds obscured the horizon and wind tore at stray clumps of tall, dead grass.

It was totally bleak, but beautifully so. I stepped down to a few yards over the waterline, and stood with my hands in my pockets, ignoring the gulls swirling around my head and trying to imagine the scene as Mia would have seen it.

This wouldn't be a frigid day at the beach for her. It would be a portal into another world. A quiet, isolated moment for her brushes and paints, happy to endure the chilling wind to capture that moment on canvas.

To immortalize, in her own way.

I slumped down to the sand, lowering my face into my hands. Wet wind caught in my throat, and I shook. But there were no tears. I listened to the waves and cries of the gulls, circling around me like a cyclone, and I thought of Mia.

Remembering the last moments I shared with her in that janitorial closet.

I felt her lips on mine, her gentle hands tracing the IED scars beneath my shirt. The smell of her hair so close to my face.

Her body warm, and vibrant. Alive.

Then my hand slipped into my pocket and closed around the revolver. My arm shook a little as I drew it out, salt spray already gleaming across the black metal. The double-action trigger felt heavy under my finger, but I was familiar with the twelve pounds of pressure it took to drop the hammer.

I had trained for years with this weapon. I knew what it felt like as the cylinder turned, the trigger clicked, and the shrouded hammer pivoted backward across a fresh round.

But I'd never felt the pressure of the muzzle beneath my chin before.

I swallowed hard and squeezed just a little. My stomach twisted and my brain screamed for me to drop the gun.

But as my eyes blurred I saw children in the school.

The dead teaching assistant next to Mia.

I heard the boom of the shotgun meld with the snap of my Glock.

I squeezed a little harder, and felt the hammer reach full cock. My hand began to shake. Voices in my head shouted a confused mix of alarms—locking my body down. I couldn't press anymore. Fear and uncertainty overwhelmed the courage I'd taken ten weeks to build.

The gun bit into my chin. My eyes watered. I pressed a little harder, only a breath away from blowing everything to black.

And then I saw the body wash ashore.

7

I jerked the Smith to the left just as the hammer dropped. It snapped against the primer of a loaded .357 magnum and the gun belched fire against my left cheek, the bullet blasting past my ear with no more than a half-inch to spare.

My head spun and my left ear rang, deafened by the gunshot. I choked and dropped the gun, disoriented and momentarily panicked.

But the body was still there. I hadn't imagined it. Rolling in on a white-crested wave, wrapped in an orange life jacket, I recognized the frame of a man almost instantly—a small guy, a little frail, with saturated blond hair.

For almost a minute I just stared, my hands shaking as an overwhelming dump of adrenaline dominated my body. I looked down at the Smith lying in the sand, the reality of what I'd almost done surging in, and my stomach convulsed. I clawed my way to my feet, vomiting into the surf. My head swam and everything felt foggy.

I wiped my mouth with one hand and looked down the beach for any sign of another human. As before, I was alone.

Just me and the dead guy. He lay face down in the sand, screaming gulls orbiting him by the dozens. I slogged forward, water washing over my tennis shoes as I dropped to my knees and rolled him over. I've seen bodies before. A lot of them, and not just as a cop. The telltale signs of a man drowned, maybe three to four hours ago, were evident. He had yet to turn stiff, but his mouth hung open and his eyes were blurry with sand and saltwater.

My left ear continued to ring and my cheek burned as I deployed my Victorinox and quickly cut through the straps of the life vest. I found myself automatically checking for GSWs, or stab wounds before attempting a few compressions of his chest. Even though I knew him to be dead by his haunted, frozen eyes, it seemed like the right thing to do.

Just to be sure.

Nothing but seawater streamed from his mouth and nose as I pumped, and I moved my hand down to his wrist to check for a pulse. I squinted at the skin as I rolled his hand over, noting faint scratching around his left wrist, barely visible, marked in blue and black.

There was no heartbeat. The guy was dead, and had been for a while.

I released his arm and knelt in the sand for a while, staring at the face. Still disoriented from my second brush with death in only a few short weeks.

Still partially longing to have had the courage to see it through.

But I couldn't think about it anymore. The mental focus and emotional turmoil it had required to draw that near to the edge was too great, and my mind now turned numb. I just stood up, folding the Victorinox back into my pocket, and thinking like a cop.

Thinking about what came next.

I scooped the Smith back into my jacket and started back

across the sand, through the dunes, to the road. It took me an hour to find a house with an occupant willing to answer the door. Another hour after calling the police, for units from Eastport PD to meet me at the body.

Then the questions began. And they were all pointed at me.

8

I sat inside the two-story mint green police building, a hot cup of coffee cradled between my hands, my damp clothes clinging to my skin. Glass walls partitioned me off from the rest of the department, where half a dozen cops scurried amid cluttered desks, talking on phones and radios, and calling to each other.

At first glance, it didn't look like a very organized operation. But then, my only real experience with policing came from the Phoenix PD, and that was a big city department, with a lot of funding. I couldn't imagine that Eastport, even with six or eight cops, enjoyed a healthy budget or very much training.

After a short interrogation at the beach, a sergeant showed up and asked me to accompany him back to the police station for "a chat." I thought it was an odd phrase to use following the report of a dead body, but I expected the invitation, and also knew it wasn't really optional. I rode in the police boat back to the mainland, then sat silently in the back of a police cruiser on the way to the station.

As soon as I stepped inside, they had me empty my pockets. I was surprised they hadn't already checked me for weapons. Another slightly sloppy oversight, but then again, small town. Small department.

I dumped my keys, wallet, Victorinox, and the Smith into a plastic container, and watched the mood of the cops around me flick from self-important "we've got a body" bustle, to semi-alarmed "we've got a gun" hustle.

Funny, to be more alarmed by a weapon than a body. But people are usually like that. A body is something bad that happened. A gun is something bad that *could* happen.

They put me in the glass cubicle, only bringing coffee on my third request, then locked the door and left me there. I wondered if they really thought glass walls would stop my six-foot-two, heavily muscled frame from escape if I decided to make an attempt.

Again, they probably weren't thinking logically. Just making decisions. I got the vibe that the boss was out of the office, leaving the local Barney Fife in charge.

It was almost an hour before the sergeant who'd met me at the beach unlocked the door and stepped in. He wore a royal blue uniform, with EPD patches on the sleeves. It bulged around his gut, and his gun belt sagged under the weight of cuffs, flashlight, radio, and what appeared to be a Ruger GP100 revolver.

That made him an old timer, I figured. More because of the choice of weapon, as opposed to the gray in his hair and the sag in his cheeks. Only long-time cops, in my experience, carry revolvers as primary service weapons.

Which meant he probably took special interest in my Smith. Revolver guys always notice other revolvers, and I wondered if he'd emptied the cylinder and found the spent round.

Probably.

"So," the guy said, scraping a chair back and settling in

with a fat-man huff. "I'm Sergeant Witmore with the East-point PD. You've got a lot of explaining to do, Mr...."

He spoke with a heavy southern accent, and trailed off as if he couldn't remember my name, but I knew it was a ploy. A designed attempt to get me talking by filling in the blank space with my name.

I chose to let him hang, leaving him no choice but to do the work himself.

"Sharpe. Right? Mason Lewis Sharpe. Of Phoenix."

I nodded. I hadn't been read my rights, because the cops at the beach weren't arresting me. But I knew the Miranda spiel as well as any cop. I could remain silent if I wanted to.

Then again, that would only prolong this irritating conversation.

"Mind explaining what you're doing in town, Mr. Sharpe?"

Odd question. A bit aggressive, and targeted. As if he expected me to respond defensively.

"Visiting," I said.

He poked out his bottom lip, peering at me with obvious suspicion. I swallowed coffee, more for the warmth than the flavor, and set the cup on the table.

"Who's the stiff?" I asked.

Witmore glared, as if I'd personally offended him. "I think I'll ask the questions."

"Okay. Well, get with it. I'm not sticking around."

"You might be," Witmore said. "You've got some explaining to do. We can start with this."

He dug in his breast pocket and produced a small brass object, slamming it hard against the table, face-up.

It was a .357 shell casing. Doubtless the one from the empty chamber of my Smith. And it said a lot about the forensics forte of this department that a police sergeant had been willing to drop it in his pocket like so much trash, fingerprints and DNA be damned.

I said nothing.

"Mind telling me why you were illegally carrying a concealed weapon in my state?" he snapped.

"It's perfectly legal. Ever heard of the Bill of Rights?"

"But where's your permit? Nothing but a driver's license and a credit card in your wallet. Or maybe it's stuffed up your ass?"

"I don't have a permit. I've never needed one."

"How you figure?"

"Because Arizona is a permitless carry state. And because I'm a homicide detective for the Phoenix Police Department."

"Is that right?" Witmore leaned back, folding his arms. "So where's your badge?"

"I left it at home," I said, quietly.

"When?" Witmore asked.

I didn't answer. I didn't like the idea of him backing me into a timeline. I still had nothing to hide, but something about his aggressive mannerism, coupled with his sloppy procedure, put me on edge.

I'd been here before, sitting across a desk from an over-eager investigator, willing to sacrifice policy and good police work in exchange for a quick conviction.

That hadn't been a civilian cop, of course. But the reckless enthusiasm felt the same.

"Let's run through the facts," Witmore said. "A body washes up on my beach, in the middle of the off-season. Only locals in town. Well, locals, and *you*. Some guy who claims to be an Arizona cop, a couple thousand miles from home with nothing but a credit card and a revolver. A revolver with one spent casing. And this guy reports the body. Sound fishy to you?"

"No."

"Why not?"

"Was there a GSW on the body?"

I already knew the answer.

Witmore said nothing, working his lips a little like a gold-fish. Irritated.

"*Gun shot wound*," I clarified.

"I know what it means, jackass."

"So did you find one?"

No answer.

"So nothing's fishy," I said. "You're just fishing. And unless you have some actual questions to ask, I'll be leaving."

I made as if to stand. Witmore bolted, placing one hand on the grip of the Ruger and shoving a fat finger at me.

"*Sit down*," he snarled. "And stay there."

I didn't move, just staring him down. His eyes blazed and he worked his lips like a fish again. It was a bizarre tic, and it made me want to punch him in the face.

I could see another question—or maybe a threat—boiling up from his chest, but just then the glass door swung open, and another old cop walked in.

Unlike Witmore, this guy was slender and clean shaven, with neat gray hair and a pressed uniform. He wore a gold badge on his chest, with no gun belt or gear around his waist. His skin glistened a little, but by the cherry red of his cheeks and the clean uniform, I figured it wasn't rain. He'd probably just showered.

So the boss had showed up, then.

The new guy set a plastic bin on the table, a folded paper in his free hand. Then he tilted his head toward the door.

"I've got it, Witmore. Thanks for bringing him in." He spoke with a gentler southern accent than the sergeant, but there was no doubt the new guy was also a North Carolina native.

Witmore jabbed a finger at me. "He's obstinate, Chief. Trouble. Ask him about this!"

He held up the shell casing, but the chief seemed unimpressed.

"Go get yourself a cup of coffee, Sarge. It's cold out."

Witmore's eyes bulged and he glowered at me again, but he left the room.

As soon as the door closed, the new guy settled into Witmore's chair and smoothed his uniform, surveying through gray, weathered eyes. For a while he didn't say anything. Then he unfolded the single sheet of paper and slid it across the table.

I accepted it without comment, scanning the top half.

It was a black and white printout of a news story from the *Arizona Republic*—Phoenix's primary newspaper. I didn't need to read the body of text. The headline said enough.

HERO COP GUNS DOWN SCHOOL SHOOTERS, LOSES FIANCÉE

I looked up and saw a shade of sympathy cross the chief's gray eyes. I pushed the sheet back, and leaned into the chair, but I still didn't comment.

It might be sincere. Or it might be the age-old good cop, bad cop routine.

"I'm Chief Lowe," he said. "Welcome to Eastport."

I remained quiet.

"Sorry about Witmore. He's an old crow, but good help is hard to find."

So bad help is better?

I thought it, but didn't say it.

Chief Lowe pushed the bin across the table, and I looked inside to see my wallet, keys, and Victorinox waiting for me.

"Strange knife," Lowe said. "Can't say I've seen one before."

"It's a Swiss army knife," I said, rolling the Victorinox in my hand and tracing the outline of its multiple tools with one thumb. It felt good in my palm—another worn and familiar tool, like the Smith.

"Doesn't look like a Swiss army knife," Lowe grunted.

"They make a lot of models. This is the Locksmith."

Lowe nodded, appearing genuinely interested, but not commenting further. I scooped the stuff into my pockets, then pushed the bin aside.

"What about my gun?"

"Can't give you that," Lowe said. "It's in evidence."

"I don't see why. I didn't shoot anybody."

"But you did shoot."

I said nothing. Lowe traced his left cheek with one finger, mirroring the burn mark on my own face. A knowing glint shone in his eye, but he didn't say what he had to be thinking.

I didn't offer any clarification.

"You in town for long?" he asked.

I didn't comment.

"Why don't you stay a day or two?" he said. "Enjoy the beach. Stick close...just in case we have questions."

Ah yes. The old "don't leave town" spiel.

"Am I gonna get my gun back?" I asked.

"Sure. In a day or two, after the medical examiner has a look at the body."

"You have an ME in this town?"

"No. But the county has a coroner, and he can be here tomorrow."

I looked through the nearest window. The sky outside was darker than before, and rain washed against the glass.

Enjoy the beach. Yeah, okay.

As much as I wanted to tell Lowe to shove it, the thought

of a hot shower and a warm bed was tempting. And I wasn't leaving town without my gun. It just didn't feel right.

"Someplace to stay the night?" I asked.

"There's some hotels near the Walmart. Or, if you want something with a little more charm, you could stay at Marley's. Little pub down the street. Couple rooms and a bar."

Good enough.

I stood, pocketing my hands. The chief tilted his head back to watch me, arms crossed. He looked neither suspicious nor trusting. An old cop, but one who had clearly learned more in his time than Witmore.

"Give the desk clerk your cell phone number," he said. "Just in case we need to reach you."

"Haven't got a cell phone."

He squinted. "Is that so?"

"I'll be back tomorrow," I said. "You better have my gun."

9

M arley's Inn and Pub was a ramshackle, cedar-shingled cabin sort of structure that looked as though it would be more comfortable near a ski resort than a beach. It sat a mile from the police station, but I declined the offer of a ride from the chief and walked instead. The Corolla was still parked at the ferry.

Out front a couple SUVs, a nineties model Ford Bronco, and a plain sedan with the bare essentials look of a rental sat in front of the slouching porch. The building was two stories, and I figured the second must be for the rooms.

A quaint kind of place. Not the re-manufactured, look-a-like imitation that millennials from California might build. This was the genuine article. Mia would have liked it.

I kicked muck off my shoes at the door, pausing to take note of a small yard littered with junk to one side of the pub. In addition to a stack of empty beer boxes and a couple aban-doned barrels, an old pickup truck sat, its tailgate pointed toward the street, a North Carolina antique vehicle license plate hanging from one screw. It looked to be an old GMC—

late sixties, probably—with grimy windows and dry-rotted tires. But, despite the disrepair, I liked the look of it. I've always liked old trucks. Back in the day I owned a '72 Chevy K10, and drove it all over Arizona camping and exploring.

I sold it when Mia and I got engaged and began to house shop. Didn't think twice about it.

Inside the pub sat a disorganized arrangement of tables surrounded by mismatched chairs. Dim lights shone from overhead, illuminating five occupants—four guys at the bar in the back of the room, dressed in grimy work clothes and knocking back bottled beers, and a lone woman sitting in the corner, dressed in jeans and a black leather jacket.

She would be the driver of the rental, I figured. She didn't look like a local.

I made my way to the vacant end of the bar and settled onto a stool, taking note of a large display case leaned against the wall above a row of coolers. It contained a folded American flag, a row of military medals, and the image of three soldiers standing beneath the blazing desert sun.

I recognized Iraq immediately, and I also recognized the utility uniforms of the United States Marine Corps. Two men and a woman, holding rifles, half smiling, half grimacing.

The Iraqi grin, we used to call it. The look you forced on your face when it was time to send pictures back home, but it was a hundred and ten degrees outside, and you hadn't showered in four days.

The doors to the pub's kitchen blew back and a woman rushed out, carrying two trays of bar food. She was brunette, maybe thirty-five, lean and good-looking without a hint of makeup. Strong arms accentuated her tank top, and I caught the hint of an Eagle Globe and Anchor tattoo peeking out from just to the side of one shoulder blade.

The woman in the picture, I guessed.

She deposited the food and exchanged a laugh with one

of the local guys, then pivoted toward my end of the bar. But instead of asking for my order she slouched against the counter and shot me a wink.

"Well, howdy, stranger. How's it going?"

The overly warm greeting felt coy, at first. Almost flirtatious. But there was nothing sly in her smile. Just friendly.

"Fine," I said, preferring to lie than disclose my train wreck of a life to a total stranger.

"I'm Marley," she said. "Thanks for stopping by."

"Mason. You a Marine?"

I gestured to the photo instead of the tattoo.

Marley glanced at the display case, and a sad sort of shadow passed across her face. But she nodded.

"Six years. Three deployments. You? You've got the look."

I shook my head. "Army. Seventy-fifth. Two deployments."

She whistled softly. "Ranger, huh? Well, in that case, first round's on me. What are ya havin'?"

"Beer, I guess. Whatever's handy. And a menu."

She slid me a Miller Lite and pointed to a chalkboard with a short list of "daily specials"—apparently the only sort of menu available. I ordered a burger and fries and leaned against the bar, sipping my beer and watching the other occupants of the pub.

The guys were typical bar creatures. They laughed a lot and told jokes loud enough for everybody to hear. Marley flirted with them and they flirted right back, dropping tens and twenties on the table as the beer bottles stacked up.

The woman in the corner was altogether different. She leaned over her plate, working her way through a trio of chicken fingers, and seeming lost in her own little world. A notebook and a cell phone lay next to her, and a backpack occupied the chair opposite her.

But she didn't engage with the room, or make much comment when Marley came to check on her. She was small, and a little pale. Had a sort of New England look to her, I thought. I wasn't sure why.

A tourist, maybe. But a disappointed tourist. It wasn't any warmer outside than it might be in Massachusetts.

I finished the burger alongside four beers, then paid my tab with a generous tip.

"Got a room for the night?" I asked.

Marley laughed. "I've got five. Queen bed okay?"

"Sure."

I handed her my credit card, and she returned with a brass key.

"Top of the stairs, third room on the left. Let me know if you need anything."

I nodded my thanks and climbed the stairs, finding six rooms filling the second floor. Mine featured dusty hardwood floors, a tiny bathroom, and a window overlooking the street with the stormy waters of the Cape Fear River barely visible in the distance.

I stood at the window, watching the rainwater drain across the glass, and barely thinking about the dead guy on the beach. My mind drifted instead to Mia. I tried to imagine her as a little girl, and wondered if she'd ever had lunch at Marley's pub.

It wouldn't have been called Marley's then. Marley was too young. But the building was old enough. Old enough to remember my beautiful fiancée as a child.

After a long while I shut the blinds and stripped out of my shirt and shoes, leaving both on the floor. I climbed into bed and thought of Mia's worn Bible, still in the Corolla back at the ferry. I wished I had it with me.

When I closed my eyes, I saw myself on the beach again. I felt the gun in my hand. I imagined Mia just on the other side of an impenetrable glass wall, beckoning to me. Longing for me to touch her.

But just out of reach.

When I woke up, I'd return to the police station. Get my gun.

And then I'd reach deep inside and look for the courage again. Because I needed her in my arms.

10

I awoke the next day with a jarring thought on my mind —the lacerations on the dead man's wrists. I'd noted them as faint black and blue scratches at the time, and hadn't really given them much thought. After ten hours of sleeping like a rock, the memory clicked in my mind and the investigator in me took over.

Why were there lacerations on his wrists?

I stripped out of my clothes and took a long, hot shower, utilizing the provided soap and towels, then redressed in the same clothes. I hadn't really brought anything with me. I hadn't expected to need anything.

The burn mark on my left cheek had swollen into a red welt. It was sensitive to the touch, but the bullet hadn't broken the skin. My left ear still rang, and I could barely hear on that side of my face. But I was alive.

For now.

Downstairs, I found the bar empty and Marley nowhere to be seen. Apparently breakfast wasn't on the menu. So I left the pub and walked the one mile back to the police station, my hands in my pockets.

It was just as cold as the day before, and just as gray, but the rain had stopped. I passed more small houses and a couple restaurants, both locked up with "Closed for the Season" signs in the windows.

The police station was just as mint green as before, but with twice as many patrol cars parked out front. As I pushed through the doors into the welcome warmth, a scuffle at the far end of the room caught my attention. Two EPD cops were busy corralling a middle-aged woman with streaks of gray in her disheveled brown hair. She was crying—or had been crying—and was clearly distraught. I couldn't hear her outbursts as they ushered her into a glass office and closed the door, but there was some manner of argument underway.

Whatever they were saying to her, she wasn't satisfied.

I approached the desk clerk. He looked up at me with no more enthusiasm than any of his numerous colleagues around the country. Desk clerks are like that. They always seem to endure their jobs, but never enjoy them.

"I came for my gun," I said.

He picked up a phone, hitting a button without replying. He mumbled a couple words, then set the phone down and turned to his computer.

I rapped my knuckles on the counter. "Hey. Buddy. I'm talking to you."

He gestured toward the back corner of the room without looking up from his screen, and I turned to see Chief Lowe approaching. He wore a fresh uniform and glistened with the warmth of a recent shower, as before.

The dude must shower three times a day.

I met him halfway across the room, in the midst of the bullpen, but he gestured me into an office.

Inside, he sat behind a desk heaped with reports and trinkets. The kind of things a cop collects over years in public service—photographs with politicians, little plaques with lame one-liner jokes on them, and a dusty wooden display laden with fly fishing lures.

Junk.

I remained standing, allowing the door to close behind me. The chief gestured to a seat, but I didn't take it.

"I'm here for my gun," I said.

He leaned back, crossing his arms behind his head, and looking like he'd just pulled third shift. Maybe he had. Maybe he hadn't slept all night, with a body in town.

"Coffee?" he asked.

"No thanks."

"Okay, well, I'm having some."

He lifted a phone and mumbled to somebody, then rubbed his face.

"Sit," he said.

This time I acquiesced, mostly because I was tired of arguing.

Some junior cop walked in with a cup for the chief, then the room fell silent again as the door closed.

"Daniel Porter drowned," the chief said, cupping the coffee.

"Porter?"

"The dead guy."

"Okay."

"Lungs full of water. Stomach, too. Bruises on his head where he hit something, maybe falling out of the boat."

"What boat?"

The chief shrugged. "I guess it's no big secret. I'm only telling you as a professional courtesy, you understand."

"So you checked up on me."

"Sure I did. Called Phoenix. They said you were on leave. I'm sorry."

I didn't answer. The chief sipped coffee, seeming to regain his train of thought.

"Anyway. Local guy reported a missing boat. Eighteen-foot, center-console fishing skiff. Water was rough, yesterday. Daniel must have fallen out."

I narrowed my eyes. "What makes you think he would have stolen a boat?"

Lowe shrugged. "He liked to fish."

"So do you," I said, tilting my chin toward the dusty lures. "You don't steal boats."

He grunted. "I've known Daniel Porter for years. Since he was a kid, really. Local guy. Trust me, Sharpe. He's that kind. Unstable. Unpredictable."

I looked out the glass toward the office across the bullpen where the woman was still busy arguing with a couple officers. The discussion didn't seem to have cooled any.

"That his wife?" I asked.

Lowe only grunted again.

"She seems upset."

"Her husband just drowned," he said. "That's how people act when they lose somebody."

I winced, a harsh lump welling up in my throat. Lowe noticed and his gaze dropped.

"I'm...sorry."

"What about the lacerations?" I said, changing the subject.

"What lacerations?"

"The ones on his wrists," I clarified. "Black and blue, like restraint marks."

The chief scratched his chin and looked to the corner above my head for no reason.

"Can't say I remember those."

"Your coroner should have caught them."

He shifted, sucked his teeth, then nodded suddenly. "Oh, right. The wrist marks. He said it must have been some line, or something. Must have got caught up falling off the boat."

I shook my head. "No. It takes at least a day for bruises to turn black or blue. If he got caught up in some line falling off the boat, those marks should have been red. Purple, maybe. He died only a few hours before I found him."

Lowe frowned and his tone changed, assuming an edge. "How you figure?"

"Rigor mortis," I said. "It begins in the face, maybe a couple hours after death, then spreads through the body. Porter's face was stiff—his mouth frozen open. But his arms and legs were still limp."

"You an ME, too?" Lowe snapped.

"No. I'm just a good investigator."

He sipped his coffee, slowly. Watching me over the rim. I stared right back.

"I don't know what the lacerations are about," Lowe said at last. "But our ME said Porter drowned. So that's that."

"I don't doubt that he drowned. I wonder why. Especially with a life jacket. And I thought you said the coroner wouldn't be here until today?"

"He got here *early*," the chief said, dropping his tone.

I held his gaze, and didn't answer. Part of me wondered if he was lying, or simply incompetent. In my limited experience, most small-town cops were great people who cared more about their community than their own ability to make a lot more money doing almost anything else.

But they were also usually under-trained, and definitely under-equipped. Maybe this guy didn't understand rigor mortis. Maybe it had never occurred to him to google it.

In the end, I didn't really care. I wanted my gun back, and then I was going to get my car, and then...

"I'll take my gun," I said.

Lowe's lips twitched. "Let's say we ship it to you. So you can get back on the road."

"If the coroner came, you know I didn't shoot that guy. So why keep it?"

"Let's say I don't feel comfortable with some stranger waltzing around, heavily armed."

"A snubby revolver is hardly heavily armed. And, back to our discussion about the Bill of Rights yesterday—that isn't your call. I guarantee you there's two dozen guns scattered around this block, and none of them are owned by your cops."

Lowe just glared at me, his mouth working as though he were evaluating something. Whatever it was, it wasn't me. But it might be *about* me.

"We'll be keeping the gun, for now," he said. "I think it's time you hit the road."

"Is that so?" I raised both eyebrows.

"Yeah. I think so."

I stared him down, contemplating the idea of slamming his face into the desk before driving my knee into his groin.

But I kept my hands loose at my sides. Because knocking him around wouldn't get me anywhere—I'd already lost this round.

"Need a ride to your car?" Lowe drawled with a sarcastic lilt.

"No," I said. "I'm good."

I plowed through the glass door. It was a lot quieter outside than it had been when I entered, and I noticed that the dead guy's wife had left. Half a dozen cops scattered around the room were busy drinking coffee and muttering irritably under their breath. They barely looked up as I breezed past the desk clerk and back into the chilled air.

I stood for a moment on the sidewalk, breathing slowly and allowing my blood pressure to ease. Lowe's pointless obstinacy made me want to throat punch him, but more than that, it sidetracked my plans. I hadn't thought about what would happen next after I recovered the Smith—not since the previous night. Now that Lowe had derailed those subconscious intentions, I wasn't sure what to do with myself.

I started to turn toward the ferry, figuring that I might as well recover the Corolla. Then I heard a soft sob and looked to my left to see the dead man's wife sitting slouched over the steering wheel of an aged and rusting minivan. She sobbed uncontrollably, her face in her hands, oblivious to the outside world.

The image of consuming grief was so visceral it made me stop cold, and stare at her. The gasping sounds she made between shaking, silent sobs were audible through her partially opened window, and they hit me like bullets. Reminding me of the similar sounds I had made over the past ten weeks.

I hesitated, thoughts of my car now fading into the back of my mind. And then, before I could stop myself, I stepped across the parking lot and tapped on her door.

11

The woman looked up, startled by the rap of my knuckles on the metal. Momentary fear crossed her face, and she looked to the police station. Then she just stared at me, her eyes red and haunted.

"Mrs. Porter?" I asked.

The woman swallowed, looking again to the station. Then she nodded.

"I'm Mason," I said. "I'm...I'm the one who found your husband."

Her bottom lip trembled as though she were holding back a new flood of tears. Then she reached for the latch, and I stepped back to allow her room to open the door.

She was small. Not frail, but not more than a hundred pounds, either. The gray and brown hair I had noticed earlier was pulled back into a ponytail, stretching the skin around her eyes and doing nothing to take the sag out of her cheeks.

On a good day, not consumed by grief and exhaustion, she was doubtlessly a bright personality. I don't know how I knew that, but I could feel it radiating off of her, somehow.

It made the agony in her eyes all the more painful.

"I'm very sorry," I said.

She blinked a few times, seeming to get control of herself, then offered a hand.

"Trudy," she said. "Trudy Porter."

"Detective Sharpe," I said, before I could stop myself. It was my standard response when meeting most people, but I instantly regretted it as hope flooded her face.

"You're a cop?"

I hesitated. "Kinda. I mean...not here. I'm from Arizona."

Her face fell. "Oh."

I looked over my shoulder to the station, a sudden tingle in the back of my mind rising into a conscious thought. I wasn't sure if the local cops had just pissed me off, or if the pain radiating from Porter's widow resonated with me a lot deeper than I wanted to admit. But either way...

"You hungry?" I asked.

———

I RODE with Trudy down the main drag to the diner I had seen when I first arrived. It was a lot smaller than Marley's place, but the parking lot loaded with trucks and SUVs indicated that breakfast was served.

Trudy's van squeaked a lot as she turned in. It was maybe twenty years old, and as I looked over my shoulder I noticed an elaborate metal contraption bolted to the floor where the back seats should be. That contraption seemed to correlate with the passenger-side sliding door, and I figured it must be a mechanism built to accommodate a motorized chair.

I made note of it, but didn't comment as Trudy parked and sat motionless in the driver seat, staring through the mucky windshield.

"I'm...I'm a mess," she mumbled.

I offered the warmest smile I could muster. My cop, comforting smile, usually reserved for scared children.

My mind was clicking into the victim management routine I'd learned during my early months as a homicide detective—get the person comfortable and give them something to focus on. Something tangible, and safe.

"Let's get you some coffee," I said. "It'll help."

She chewed her lip, working the car keys in one hand, then nodded. I got out and held the door for her before ducking into the small restaurant.

The smell was irresistible. My stomach growled as we entered the crowded space, stepping over a saturated doormat and waiting for the hostess to point us toward a small table in the back of the room. The diner was packed with locals, all huddled around tables and booths, chowing down on late breakfast. A low murmur of conversation filled the room, but it died off as Trudy was noticed.

A hushed calm fell across the crowd, and Trudy dropped her head as she hurried to the table. I knew the look, and shot my "mind your own business" glare around the room.

Another cop look.

The chatter resumed, and I found my way to the table, sliding back a chair and sitting across from Trudy. The waitress came and I ordered coffee—Trudy ordered water. Then I scanned the menu to give Trudy time to relax a little.

It was a fruitless effort. I could feel the strain and fear radiating off of her like the cold from outside, and it confused me a little. The signals I detected from her reminded me of kidnapping victims. People who were missing somebody.

Not people who knew they had lost someone.

Maybe she was simply in the denial stage of grief.

"The pancakes are good, right?" I asked.

Trudy looked up, as though she were startled by the question. She nodded.

The waitress returned and we both ordered, then I signaled for there to be one check. She retreated to the kitchen, leaving our corner of the diner quiet.

I watched Trudy fiddling with a napkin, wrapping it around her hand and pulling at it until her fingertips turned white, then twisting it back the other way.

She wasn't just grieving. She was distressed. And confused. I knew the feelings all too well, and saw the same devastation in her eyes that I'd seen in my own any time I bothered to look into a mirror over the past ten weeks. It was visceral and it took me back to those first few days after the hospital. In the house...alone.

"I'm...very sorry," I said, quietly. I knew the words bounced like a bad check, but I didn't know what else to say.

Trudy blinked. I gave her time, sipping coffee.

"Did he go out on the water often?" It wasn't an important question, but I thought she needed something to focus on.

Trudy smiled, just a little. "Danny loved to fish. He used to go whenever he was free, with his friend."

"What friend?"

She shrugged. "Mr. Sherman, up the river. Retired guy. He...he's the one who reported the missing boat."

"Daniel took his boat?"

Trudy looked away, chewing her lip. Maybe it was a sensitive question, or maybe it hit too close to the heart of the tragedy.

I decided to change tack.

"What did your husband do for a living?"

"He worked for the social security administration," she said. "In Wilmington."

"That's a long ways," I said, prompting her to keep talking.

"Forty-five minutes, one way. Not bad. The health insurance was good."

Health insurance.

I thought about the contraption in the van, and decided to probe.

"You have a lot of medical bills?"

She nodded. "Our son has cerebral palsy. It's...it's very expensive."

"I'm sorry. Is he okay?"

Trudy shrugged. "He's only eight. It could be a lot worse."

I couldn't imagine. For most of my life I'd enjoyed pretty robust health, sponsored by a clean diet and an extensive amount of time spent working out in a martial arts gym near the police station. Mia was healthy, too.

I probably had bills waiting for me from the shooting, but they couldn't be anything like having a child oppressed by a severe illness.

"That must be difficult," I said.

Trudy shrugged again. "We have some help. My sister lives in Lowberg...she's keeping him now. So I can...you know..."

She looked away, tears clouding her eyes. I knew I was pressing her, but in my experience asking direct questions could sometimes minimize the pain. Like putting everything out in the open, so there's nothing to bottle up.

"When did your husband go missing?" I asked gently.

Trudy hesitated, and I thought it was strange. The cops would have asked her this, and I expected her to have an answer ready.

"He never came home from work, Friday. But he's been working overtime, so I thought..."

She choked, and I subtly checked my watch. I really had no idea what day it was, but my watch read Sunday, meaning that I had found Daniel's body Saturday afternoon.

No wonder the diner was this busy after ten.

"He never called?" I said, prompting her to continue.

Trudy shook her head, lip trembling. The food came, and the waitress set the plates on the table, but Trudy ignored her pancakes, working the napkin around her fingers again.

There was something here. Something deeper than shock and loss. Something she wasn't telling me.

I kept my voice low. "Trudy?"

She faced me.

"You can trust me," I said. "I'm trying to help."

Her eyes watered.

"They...they're saying he stole the boat and fell off. But Daniel would never take a thing! He wasn't like that. He was a stable guy. Active around the house, helping with the dishes, looking after things. Sure, he took off fishing now and again, but that was only to blow off steam. He was under a lot of stress, same as me. With the bills and all. But he would *never* take Sherman's boat. He's never stolen a thing in his life!"

I noted the blatant discrepancies between Trudy's description of Daniel, and Lowe's, and I focused on her body language. She was too convincingly distraught for me to seriously suspect her of lying.

"Why do the cops say he took the boat?"

She raised her hands. "I don't know. They just say so. They say Sherman reported it missing."

"Sherman says Daniel took it?"

"I...I don't know."

I sipped coffee, giving her time to calm. My next series of questions would be a little more challenging.

"Was Daniel in any kind of trouble?"

"Trouble?" She looked confused. "Like with the cops?"

"With anybody."

She shook her head. "Daniel was a rule follower. He wouldn't change lanes without signaling. Wouldn't park without paying the meter. Everybody loved him. He was a servant."

She ducked her head and her eyes began to water. Once again the pain radiating off her hit me in the gut, and I swallowed hard. I remembered sitting on the end of my bed, back in Phoenix. Sobbing by myself.

The little noises she made sounded like mine. The faint tremor in her hands felt like déjà vu.

"It's...it's okay," I said, gently touching her arm. "I know what it feels like."

She just stared at me a long time, then ducked her head again.

We ate barely half the food, my appetite having left me, and hers having never arrived. Then I paid the check and asked Trudy to drive me to the ferry to collect the Corolla.

As we exited the diner, I sucked down a crisp breath of January air, and looked down the street. My gaze settled on a two-tone, blue and white Ford Bronco parked a block from the police station, exhaust fumes bubbling from the rear bumper. It was the same one I'd seen the night before, parked in front of Marley's. A battered, but still noteworthy vehicle.

Trudy drove in silence all the way to the ferry, parking outside the lot and doing the thing with her fingers again, this time wrapping the tail of her shirt around them.

"Thank you for breakfast," she said. "And...for listening."

I simply nodded. The van fell silent, my mind still spinning. Something still nagging at the back of my brain, like a worm burrowing through the dark recesses of my mind.

It was those lacerations on Daniel's wrists.

I felt the sting of the burn on my face again and recalled Chief Lowe touching his cheek when he asked about the spent bullet in my gun.

He knew I almost shot myself. He connected the burn mark to the missing bullet almost immediately.

How did a cop that observant miss the marks on Daniel's

wrists? Sure, they were minor, but they mattered. They might matter a lot.

And yet Lowe had dismissed them, and if he was to be believed, so had his coroner.

Which meant something was wrong, here. Something significant.

"Where does Sherman live?" I asked.

Trudy frowned. "Why?"

"Just thought I'd stop by. Ask some questions."

"Are you...investigating?"

I shrugged. "I just like to meet people."

She hesitated, then peeled off a scrap of paper from the van's console and scratched down the address. After making the note, she seemed to hesitate, then added her phone number.

"Go that way," she pointed. "Up the river. He lives down a long gravel road, alone. Make sure you go straight to the door to knock."

I folded the paper into my pocket. Then I gave her a gentle smile. "It's gonna be okay."

Trudy stared at me, her gaze fixated on the red welt on my left cheek. I doubted she could guess where it came from, but it still looked nasty.

"If...if you learn anything...call me?" she asked.

I promised, then got out and watched her drive away, fingering the paper in my pocket. Thinking about those lacerations, and what would be required to steal a boat.

Then I headed for the Corolla. I had questions, and I wasn't taking Lowe's word for anything.

12

The man called Sherman did indeed live down a long gravel road. It took me some time to find it, fighting with the built-in GPS in the dash of Mia's Corolla. The navigation software was probably outdated, and the roads north of Eastport were rural.

A quick survey of a map confirmed that the Cape Fear River spilled south out of Wilmington, framed by Carolina Beach to the east and the rural North Carolina countryside to the west. Then it traveled south, before reaching Eastport and Saint Ellen Island, and spilling into the Atlantic.

Sherman's place resided in a portion of that rural North Carolina countryside, north of Eastport by about ten miles. I drove up progressively more isolated county roads before finding a rusting and battered mailbox reflecting the correct street number standing next to a gravel drive.

No Trespassing and *Private Property* signs hung from trees on either side of the entrance, but I turned in anyway and piloted around potholes and ruts toward the river.

The drive was at least half a mile long, and by the time I

saw the house, a dense forest of trees had isolated me from the county road.

It was a nice home. Two stories, with dormer windows pointed toward the forest, and a wide, tree-less backyard spilling down toward the river a hundred yards away. I saw a pier and a boathouse, and an old Dodge pickup parked in the drive.

But no people.

Stopping the car a few yards short of the Dodge, I stepped out, my face stung by the cold again. My left shoulder ached endlessly, and it hurt to fully extend my arm. But I stretched anyway to loosen the kinks in my muscles, then pocketed my hands to avoid appearing aggressive, and started toward the front porch.

Another *Private Property* sign decorated a post at the edge of the driveway, followed by a worn footpath to the base of the steps. I made it halfway up before the front door squeaked open two inches, and a voice barked for me to stop.

I complied, sensing the probable presence of a firearm on the other side of that door.

"Who are you?" an old man's growl demanded.

"Mason," I said. "Mason Sharpe. A friend of Trudy Porter's."

A pause.

"Trudy ain't got no friends."

"I'm a new friend."

Another pause. Then the door eased back to expose a grizzled old man with a graying beard and a bald head. Jeans and a plaid shirt were joined by flip-flops, and a Colt Python revolver dangled from his hand.

Four inches of cold barrel, six rounds of .357 magnum.

Bingo.

"What do you want?" he said, his voice softening. I

noticed tired, slightly bloodshot eyes, and thought I detected the hint of liquor drifting from his breath, but maybe I imagined that. He hadn't slept or showered recently, that was for sure.

"I wanted to talk about Daniel," I said. "And your boat."

He wiped his nose with the backside of his left hand, the Colt still riding in his right. "You a cop?"

"Yes, but not from Eastport. I was just visiting town. I found his body."

Sherman thought about that a moment, his gaze drifting away from me and into the trees, his face blank. Then he stepped back and tilted his head inside without a word.

I followed him in, wiping my shoes on the doormat before I crossed the threshold. Sherman may have needed a shower, but his home was immaculate. Clean wood floors led down a hallway past a parlor on the right, and a library laden with a couple thousand books on the left. I noted flowers on a table next to the door, and framed photographs of a couple adults surrounded by small children. Sherman's grandchildren, I guessed. He looked to be in his late sixties.

There was a lot of decor, also. Knickknacks and elegant decorations—the kind of thing a woman would buy, but there had only been one vehicle outside, and there was no ring on Sherman's finger.

He shut the door and stomped past, still carrying the Colt. I trailed him through a kitchen and a sliding glass door. The back porch beyond was lovely. A little cool, with the icy January wind pouring through the screens, but there was an electric heater in one corner pumping heat toward a couple rocking chairs, both facing the river. A table lay between the chairs, with an open bottle of Jack Daniel's and a single glass.

Sherman motioned to one of the chairs, then walked back inside, keeping the Colt with him. When he returned he set an additional glass on the table and poured two fingers of Jack without asking about ice, or whether I even drank.

Then he sat down with a soft grunt, laying the pistol in his lap, and looked out to the river.

Well, it might be called a river, but it was really more of an inlet. This far south of Wilmington, the waterway had already widened to over a mile in front of Sherman's house, looking more like a lake with a gentle current than a river. The pier I'd seen before was now fully exposed, and for the first time I noticed the thirty-foot fishing trawler tied off on the sheltered side of the boathouse. A tuna tower was built over the cockpit, and an American flag fluttered from the bow.

So Sherman had two boats, then. Lowe had said Daniel took a small, center console. Why would he take the small one?

"I'm Pat," Sherman said. "But folks just call me PJ, or Old Man Sherman, depending on who they are."

You mean depending on whether you answered the door with a gun the first time they met you.

I thought it, but didn't say it.

"I'm Mason," I said.

Sherman grunted and swallowed Jack. I followed suit, enjoying the burn on my throat. I've never been a big whiskey man, preferring Kentucky bourbons. But I've never been known to turn down a free drink, either.

"You said you found the body..." Sherman's voice softened.

I nodded. "Yeah. On the island."

He stared at the boat, his glass resting on one arm of the chair, the revolver lying in his lap. I decided to press ahead.

"Chief Lowe says Daniel took your boat. Trudy said he never would."

Sherman sipped. He didn't answer.

"I guess I'm just trying to put it all together," I said. "The whole thing looks a little wall-eyed to me."

Sherman turned. "What's your angle?"

"Pardon?"

"*Why are you here?*" he clarified.

I hesitated, hoping I wouldn't have to answer that question. I knew of course. I knew why I was still in town. But I wasn't sure I wanted to say.

Sherman wasn't talking, though. I could tell that much by his blank stare.

I looked out to the river. "I'm visiting town. I found the body, and the cops had questions. I'm a cop myself, like I mentioned. A homicide detective in Phoenix. Some of their procedures didn't add up to me. Then I met Trudy and...well, I guess I feel for her."

Sherman swallowed more whiskey. "What happened to your face?"

I flinched, feeling the burn on my cheek, and resisting the urge to touch it.

"Long story," I said.

He grunted, mopping whiskey off his lips with his tongue. Then he reached for the bottle and topped us both up.

"I met Daniel at the tackle shop, couple springs ago. He was buying all this crazy dumb crap and kept asking me questions. Clearly didn't know a fishhook from an earring, but he sure wanted to learn. I told him to meet me at the river, five in the morning. Didn't figure he'd show. But he did, so I took him out."

Sherman tilted his glass toward the trawler.

"Catch anything?" I asked.

Sherman's face flashed into the hint of a smile, the first real expression I'd seen since arriving.

"I did. He caught seaweed. But you know what?"

"What?" I asked.

"He didn't say a word. Just sat in the fighting chair all day, line in the water, a smile on his face. Enjoying the sun."

Sherman grunted softly. "That kid didn't know jack about angling. But he sure knew how to fish."

I've never been much of a fisherman, but I thought I knew what he meant.

"So we get back to the dock, late in the afternoon. And he shakes my hand and tells me thanks, it was the best day he'd had all year. I saw something in his eyes...I don't know. He was tired. Something was really eating at him. So I told him to see me next Saturday, same time, same place. And he was there."

Sherman swirled his drink. "We've fished three or four Saturdays a month ever since. Sometimes just off the dock. Most times never catchin' anything. But Daniel needed the time. I guess you heard about his kid?"

I nodded. "Cerebral palsy."

"Yeah. Lots of bills. Lots of stress. Daniel didn't have anybody to share that with, just bottled it all up inside. Wouldn't talk much about it. But I like to think the fishing helped. Gave him a safe place, you know?"

"What about the boat?" I asked.

Sherman rolled his eyes. "It went missing last Friday. I called it in. Never told nobody Daniel took it."

"Do you think he did?"

Sherman hesitated. "Maybe. I wouldn't think so, but I've been around long enough to know that people are capable of just about anything. He knew where the keys were, anyway. But, I will say, Daniel wasn't impulsive. If he took it he had a reason."

I sipped whiskey, weighing my next question.

"Was Daniel in trouble?"

Sherman cocked his head. "Trouble? Like with the cops?"

That's what Trudy said.

"Maybe. Or just in general. Did he cross somebody?"

Sherman thought about it, then shrugged. "I wouldn't know. He never mentioned anything, but like I said. We didn't talk a lot. Why do you ask?"

I wasn't sure if I wanted to show my cards. Something about the grizzled old salt was reassuring, though. He felt trustworthy.

"There were lacerations on his wrists," I said. "Blue and black, bruised. Older than time of death by a few hours."

Sherman raised both eyebrows. "The cops say so?"

"No. I found them myself. The cops say he hit his head and fell off the boat."

"But you told them?"

"I told them."

Sherman sucked his teeth, then shook his head. "I don't know, kid. That boat weren't but eighteen foot long, and Daniel wasn't much of a sailor. If he took it past the island... well. They call it Cape Fear for a reason. The currents out there can be treacherous. Swamp a little boat like that in a heartbeat. Life jacket or no life jacket, if he was unconscious and face down...that's all it would take."

"You know where he may have hit trouble?"

Sherman exhaled a long breath. "Couple likely spots. Places where the rip current could turn your flank to the waves. Water ain't that deep, but it's nasty. I could see it."

I looked into the amber depths of the whiskey, weighing Sherman's comments and thinking about Daniel. Thinking that the how of it all mattered a lot less than the why.

Why would a dedicated husband and father steal a boat and plough it into treacherous waters?

To commit suicide?

There were better ways. And if he were trying to take his own life, then why the life vest?

And why the lacerations?

"You military?" Sherman asked, startling me from my daze. I looked up.

"Why do you ask?"

Sherman smiled. "You don't look like a cop. Too relaxed. Too loose, even when you saw my gun. I'm guessing you've seen combat. A lot of it, maybe."

"Or maybe I just expected the gun."

He shrugged. "Maybe."

I drained the glass, deciding there was no reason to lie. "Army. Seventy-fifth regiment. Two tours."

Sherman raised his eyebrows at me. "Impressive résumé. But you're a little young to have got your twenty. Must have retired early..."

There was a question in his voice, but I didn't answer it. It wasn't something I wanted to talk about.

"I was in the Coast Guard," Sherman continued, detecting the resistance in my silence. "Twenty-eight years. Search and rescue all up and down the east coast. Finished up as Command Master Chief of Sector North Carolina."

I ducked my chin, genuinely impressed. I'd only met a few Coasties in my time, but I liked them all. They were a little crazy. A lot of fun. And very dedicated to their mission.

"Thank you for your service," I said. It was a trite saying, but it meant a little more, one service member to another.

Sherman lifted his glass. "Likewise."

We finished the drinks in silence, enjoying the beauty of the passing water, and ignoring the cold. It was easy to understand why Sherman wanted to settle down in a place like this.

It was perfect.

I shook his hand on the way out, and complimented his revolver. Sherman asked me to call him if I learned anything, and wrote his number on a scrap of paper. Then I climbed back into the Corolla and turned toward Eastport, no less confused than I'd been when I arrived, but more convinced than ever that something wasn't right.

Those feelings were only reinforced when I turned a corner and slammed on my brakes.

The two-tone Bronco I'd seen twice in Eastport sat parked in the middle of the road, blocking my path.

And two beefy guys carrying baseball bats waited near the front bumper.

13

I sat with my foot on the brake, watching the two hulks softly swinging their bats, glaring at me through the frosty glass.

I'd seen them before—both of them, the previous night at Marley's. They were the ones knocking back beers and making loud, unfunny jokes while Marley pretended to laugh.

I knew the type. Meatheads; overconfident in their muscle and under-equipped in the mental faculty department. These sorts of guys were everywhere in the world. In the Army. In the PPD. On the streets of Phoenix.

And, apparently, here in Eastport.

I could hit the gas and slide around their right side, scraping the ditch with my back tires and maybe knocking the right-hand guy to the ground. Maybe blowing out his knee with my front bumper.

But I didn't like the look in their eyes. I didn't like the idea that, for whatever reason, they thought they could just block a road and shake somebody down.

So I got out of the car, leaving it running, and pocketed my hands next to the front driver's side wheel.

"How's it going, guys?"

"You the cop?"

The left-hand guy spoke, spitting and letting the bat dangle next to his foot. The right-hand guy glared at me above a tangled black beard, a cigarette dangling from his lips, cradling the bat with one meaty hand.

"I'm a tourist," I said.

Lefty snorted. Tangle Beard fingered his bat. It was a little perverted looking, somehow.

"Look," Lefty said. "We knows who you are. And we've been asked to escort you *out* of town."

"Is that right?"

"That's right. And we can do it the easy way...or the *hard way.*"

How many times did you practice that one in front of the mirror?

I thought it, I didn't say it.

"So you're telling me Eastport is off limits?"

"Eastport. The island. The whole county. You gots to go."

"But it's a free country."

Lefty spat a long stream of brown tobacco juice. "Not here it ain't."

I grimaced. "Well, guys. That's gonna be a problem."

"You figure?"

"I do figure. But not just me. The Constitution figures. The Declaration of Independence. The entire American philosophy. You see—" I took a step forward, unpocketing my hands "—a lot of good people died to make this place free. And me, being a citizen...well, I find myself obliged to honor their memory with the defense of that freedom."

It was a lot of big words. I didn't blame them for not understanding. Lefty looked to Tangle Beard. Tangle Beard dropped the bat from his free hand and clutched the grip with both fists.

I took another step forward.

"Move the truck, guys."

Lefty's bat twitched, and his shoulders bulged. Classic big guy bristling, just bucking for a fight. A grin crept across his face, broken and rotten teeth oozing with tobacco juice.

"So it's gonna be the hard way."

You're damn right it is.

I've spent most of my life learning how to fight. From the school yard in Phoenix, to the Army Rangers at Fort Benning, to the martial arts school I used to stay in shape while working as a cop.

I know how to break bones. And, if I'm honest, I rather enjoy it.

Lefty moved first, raring back with the bat and charging me like a bull. I didn't move, hands at my sides, shoulders loose, just watching him come. He swung, and I dropped right, the bat whistling over my head and his hulking, over-weight body hurtling past as momentum took over.

His shoulders flashed by my face, and I twisted, catching the back of his neck with my left arm and propelling him forward. He lost balance and began to fall, but I was already striking with my right foot—driving it into his left knee with enough force to bust a cinderblock.

The joint shattered. I heard it like a gunshot, mixed with a blood-curdling scream. Then he was on the ground with the bat spinning across wet pavement, writhing and reaching for his leg.

I left him, wheeling to confront Tangle Beard as he hurtled toward me like a freight train. He was smarter—he swung from the right instead of from over his shoulder, making the bat impossible to miss by swerving.

I stepped right, leaning out as pain from my bullet

wounds seared in my left shoulder. The tip of the bat brushed against my stomach, only a half-inch away from being a real problem, but pretty harmless as it was. As the weapon completed its arc I grabbed it and pushed right, again using the momentum of the swing against my attacker.

Tangle Beard stumbled, momentarily losing his balance, and I drove a right hook right into his jaw. Teeth crunched and blood sprayed, but he didn't let go of the bat. He wrenched it free and staggered back, fighting for footing on the slick asphalt.

I never gave him the chance. Lowering my shoulder I rushed in like a charging linebacker, catching him just below the rib cage and driving him against the front corner of the Bronco. The wind rushed from his lungs and the bat fumbled.

He crumpled down, slipping down the front left fender. I grabbed his head on its way down with my right hand and slammed it against the body panel, hard enough to leave a dent and send his eyes rolling back in his head. The bat dropped free and I scooped it up as it fell, turning to confront Lefty as he staggered toward me. I had heard him regain his footing—the effort marked by a lot of curse-filled grunts.

Not to my surprise, he was clawing a handgun out of his pocket, as he leaned against the Corolla with his eyes bulging in pain.

I walked casually toward him, the bat swinging freely from one hand. He drew a revolver, and I batted it to the ground with a quick flick, busting his knuckles along the way. He staggered back. I shoved him with the tip of the bat, knocking him to the ground. He hit and tried to scramble backward. I snapped the bat against his shattered knee, fast and hard enough to further obliterate the joint.

Lefty writhed on the ground, actual tears spilling down his face as I pushed the tip of the bat beneath his chin.

"Who sent you?" I asked.

He sobbed. I nudged his knee with one shoe.

"We can do this the easy way or the hard way," I said with a little grin.

He looked at me through blurry eyes, his face cherry red.

"Who sent you?" I repeated.

"I dunno, man..." he spluttered. "We just got a call. Some guy says he'll give us a hundred bucks each to run you out of town."

"That right?"

"Yeah."

I stopped, thinking for a moment. Trying to decide if I wanted to believe him. I nudged his knee again and he screamed.

"I swear! It's the truth."

I rested the bat on my shoulder and watched him writhe for a while. I couldn't deny finding satisfaction in his pain— another bully, confronted by swift and absolute justice.

I tilted my head toward the Bronco.

"Can you drive?"

He nodded quickly. "Yeah!"

"Okay then. Take your buddy and get out of here. And think twice before you harass somebody again. You hear me?"

He spat blood from his mouth, probably from where his face had collided with the asphalt. I slung the bat into the woods, then knelt to retrieve the handgun. It was a Rock Island Armory M206—a cheap Filipino piece available brand new for a couple hundred bucks, and used for a lot less. Not a bad gun, really. It would kill as well as anything.

I felt the weight in my hand, and my mind flashed back to the beach. The moment the Smith spat fire next to my face.

Lowe still had my gun, but the Rock Island would do. I thought about slipping it into my pocket...returning to the coast. My heart began to pound as I fingered the parkerized cylinder. I imagined Mia again, on the other side of that impenetrable glass wall.

Then I thought about Trudy. I saw the pain in her eyes. The agony she felt, not knowing what had happened to Daniel.

I knew how Mia died. I couldn't change it, but at least those responsible had been brought to justice.

Didn't Trudy deserve as much?

I rolled the Rock Island in my hand. Almost pocketed it. Instead I dumped the bullets, then dropped the gun on the asphalt with the cylinder open and stomped down with one foot. The crane bent, rocking the cylinder out of alignment like a crooked tooth and effectively destroying the weapon for any future use. I scooped it back up and flung it into the forest.

My own problems could wait—at least long enough to find whoever killed Daniel Porter. By then I'd have my Smith back, and in the meantime I didn't want to be caught with what was likely a stolen gun.

Stepping over Lefty, I returned to the Corolla. He scrambled to the side as I circled Tangle Beard, and then I sped away, leaving them in a wrecked heap next to a dented Bronco.

14

I found my way back to Eastport and parked the Corolla at the end of the main drag, in a little parking lot facing directly into the mouth of the Cape Fear River.

It was as gray and cold as ever, and my shoulder and back ached as I left the car. My encounter with the two thugs on the road had been relatively brief, and entirely one-sided. But I was still a long way from one hundred percent after being shot three times, and each breath sent waves of pain through my left shoulder.

A boardwalk lay in front of the parking lot, running along the face of the river with park benches lining it, and a long pier shooting out over the water. Ornate lampposts glowed in the midday haze, and more gulls swooped over the water and landed on the benches to squawk at one another.

It was a nice spot. Very calm. If I squinted over the water I could see the faint outline of Saint Ellen Island on the horizon, but the funny old lighthouse was dark. Maybe out of service entirely.

It wasn't hard to understand why Mia loved this place. It was peaceful. Quaint, in a very natural way.

In the summer it was probably paradise.

My stomach twisted and I turned away from the water, starting into town instead. Shooting off the main drag were a number of orderly little streets, each lined with brick buildings that probably dated back to the founding of the town, maybe two hundred years ago. At the time, they must have been blacksmith shops, mercantiles, and warehouses. Now those buildings were occupied by cutesy shops, banks, boutiques, a couple restaurants, and a number of jewelry stores.

The shops and boutiques were closed for the off-season, and the banks were closed because it was Sunday. But the jewelry stores all had their lights on, with *Open, Please Come In!* signs proudly displayed in their front windows.

I walked past a few, noting displays of fine diamonds, pearls, and expensive watches encased behind glass. Hawkish store clerks watched me as I passed, their dark eyes a little cold and not at all reflecting the hospitality of their welcome signs.

I noticed the woman I had seen at Marley's shopping in one of them. She talked quietly to the clerk and admired a watch, maybe as a gift for a husband or boyfriend. There was a guy there also, dressed in a heavy overcoat and carrying a duffel bag. He appeared out of the back of the store, made a comment to the clerk, then bustled outside to climb into the driver seat of a waiting Cadillac Escalade.

The big motor roared, and he drove around the street to a similar shop, and went inside.

An owner, I figured. Some kind of multi-property businessman. Which meant that, other than the woman from Marley's, I appeared to be the only outsider in town. It seemed strange at first, with so many local shops and businesses set up to cater to tourists, but spring break wouldn't start for another six weeks. This time of year, they were probably used to being slow.

I paused at the end of the street and looked both ways. Eastport was dead quiet, with only a couple cars parked in front of a few cafes, and some kind of municipal building. I could see the police station, several blocks away and barely visible over a hump in the road. The Escalade purred on the street nearby, staying warm while the business guy was inside, but otherwise only the dull whisper of icy wind broke the stillness.

The businessman returned to the SUV, depositing his duffel, then the motor grumbled and he drove away down a side street, into the heart of town. Maybe going home.

It was too cold to be out. I was chilled to the bone, and now that I thought about it, I was hungry also. I'd only eaten half my pancakes at breakfast, and breaking bones makes me hungry. I returned to the Corolla and steered it toward Marley's, parking out front, where I noted the absence of any two-tone Ford Bronco before stepping into the quiet warmth of the old structure.

Marley was the only one inside. I sat down at the bar and looked up to the chalked menu, noting that yesterday's selections had completely changed. Now there was a rib eye on offer, with fries and green beans.

"Hungry?" Marley asked, catching me eyeballing the menu.

"Yeah. How about that steak?"

"My cook's not in, yet. I can grill it myself, but it'll take a minute."

"No rush."

She took her time fixing the meal, and I didn't complain. When the plate hit the counter, I was already three beers in and feeling a little buzzed. The alcohol helped to ease the pain in my shoulder, and numb the ache in the back of my mind.

It helped me not to think of Mia.

I focused instead on the steak, which was incredible—both juicy and tender. I sawed through it like it was my last meal, leaving the green beans and fries as a sort of dessert.

Marley placed another beer next to my plate.

"How long you in town for?" she asked.

I paused over the steak, pondering the question. It hadn't really entered my mind. Not much of anything had, except whatever was laid right in front of me.

I wanted to find Daniel's killer, on Trudy's behalf. But I didn't know how long that would take.

"I don't know. Got the room for another night?"

Marley laughed. "You can have it all month. This is the dead season."

I wiped my mouth on a napkin. "Yeah, about that. I noticed a lot of shops around here. Seems like a retail-heavy town."

She shrugged. "Eastport is a tourist place. In the spring and summer we're packed. Yankees and Midwesterners, mostly. Some west coasters, like yourself."

"You don't sound like any of the above."

"Nah. I was born here. Probably die here, I reckon. Could be worse. Tourist business can be profitable."

"Tourists buy a lot of high-end jewelry?"

She frowned. "What do you mean?"

"There's like five or six jewelry shops down by the water. They're open, too."

"Oh, you mean the development thing."

"Development thing?"

"Yeah, the investment firm."

"I don't follow."

Marley slouched against the bar. "Couple years back,

some equity firm out of New York or Boston or some such place came down here. They had all these ideas about turning Eastport into another Panama City. Big tourism, lots of shops, that kind of thing."

"An equity firm?" I asked, barely disguising my suspicion.

"I think so. I really don't remember what they called it. Bunch of millionaires looking for a place to park their money, I guess. They wanted to invest in the town and open those jewelry shops. Even offered the locals grants to fix up their properties. I got a new roof."

Marley jabbed her thumb toward the ceiling, and I thought about the cedar shingles outside. Not cheap.

"So they just opened some shops and...nothing?"

She shrugged. "I guess it never took off for them. The stores are still there, but we're a long ways from becoming the next Panama City. Thank God."

She chuckled and I looked at my plate, lost in thought. The story was almost believable. But something felt out of place.

"What happened to your hand?" Marley asked.

I glanced down at my right knuckles. They were battered and red, from knocking Tangle Beard out. I hadn't even thought of them in context of the pain in my left shoulder, but the knuckles were a lot more visible.

"Hit a wall," I said.

"Uh-huh." Marley wasn't convinced, but I wasn't interested in discussing it. The last thing I wanted was another conversation with Chief Lowe. She disappeared into the kitchen to clean up the dishes, and I sipped on my beer, staring at the display case of her Marine memorabilia on the wall, and thinking about Daniel Porter.

The red flags I'd noted after finding his body left plenty of questions. Talking to Trudy and to Sherman added to my suspicions.

But being confronted by the two thugs on my way back to Eastport sealed the deal for me. Whatever had happened to Daniel, somebody didn't want me poking around. Somebody had rushed his autopsy, quick to label the death an accident. Whether that was one of the Eastport cops, Chief Lowe himself, or a third party, I didn't know.

But Lefty hadn't been lying, back on the road. Somebody had offered him a hundred bucks to run me off, and that irritated me. Because I meant what I told him—a lot of good men and woman have died to protect freedom, and it wasn't his right to infringe on that.

But it also irritated me because of Trudy. The pain in her eyes. The extreme loss she felt, that so clearly mirrored my own.

Somebody had taken Daniel from her, and I had no place to be and nothing better to do than uncover the truth.

"Mind if I use your phone?"

"It's on the counter!" Marley called from the kitchen. I left my stool to retrieve it, then dug Sherman's number out and punched it in. The old Coastie answered almost immediately.

"Who is it?"

I wanted to smile at his abruptness, but I was too focused.

"Mason. You free tonight?"

"Why?"

"I was thinking we could ride down the river a ways. You could show me that spot where you think Daniel may have hit trouble."

"Why?" He repeated the question, but the tone changed, dropping a notch. Pushing for the real truth.

"Couple locals tried to rough me up after leaving your place. Seems they're eager to silence any questions. I guess you could say I have a problem with that."

A long pause. "I guess you could say I do too."

"Great. So your place, around ten?"

"See you then."

I moved to hang up.

"Hey, Mason?"

"Yeah?"

"Bring Jack."

This time I did smile. "You got it."

15

I drove the Corolla into the shopping district outside of town to pick up some basic essentials—a change of clothes, ointment for my face, a toothbrush, and Sherman's whiskey. Then I returned to Marley's and showered again, cleaning my cheek and applying the ointment.

The left side of my face was now swollen to the point of being impossible to ignore. A little soap helped to wash the burned gunpowder away, but anybody who knew anything about guns would probably still be able to guess.

I stood in front of the mirror staring at myself, and suddenly felt deeply ashamed. Like a quitter. A failure. Over the years I'd seen plenty of fellow soldiers and even a couple cops take the easy way out. In our business it was inevitable. PTSD, survivor's guilt, and the simple grit of the daily grind was more than some could take.

But not me. I'd never been that guy. I'd always reached a little deeper, and found something to keep me moving.

Over the last eighteen months, that thing had been Mia.

And now...

I left the bathroom and cracked Sherman's whiskey open,

knocking back two or three shots before stretching out onto the bed with Mia's Bible resting next to me. It was quiet in the room, with only the dull patter of fresh rain against the glass.

I laid my head against the pillow, closed my eyes, and saw her again. Not as she lay dying in a pool of blood, but as I remembered her from before. In the park. Or in the city.

Alive. Vibrant.

The only woman I had ever loved.

I MET Sherman at his dock, exactly at ten PM. The clouds overhead were finally beginning to clear, exposing large swaths of black sky speckled by stars, so I was surprised to find the old Coastie decked out in rubber boots and a full rain suit.

He only grinned when he saw me, the thick stub of a cigar protruding from one side of his mouth, and nodded me toward the back. The grin was friendly, but he appeared more privately amused than enthusiastic. I handed him the bottle of Jack and found my way to a seat near the stern, settling in and crossing my arms to stay warm. Sherman poured himself a plastic cup of whiskey, then fired the big diesels and backed us away from the dock. He spun the thirty-foot boat like it was a jet ski, snapping the bow around in the gentle current before pointing us down river, the cigar clamped in his teeth the whole time.

An old salt. No doubt about it. A man who knew boats better than he knew cars. I liked that.

For half an hour we churned south at about ten knots, leaving a muddied wake, but keeping most of the big engines' power in reserve. I watched the North Carolina coast drag by, marked on occasion by yellow specks of light against the black sky, and tried not to think about Mia.

I wanted to remember her. I wanted to lose myself in the image of her smile and imagine her head resting against my chest. But right now I just couldn't take the pain.

It was easier to think about Daniel, and who had killed him. Because I was about ninety percent sure his death hadn't been an accident.

As downtown Eastport passed our starboard side, Sherman waved me to the cockpit, and I climbed two steps to stand beside him. He held out an empty cup and I refreshed him, then he pointed to a spot dead ahead, deep in the black horizon.

"If Danny hit trouble, he went that way," Sherman called over the growl of the engines. "Hang on to somethin'. We're gonna haul!"

I grabbed one leg of the tuna tower and braced myself as Sherman advanced both engines to full throttle. The bow of the trawler lifted skyward and the air filled with a mechanical roar. Then we were off, plowing through the waves like a rocket.

It didn't take me long to understand why Sherman wore the rain suit, or why he had grinned at me as I came aboard in jeans and a cotton jacket. Salt spray exploded over the bow like a hurricane, washing over the puny windshield and saturating my clothes. The thunder of the engines was so loud I couldn't hear myself think, and I had to swab my face just to keep my eyes open. With every bound of the trawler through a rolling wave, a fresh shower drenched us both, leaving me colder than I'd felt since a winter deployment in Germany, four years ago.

It was brutal. Mind numbing. Endless.

But I didn't mind. I ignored the numbness and focused on the rush of it all, enjoying the speed and the noise. The roar of the wind and endless pound of the motors reminded me a little of riding a Black Hawk into combat. Not as fast, and not as smooth. But just as visceral.

Sherman guided us around the western shore of Saint Ellen Island, then turned out to sea and drove straight into the oncoming waves. Maybe the waters were rougher that night, due to the recent storms, but it didn't take me long to understand how quickly a small boat could be swamped. The trawler handled the stress well, cutting through the breakers and smacking the resulting troughs like an axe. But in a smaller boat—a completely open boat, only eighteen foot long—it wouldn't take much of a misstep for the bow to swing wide, and the next wave to take the craft broadside.

At which point, it would be over for the pilot. Even with a life vest, you might hit your head. You might black out, or temporarily become trapped beneath your craft, whereupon you would drown.

But you wouldn't develop blue and black lacerations around your wrists. That part I still couldn't swallow.

After ten minutes of full throttle, Sherman eased the trawler back to a slow cruise, and the waves rocked us instead of washing over the bow. Over my left shoulder I could see sporadic lights across the east face of Saint Ellen Island, but directly ahead and to my right nothing but endless miles of the Atlantic filled my view.

"There's a spotlight under the seat," Sherman shouted, pointing to a bench on the other side of the cockpit. "Oh, and a rain suit. If you want it."

I shot him a glare. "*Now* you tell me?"

He laughed, a deep, rolling sound melded with cigar smoke. I moved to the bench, pulling the seat back to expose the spotlight—a giant, hand-held unit equipped with an independent battery pack and a cable. The rain suit was there, also, but I didn't bother with it. It looked too small, and I was soaked anyway. Might as well just deal with it.

Sherman backed off on the throttle and motioned me to the tuna tower. We both swung up the aluminum frame, climbing to ten feet off the deck where Sherman resumed control of the trawler with the overhead controls, then pointed off the port bow.

"There's a reef over there. Breaks the surface sometimes, during low tide. Let's give it a look."

I flipped the light on, and he steered the trawler with practiced ease. From the top of the tuna tower I was amazed how easily I could see into the water. It was murky with disturbed silt from the storms, but the spotlight penetrated two or three feet beneath the surface, illuminating the shadowy silhouettes of big fish on occasion.

Sherman guided us around the reef, then churned back and forth across the mouth of the bay in zigzag patterns, like a drunk cutting grass. I used the light to scan the water, following Sherman's direction, and we searched for a solid two hours.

We found nothing. More fish, a lot of plastic bottles, and what may have been a sea turtle. But no eighteen-foot, center console boat, busted and submerged just beneath the surface. The fish finder on the dash reported the water at only twelve feet deep, and Sherman said the missing boat was equipped with a little roof, rising about eight feet off the deck, which meant ten or eleven feet off the keel.

In only twelve feet of water, I would have expected to see it, but there was nothing. No debris. No wreckage.

Just empty water.

As midnight slipped by and we neared one AM, Sherman steered the trawler away from the rough waters of the inlet and into a calmer patch a couple miles off the coast. Then he motioned me to cut the light, and led me out of the tuna tower and back to the deck.

"It was a long shot," I said.

Sherman only grunted and retrieved an additional cup from the cockpit, cutting the engines before taking a seat near the stern. He poured us both a drink, and I accepted with a nod, sitting across from him.

"Cigar?" he asked, holding up a box.

"Sure. Thanks."

I lit up and puffed, recognizing the deep and oily texture of a Maduro. I couldn't read the label, but I'm not much of a cigar aficionado anyway. I just know what a good stick tastes like, and this was a great one.

For a long while we sat quietly, knocking back doubles of Jack and enjoying the cigars. Smoke clouded around my head, but if I leaned back I could make out a million pinholes of light breaking from the heavens, far above.

The clouds were almost gone now, and the waves were just strong enough to give the big boat a gentle rock.

It was perfect, and I kept my mouth shut, remembering what Sherman had said about not ruining the moment. The longer I sat there, puffing on the cigar and admiring the galaxy, the better I understood.

It wasn't a moment to ruin with pointless conversation.

"He was a good kid," Sherman said at last. I detected a slight hitch in his voice, and squinted at him through the smoke. Maybe it was just the Jack—he'd had a few at this point.

Sherman looked out at the water, the drink resting on his knee, his cigar now cold in one hand. I remembered the picture frames at the house, and the ring on his finger, contrasting with his lonely eyes.

We might have more in common than I first thought.

"You gonna find who done it?" he asked.

I assumed he was referring to Daniel. I sucked on the cigar, considering the question.

"I'm gonna try," I said.

"And then?"

"And then?"

I didn't answer. Didn't know how to answer. This wasn't my fight, technically. Not my circus, and not my monkeys.

But I thought again of the haunting loss in Trudy's eyes—and, I realized, I was angry. Not just because Mia died, but because her killer died too.

Quickly.

Before I had the chance to throttle him slowly, the way he deserved.

Maybe I was feeling noble, thinking about Trudy. Or maybe Daniel's killer was just my surrogate victim. It didn't matter.

"I'm going to deal with them," I said, simply.

Sherman relit his cigar and puffed for a while. Then he lowered it, and spoke softly without making eye contact.

"Let me know when you do."

I felt a deeper burn in my gut than alcohol alone could bring—strong enough to make me forget my wet clothes and chilled skin. It was anger. And loss.

And bloodthirst, maybe. All at once.

I looked out to sea, smoke clouding around my mouth. Then I saw the boat.

It was smaller than the trawler, but not by a lot. Maybe twenty-five foot, without a tuna tower, and old. Dull lights in the cockpit marked it, two or three hundred yards away, and it churned out to sea directly across our stern.

Sherman saw it too, and he squinted.

"You know it?" I asked.

He shook his head. "No..."

We both watched as the boat plowed on another half-mile, vague figures moving across the deck. Then Sherman reached beneath his seat and passed me a pair of binoculars.

"My eyes are 'bout worthless when I'm sober."

And you're a long way from sober.

I took the binoculars and leaned toward the stern, focusing on the craft. They hadn't seen us. That much was obvious. Framed against the black sky, without a light on board, Sherman's trawler would be almost invisible.

There were three men on board. All overweight and moving like cows—slowly, and with a lot of production. I couldn't make out faces, but the third guy appeared familiar. It was his frame—the way he carried himself.

When he turned toward me, and I detected the outline of a large beard, my suspicions were confirmed. It was Tangle Beard. Apparently, he had recovered from being knocked unconscious against the side of a two-tone Bronco, and was back on his feet.

Remarkable.

The guy in the cockpit seemed to be in charge. He pointed toward the water as he killed the engine, then Tangle Beard and his associate moved around in the stern, bent over, and lifted something.

I stopped breathing as the object cleared the side and fell toward the water. It was a bag—oblong, and black, about six feet in length.

A body bag.

16

"**B**ody!" I hissed.

Sherman sat upright, but I held up a hand. The bag hadn't been rigid, and it hadn't been moving. Whoever was inside had already been killed.

No point in blowing our cover.

The driver fired the engines again, then turned the boat and churned back toward shore. I held my gaze on the spot where the bag went overboard, and as soon as the second boat had distanced itself by a few hundred yards, I motioned for Sherman to start our engines.

"Slow," I urged him, almost silently.

Sherman staggered a little as he resumed position in the cockpit, and I thought about the Jack. Bringing whiskey for my designated driver hadn't been one of my smarter moves, but I also figured this wasn't Sherman's first rodeo.

He wound the trawler around, keeping the lights off, and I maintained my visual of the spot as he churned for it.

In open waters, it was really anybody's guess where the bag had fallen. Finding it would be a shot in the dark. But it was a shot worth taking.

Once we were near the spot, I left the stern and joined Sherman in the cockpit. The fish finder marked the depth at fourteen feet, with no fish in sight.

"Think it'll pick up a body?"

Sherman shrugged. "Never been looking for one."

We churned back and forth across the general vicinity of where Tangle Beard and his buddy had dropped the bag, using the fish finder to scan the murky depths. I knew almost nothing about fishing, but I knew something about sonar, and that's all a fish finder is, really. Cheap sonar.

On the eighth pass, we got a hit.

"Tuna," Sherman said, with a dry grin.

The screen did indeed display a tuna reading, but the fish wasn't moving. It lay just off our starboard side, thirteen feet down. Resting on the bottom.

"That's it," I said, moving to the stern.

Sherman killed the motor and dug through a hatch, producing a recovery hook on a rope. I waved him off and peeled my jacket over my head.

"I'm going in," I said.

"It's freezing!"

"I'm wet anyway. Thanks to you."

Sherman snorted and slammed the hatch. I stripped down to my boxers and advanced to the swim platform at the back of the boat. The ocean beneath was gray, murky with silt, and invisible beyond six or eight inches down.

Not your average swimming pool. But I grabbed the swim ladder and eased in anyway.

The water was frigid, driving the air from my lungs like I'd been punched in the chest by a giant. I resurfaced and gasped, my muscles spasming in objection. But I didn't clamber back aboard the trawler.

"Here!" Sherman said. "It's waterproof."

He tossed me a plastic flashlight, and I caught it just

above the surface. Then I drew in the biggest lungful of night air I could and dove, switching the light on and kicking hard for the bottom.

Even with the light, I couldn't see beyond eighteen inches. I reached the bottom and panned around with both arms, finding a couple rocks and watching a crab scuttle off before I needed air.

Breaking the surface for only long enough to suck down a fresh lungful, I repeated the procedure five times, working my way up and down the side of the trawler in search of our elusive tuna.

I found it on the sixth attempt, stretched out across the mucky sand and rippling in the current. It wasn't a body bag —it was more of a body net, made of fine black mesh with a zipper running down the middle. I returned for air, gasping it down and calling to Sherman that I had found it. Then I was down again.

Finding the zipper took longer than it should have, due to the tangle of the mesh tugged by the current. I held the flash-light in my teeth, holding my throat closed and kicking to keep from floating to the surface.

The mesh closed around my fingers and I probed down, searching for recognizable appendages.

I felt nothing.

At last I found the zipper and yanked it down, exposing the inside of the bag. My lungs burned, begging for air, but I didn't kick for the surface. Grabbing the bag with my left hand I pulled myself down, gritted my teeth around the light and reached inside.

What I felt wasn't a body. It wasn't flesh at all. It was a mess of soft particles and hard edges—a giant pile of some-thing both loose and tangled.

I grabbed a fistful of whatever it was and struck out for the surface, my head thundering. I gasped as I broke through, spitting the flashlight out and barely catching it as it slipped under.

Sherman hauled me aboard with large and powerful hands. I landed with a thud, and he patted me on the back, helping to expel gunky seawater.

"No body," I coughed, dropping the stuff onto the deck.

"What's that?"

I panned the flashlight over the mess. What I saw was so out of place that it took us both a few seconds to even realize what it was.

The soft stuff I had felt were paper shreds—like the kind you dump out of an office shredder. The hard stuff were plastic shreds, the same size and general shape, all mixed in with the sodden paper.

I spluttered more water and rolled onto my knees, sifting through the mess and spreading the plastic shreds across the deck.

I recognized the markings of credit cards, but the seawater flooding through the mesh bag had already saturated the paper enough to blur any printed text.

I sat back, shivering in the cold, my lungs still burning.

"You kidding me?" I muttered.

Sherman squatted next to the pile, running a hand over his bald head. He grunted.

"People dump trash out here all the time. Been doing it since trash was invented."

"In a body bag?"

"In any kind of bag. Or in no bag."

I muttered a curse and reached for my clothes. They were still damp, but at least they helped with the wind.

I glanced over my shoulder to see Sherman eyeballing the fresh scars on my back, but he didn't say anything. He just relit his cigar for the second time and offered me a rough blanket before returning to the cockpit.

"Let's call it a night. We're way past this old codger's bedtime."

Sherman drove the boat back to his dock, and I helped him tie it off and clean up. Then he bid me goodnight, reminding me again to call him if I learned anything. I promised I would, and returned to the Corolla.

The flood of heat pouring out of the car's vents felt like the breath of Heaven, slowly loosening my tight and throbbing muscles. I fantasized about a hot shower back at the hotel, and drove a lot faster than I had since leaving Arizona on my way back to Marley's.

The pub was dark, and the front door locked. I moved to the exterior stairs built along one end of the building and took them to the second floor, where a rickety door opened into the hallway of the little hotel. I shivered as I found my way to the third door on the left, fishing in my pocket for Marley's brass key.

Then I stopped, my gaze falling on the lock. Fresh scratches gleamed against the brass of the knob, near the keyhole, and as I placed my fingers on the latch it gave without any resistance.

I had locked the room when I left. I knew I had. And now, as I leaned close to the door, I thought I heard a scuffling inside.

I retreated around the corner to the interior stairs leading down into the pub. Held back in the shadows, I couldn't see my door. But I could hear—clearly. And, as I pressed one cheek against the wall and waited, I was rewarded with footsteps, followed by the soft creak of hinges.

It wasn't Marley. It couldn't be. She wouldn't have used picks—she had a key. But it was a woman, or a very soft-stepping man. I could tell that long before I leaned around the corner, stealing a glance into the hallway.

It was a woman, all right. It was *the* woman. The one I had seen downstairs from before—the tourist in the cheap rental car. She walked away from me, stooped low and obviously attempting to sneak, but instead of proceeding onto the exterior stairs she turned left, and entered another guest room.

The door closed and all was silent. I squinted, then stepped across the hallway and tried my door. It was locked again. She must have flipped the thumb latch as she left.

I withdrew Marley's brass key and let myself in, stepping cautiously over the threshold.

A pool of dim light spilled over the hardwood as I hit the switch. The bed lay just as I had left it—unmade, with yesterday's clothes strewn across the floor and the Walmart bags from my shopping trip wadded up in the corner.

I locked the door and conducted a slow search of the entire room, checking the drawers, bathroom, my personal items, and beneath the bed.

I found nothing. No hint that anyone had been there, save for the scratches on the knob outside. Everything was just as I'd left it.

Proceeding to the window, I opened the blinds and looked out over the parking lot.

The rental car sat right where I'd last seen it—on the extreme left side of the lot, facing the building. It was muddy, but I could make out the Virginia license plate bolted to the bumper.

I memorized the number, chewing my lip and thinking again about the woman. What I remembered of her.

Then I shut the blinds and peeled out of my clothes. I'd take that hot shower I was dreaming about, then cut the lights and lie across the bed.

With some luck, I might even sleep.

17

I didn't sleep. Not well, anyway. Every time I faded into black I saw Mia again—vibrant and beautiful, like the first night I met her. Dressed in that little black cocktail dress, laughing and drinking Manhattans on the dance floor.

And then I saw the school. I saw shells on the floor, and heard people screaming. I saw Mia pinned against the wall, pleading for her life.

Begging me to save her, only moments before the shotgun thundered.

I woke up then, sweating and gasping for air, my shoulder alive with pain. Twice, I took showers and returned to bed, trying to sleep.

Both times the dream repeated.

By five AM I gave up trying, even though I was still exhausted. A fourth shower, followed by morning news on the TV ate up another hour, and at six I dressed in the driest clothes I had and left the room.

The pub was closed, so I pocketed my hands and walked to the diner, leaving the Corolla at Marley's. Eastport was as quiet on a Monday morning as it had been the previous

Sunday, and just as gray. But I was growing accustomed to the stillness, and even coming to enjoy it. Despite the dead body on the beach and the attempted beatdown outside of Sherman's place, I didn't miss the bustling chaos of a big city.

It was nice to be someplace without the traffic and noise, at least for a while.

When I reached the diner I saw the rental car. It sat in the back of the lot, almost invisible beyond a row of pickets. But I recognized the Virginia license plates, and quickly located the woman inside.

She sat in the back, by herself at a booth, her face buried behind a menu. I plowed right toward her, weaving between the tables and sliding onto the bench across from her without waiting for an invitation.

She lowered the menu, looking up with a lot of surprise but not much alarm.

Interesting.

"Uhm. Can I help you?" she asked.

It was an east coast accent. Maybe Jersey, or Philly. Someplace like that.

"Just need some breakfast. Had the pancakes yesterday. I recommend them."

I laid both hands on the table, relaxed and unthreatening, but didn't break eye contact. She hesitated, either unsure or simply undecided about how to react.

"Do I know you?" she said, at last.

"You ought to. You had a good look at my hotel room last night."

A flash of surprise and maybe discomfort passed across her face. She hesitated again.

"I don't know what you're talking about."

"Sure you do," I said. "Last night, about two AM. I saw you leave."

Her tongue darted across her lips, but before she could answer the waitress appeared.

"What are you drinking, sir?"

"Coffee," I said, still not breaking eye contact with the woman. "Two creams, one sugar. Pancakes with butter, bacon, and two eggs over medium."

"Sure thing. And you, honey?"

The woman made a show of looking at her menu. "I'll have the French toast. Eggs scrambled. Water to drink."

"You got it."

The waitress shuffled off, and I kept staring.

"I guess I wandered into the wrong room," she said. "Late night. Too many drinks."

I nodded, considering whether I should mention the lock picks. I decided to hold that card, for now.

"I'm Mason," I said, keeping my tone casual.

"Cassandra," she said, offering her hand. I shook it gently, then leaned back into my booth.

"What brings you to Eastport?" I asked.

"I drove down from Philadelphia. I'm a photographer. I wanted to shoot some coastal sunrises."

"Rough weather for that," I said.

She forced a laugh. "No kidding."

The waitress returned with my coffee. Cassandra sipped water while I stirred in my sugar, and for a while we didn't speak.

"What about you?" she said.

I shrugged. "Just passing through."

"You're traveling?"

"Something like that."

"Not much luggage..."

I cocked my head, and she blushed.

"Well. I mean, I did bumble into your room."

"I pack light," I said. "Speaking of which. Where's your camera? I've never seen a photographer without a camera."

"Oh, I left it in the room. Too ugly to shoot today."

I grunted, glancing out the window as though I agreed. I didn't doubt this wasn't ideal photography weather. But the forecast I'd seen on the morning news called for rain on and off for the next three days. If she wasn't interested in photographing the rain, why was she still here?

And why was she in my room?

The food came, and we ate mostly in silence. I asked a few more probing questions, but Cassandra gave me nothing more than she already had. I learned more from her questions, and her general behavior. I found it odd that she so quickly relaxed to the intrusion of a complete stranger at her table. Maybe she was simply too polite to ask me to leave, but she hadn't impressed me as much of an extrovert at the pub. I remembered her sitting in the back, alone, keeping to herself every time I saw her.

And never with a camera, either.

It was odd, but for the moment I wasn't going to pry any further. If Cassandra's presence in Eastport had anything to do with Daniel's murder, I'd find out soon enough. For now, I didn't want to spook her.

I paid for us both and wished her luck, then walked back to Marley's, still thinking about Daniel. Thinking about the mesh bag from under the frigid ocean, and the chopped up credit cards.

Who dumps credit cards out at sea?

Tangle Beard's involvement linked the incident to my encounter with the Bronco, and whoever deployed the Bronco wanted me out of town because I was poking into Daniel's death.

So, in my mind, that linked the dumped garbage to Daniel, although in what way I couldn't imagine. But it kept the investigator side of my mind spinning, twisting and evaluating it like a puzzle.

A puzzle I wasn't ready to abandon.

Back at the Corolla, I sat with the heat on for a while, drumming my fingers against the wheel, and thinking. Then I called up the built in GPS and input *Wilmington* into the destination menu.

I needed fresh, clean clothes. Better than I could find in Eastport. But, more importantly, I remembered Trudy saying Daniel worked for the Social Security Office in Wilmington.

Whatever got him killed, it wasn't a prominent enough issue for either his wife or his fishing buddy to know anything about. But maybe his coworkers did.

Another long shot. But a shot worth taking.

18

Wilmington was a forty-five-minute drive north of Eastport, but I took my time on the wet roads and stretched it into an hour. The city was built right on the Cape Fear River—a shipping and industrial town, I gathered, and an old one, too. I knew that by the plethora of original Victorian homes I passed on my way through downtown. The houses were multicolored and gorgeous, built with elaborate scrollwork around fancy porches, and set just off quiet streets.

The core of the city itself was quiet, even on a Monday morning. Tall towers graced the subdued skyline, but everything felt peaceful. Almost sleepy, in a classic southern way.

I liked it.

In the shopping district I stopped at a department store to gather a new pair of jeans, a few sweaters, socks, and underwear. Then I searched for the social security office on the GPS, and navigated to Daniel Porter's place of work.

The office sat by itself on the southeast side of town, surrounded by tall trees and wide roads. Cars drove slowly, and more than a few complete strangers waved to me as I passed. I waved back, then pulled into the parking lot and stopped to consider my speech.

Who was I, anyway? Just some guy, stopping by to inquire about a dead man? No, I'd need to do better than that. In my experience, very few people lawyered up at the first sight of a stranger asking questions. Given a plausible reason, most were only too happy to engage in useful conversation, if only to break the monotony of their day. Especially people who worked boring desk jobs. But I'd still need that plausible reason.

I left the Corolla in the back of the lot and approached the front door casually. A security guard asked me if I was carrying any weapons, then waved me forward with a sleepy flick of his hand.

Inside the air smelled stale, and everybody looked as though they were hungover. Faded paint adorned scuffed walls, and the glass partitions between cubical offices were smeared with an over-application of cheap cleaning products. The carpet was worn. The ceiling consisted of suspended tiles and fluorescent lights that flickered, just a little.

A typical government building, in my experience. I'd worked in such places for years, and I knew how to handle the people who ran the desks.

Approaching reception, I focused on keeping my posture relaxed while maintaining a vague air of authority. Like I knew what I was doing here, and wasn't interested in wasting anybody's time.

"Can I help you?"

"Yes. I'm Detective Sharpe. I was hoping to speak to Daniel Porter's supervisor, please."

I didn't flash a badge, gambling that nobody would ask for one. The gamble paid off, at least with the receptionist. She glanced momentarily at my jeans and button-down shirt, probably expecting a uniform, but the pain that crossed her eyes at the mention of Daniel's name overcame her suspicion.

Word had reached the office of Daniel's death, then. People were shocked, and maybe grieving.

I hated to admit it, but that was helpful.

The receptionist lifted a phone and made a quick call, then offered me water. I declined and shuffled to one side, standing for barely a minute before a short man in a very cheap business suit stepped around the corner and offered his hand.

"Detective? I'm Gerry Polland. I manage this office."

I took his hand with a firm shake, noting his suspicious survey of my clothes. Gerry looked tired, and bored, but something about his stiff shoulders and formal handshake told me he wouldn't be like the receptionist. He'd ask for ID.

"Let's step into my office," Gerry said.

I followed him down a hall to a glass-enclosed room in one corner, heaped with paperwork and the usual desktop knickknacks. He shut the door and invited me to take a seat, unbuttoning his jacket and finding his way into a squeaking desk chair.

"Do you mind if I see some ID?" he asked.

I settled into the chair, taking my time and smoothing the surface of my jeans.

"I'm not with the Eastport PD," I said. "I'm sorry, I should have clarified. I'm a detective with the Phoenix Police Department."

He squinted. "Arizona?"

"That's right. I was in town when Daniel passed away."

He nodded slowly. Then cocked his head. "So you're not investigating the case?"

I scratched my cheek. "Not officially."

"Oh. Well, I'm not sure how I can help you."

I opened my mouth as if to speak, then stopped. Catching

myself, and taking my time. I hated to be manipulative, but long experience had taught me that dealing with a guy like Gerry required finesse. He was too smart to be lied to, and maybe a little too self-important to be bossed around. He needed to be won over.

"I'm a friend of the family," I said softly.

"Oh..." Gerry nodded a couple times. "I'm so sorry for your loss."

"We all are." I let the sentence hang, and deliberately looked away.

Gerry cleared his throat.

"Look," I sat forward, "I know this is irregular. Off the record, the guys in Eastport think Daniel died in a boating accident. But..."

"But?" Gerry's tone dropped into a conspiratorial whisper, in spite of himself.

"Trudy just...she's having a hard time with that. You know how Trudy is."

I tilted my hand sympathetically, as though Trudy were a couple eggs short of a dozen. Gerry nodded.

"She asked me to have a look. As a friend." I shrugged, leaning back. "I guess she thinks, big city cop and all...I don't know. It just makes her feel better to have a second opinion."

"Well, that makes sense," Gerry said. His gaze was now fixed on me, both elbows resting on the table. I knew I had him.

"I had a look at the 10-55," I said, referencing the radio code for a coroner's case. It wasn't the kind of thing a cop would actually say in conversation, but I wanted to reinforce my bona fides.

Gerry squinted.

"Oh, sorry. Coroner's case. I took a look at the body."

"And?"

I hesitated. "You know how it is, Gerry. I'm sure you never criticize the guys at the Raleigh office."

"So something was wrong?"

"I wouldn't say that. I mean, sure. They do things differently out here. Small department and all that. I had a few questions. Honestly, I just thought I'd drive up here and ask about Daniel's work situation. You know...cover the bases. Help out the local guys."

Gerry held both hands out, open palmed. Inviting.

Ready to spill his guts.

"What did Daniel do, exactly?"

"He worked in processing," Gerry said. "New files, predominantly."

"New files?"

"Yeah, you know. When somebody is born, or when somebody emigrates, or whatever. They need a social security number. They have to be put in the system. Name, date of birth, and SSN. Somebody has to do the legwork."

"So Daniel was responsible for assigning new social security numbers?"

"Right. Say a baby is born, they fill out the birth certificate at the hospital, then send us a copy. Local social security offices are responsible for filing the paperwork with Washington. They assign a social security number to the baby. That was Daniel's job."

"Are that many babies born around here? I mean, for somebody to have a full-time job."

"Oh sure. I mean, there were over a hundred thousand births in North Carolina last year. Over three hundred per day. And our office doesn't just cover Wilmington. We cover several rural counties, also. Daniel was actually one of four people managing new files. He was always busy."

"Sounds like a lot of paperwork. Sounds like it could have been a little monotonous."

Gerry forced a laugh. "I don't have to tell a fellow government guy about paperwork."

I smiled, sharing the moment of manufactured camaraderie.

"Was Daniel depressed at all?" I asked.

Gerry shrugged. "Of course you know about his kid."

"Cerebral palsy."

"Right. Lots of pressure there. We have good health insurance, working for the fed. But the bills still stack up. All the things healthcare won't cover. You know, he told me one time, the lifetime cost of caring for a child with CP is over a *million* dollars?"

"No kidding?"

"That's what he said. We all got together to help him out one time, when they had to spend a week in Raleigh and stay in hotels. We chipped in, did what we could."

Gerry leaned back, that self-important lift returning to his chin. I indulged him without comment.

"But it's the little things that get you," he continued. "All the small stuff, building up over time. So I guess you could say Daniel was stressed a lot, but I wouldn't call him depressed."

"I know he liked to fish," I said.

"Oh yeah. He talked about that a lot." Gerry rolled his eyes. "Would stand by the water cooler all afternoon, if I let him. Don't know if he ever caught much, but he loved to be on the water."

Gerry's face dropped a little. "I guess...it didn't surprise me much to hear that's where he died. I won't set foot on a boat, myself. No, sir. Lost an uncle in Vietnam on a boat."

I squinted, impulsively wanting to point out that the *boat* had a lot less to do with that story than the location. But I held my tongue.

"You...you think he was killed?" Gerry asked, the conspiratorial tone returning.

I shook my head. "The guys in Eastport are solid cops. They know what they're doing. I'm just trying to take care of Trudy, you know?"

"That's good of you. I know we'd all like to help her. At least the bills are covered, now."

"Covered? What do you mean?"

"Well, the life policy."

I frowned. "What policy?"

"Daniel had a life policy, through work. It's a federal program. They give us a break on premiums, via paycheck deductions. Daniel maxed his out."

"Did he? I hadn't heard. How much, exactly?"

Gerry lifted his shoulders and looked away, playing hard to get. But I knew he would spill.

"Well. I mean, that's confidential. But, you know. It's something like the lifetime cost of caring for a kid with CP."

A million dollars.

One heck of a payout. And tax free, I knew. I'd seen people die for a lot less.

"Did Trudy know?"

"About what?"

"The policy."

Another pause. "I mean, I guess so. I would assume she was the beneficiary."

I spent the next ten minutes fishing around about Daniel's line of work, but Gerry had little else to say. He let me have a quick look into the dead man's office, but there wasn't much to see. Daniel was clean and organized, and kept his desk drawers locked.

I thanked Gerry and made my exit, smiling but remaining noncommittal when he asked me to call him if I found anything. It was colder outside than it had been when I arrived, and I tasted rain on the air. Clouds rolled in from the west, and a harsh wind tore at the trees.

But none of that was what caught my eye as I stepped onto the sidewalk.

What caught my eye was the two-tone Bronco parked on the street, forty yards away. And the four burly guys inside, glaring death right at me.

19

Tangle Beard sat in the passenger seat, glowering at me through fogged glass. Exhaust bubbled from the tailpipe and the guys in the back seat looked as though I'd slapped their mothers.

But they didn't leave the vehicle. Not here—not in public, with so many witnesses around.

I pocketed my hands and walked casually to the Corolla, taking my time. I started the engine and gave it a minute to warm, making a show of fiddling with the GPS system and adjusting the heater.

The Bronco remained next to the curb, purring smoothly. Tangle Beard pivoted his head to the windshield, still glaring, then theatrically ran a grimy finger across his throat.

I tapped my head, just above my right ear, indicating the portion of Tangle Beard's skull I had rammed into the Bronco's fender. His eyes blazed and his hand twisted into a fist. I ignored him and backed into the street.

The Bronco followed me as I wound through downtown, driving slowly and signaling at every turn. By the time I crossed the Cape Fear Memorial Bridge, I had managed to put a couple of sedans and a bread truck between my rear bumper and the Bronco, but it would be difficult to maintain that distance on the highway. Even loaded down with four fat rednecks, the Bronco's V8 would run down my undersized Japanese 4-cylinder with ease.

So I didn't try to run. I set the cruise at sixty-five, hung in the right lane, and let the Bronco ride my ass. We took 76 West through Leland, and then Maco. Fifteen miles outside of Wilmington, Tangle Beard rumbled directly behind, flashing me the bird now and again whenever I waved to him. A couple state troopers and a county cop passed, but they wouldn't be any help.

Not for four jackasses with less brain between them than God gave a cockroach. No, this was my problem. And I was going to deal with it.

I took an exit onto Highway 11, at Freeman. The Bronco swung in behind me, and I stomped on the gas. The Corolla whined but took off, spinning up to eighty miles per hour on the wide, flat highway.

Behind me the Bronco's lights flashed as a light rainfall obscured my vision. I couldn't hear over the rush of my heater and the whine of the engine, but the distance between my rear bumper and the Bronco's front was shrinking, slowly.

I thought about my gun, in the evidence locker back in Eastport. I thought about Lefty's gun—that cheap revolver I emptied and hurled into the ditch outside of town.

Maybe I should have kept it after all. But, after obliterating his buddy's knee, then busting Tangle Beard's skull, I really hadn't expected him to be hungry for more.

My mistake. These guys were gluttons for punishment.

I swerved around a minivan, the Corolla rocking a little. The driver laid on the horn, then jerked his van to the shoulder as the Bronco shoved by. I saw him struggle to regain control, and gritted my teeth.

Time to end this. Before an innocent got hurt.

I hit the wipers to fight the growing rain, and looked into the mirror just in time to brace for impact.

The Bronco made contact, sending my head smashing back against the headrest. I wrestled the wheel with both hands to maintain control, and smashed the gas. Trees and houses rushed by on both sides, with nothing but empty highway ahead. The speedometer passed ninety, but the Bronco kept coming.

Another bone-jarring impact sent cracks racing through my back glass. I could hear the roar of the Bronco now, loud enough to overcome my own engine.

And then a gunshot. Glass shattered next to my face and icy wind ripped in. I ducked as another string of handgun rounds ripped toward me, and I instinctively pulled to the right.

My left-hand mirror was blown off, and the Bronco's motor thundered. The Corolla jerked and I felt the right-hand tire leaving the road, now caught on the shoulder.

And then I saw the bridge. It shot toward me directly ahead, only a hundred yards away and closing. The guard rail built along the right-hand side was pointed right at my bumper.

The Bronco didn't stop. Instead it snatched to the left, crossing onto my driver's side, and then jerking back toward me.

There was nothing more I could do. I hit the brakes and steered right, leaving the road at sixty miles per hour and plowing across flat, muddy earth. The guard rail passed me on my left side as the Bronco raced onto the bridge, and then I hit the edge of the drop-off leading down to the water.

Everything moved in slow motion. I saw the muddy river churning by, thirty yards ahead. Trees and brush exploded over my hood as speed bled away, but I was still hurtling ahead far too fast to be stopped.

Far too fast to escape the water below.

The hood of the Corolla hit the river with an explosion of white spray. The windshield was consumed in an instant, and then a rush of brown murk surged through my busted window.

I remained calm, my heart thundering, but my mind still working like an oiled machine. Years of Army training, prepping me for helicopter crashes over water, kicked in, and I moved automatically to unlatch my seat belt.

The water reached my knees, so cold my muscles locked up. I snatched the photograph of Mia off the dash, holding it above the waterline. Then I rolled right and abandoned my seat, not even bothering with the driver's door. It was almost fully submerged now, the Corolla's front bumper buried in the muddy bottom of the river. Hundreds of gallons of heavy current rushing against the cabin would quickly overcome that mud, shoving the entire car into the midst of the river and sweeping it downstream.

I had to get out before then.

Reaching the back seat my knees hit the cushions, and I found them already soaked as water filled the rear floorboards. Water had reached the back windows also, covering the door panels and pressing hard enough to eliminate any hope of opening them from the inside.

The trunk was my only option.

I found the latch to drop the back seats, and jerked them down, exposing the trunk from the inside. Without thinking I dove through the hole, clambering over shoes, boxes of coloring supplies, notebooks, and all the other junk a second-grade schoolteacher would keep in her trunk.

It was dark, and the water pouring in through the busted driver's window had now largely flooded the cabin. But I found the emergency latch release on the inside of the trunk lid and snatched it down before pushing up hard on the lid.

The trunk was bent and mangled from impact with the Bronco. It squeaked and groaned, but I shoved upward with a powerful right forearm and forced it open.

The water was up to my waist as I crawled out, falling face-first into the river. I scrambled to my feet and reached back into the trunk, shoving coloring books aside and peeling back the false floor to expose the tire-changing kit housed beneath.

The lug wrench was fourteen inches long, built of solid steel, and crooked at one end. I grabbed it, then ran for cover beneath the bridge as I spotted the Bronco pull off the road, fifty yards up the bank, and the four rednecks spill out.

The photograph of Mia was wet. I wiped it against a dry portion of my shirt, my eyes stinging as I looked down at her gorgeous smile.

Then I heard the rednecks coming, and I braced myself for action.

I hadn't managed to knock any sense into Tangle Beard the first time. This time he'd be lucky to walk away.

20

I made it to the shelter of the bridge, scrambling over rocks and breathing evenly. Rain now fell in a steady torrent, rushing down the bank. The Corolla twisted in the current, the back end crashing into the water as the nose broke free of the mud. I saw notebooks and boxes of pencils floating free of the open trunk, and my stomach twisted.

It felt like a piece of Mia—drifting away right in front of me.

Above me, coming down the bank, I heard Tangle Beard and company headed my way. I crawled farther up the bank to the point where the bridge met the dirt, pressing myself into the shadows, still gripping the lug wrench.

I saw Tangle Beard first. He led the way with another Rock Island revolver clutched in one hand. His beard ran with rainwater, and his attention was fixed on the barely visible rear door panel of the Corolla as the car was dragged into the middle of the river.

They hadn't seen me leave the car, I realized. As fast as the Bronco was traveling, it had taken them time to stop, then turn around.

They didn't know where I was.

"Do ya see him?" somebody shouted.

"There's the car!"

Two more guys appeared to my right, only a couple yards away. Dense brush obscured my view, and the edge of the bridge blocked out the top half of their bodies. But I knew what I was looking at—more guys like Lefty and Tangle Beard. Large, overfed, and overconfident.

I tucked Mia's photograph into my sodden pocket, my knuckles tightening around the wrench.

The fourth guy appeared, sweeping a flashlight across the surface of the river even though it was barely past noon. Tangle Beard had reached the water and was poking his revolver around, following the Corolla as it bobbed to the surface, upside down now. The river was dragging it downstream, but there was no body for him to find.

"Daryl! You see anything?" the fourth guy asked.

Tangle Beard—or Daryl, I guess—shook his soggy head and maintained the search. The fourth guy stepped two more yards down the bank, his shoulder blades crossing into my view.

Completely blind to my position.

I launched out from under the bridge like a striking viper. The lug wrench crashed into the fourth guy's skull with a splitting crack, and he went down. I looked quickly to his belt for a gun, but saw nothing, and I didn't have time to search.

The third guy turned, four yards away, conscious of the storm of activity behind him. He shouted and pointed the flashlight at me.

I hurtled ahead, knocking the light aside with the wrench before driving a vicious left hook into his jaw.

The blow was weaker than it should have been—compliments of my gunshot shoulder. But it was still a lot more than he was prepared to take. His head snapped back, and I back-handed his rib cage with the wrench.

Bones cracked and he hit the bank, rolling toward the water and choking for air.

A gun cracked, and a bullet hissed past my head. I dove into the brush as the next guy hurtled toward me, a Beretta 92 clenched in both hands, spraying bullets like a drunk Marine.

He reached my spot, boots sliding over the mud. I sprang from the brush and drove my right foot into his left shin, knocking him off balance. He fell forward and I raised the wrench, clocking him across the back of the head as he hurtled toward the ground.

The blow was hard. Hard enough to break bone. If he wasn't dead, he would be lucky to remember how to walk.

More bullets snapped toward me from the bank. Daryl fired with his revolver, his shots far too hurried and panicked to represent any real threat so far away. I ducked to scoop up the Beretta, then started casually down the bank.

Daryl fired twice more, his back to the water. Then the revolver clicked over an empty cylinder, and his face washed white. I quickened my pace, reaching the torn earth of the Corolla's tire tracks as Daryl turned to run.

I fired once, snapping the gun up to eye-level and pressing the trigger instinctively. The bullet struck Daryl in his right knee and he went down with a scream, the revolver spinning from his hand.

I reached his body, wiping rainwater off my nose and rolling him over with one foot. His face was a mess of mud and tears, his teeth clenched in pain as blood spurted from his knee.

I thought he was down—and if he had any sense, he would have been. But Daryl reached for a knife in his belt, and lurched toward me.

I flipped the Beretta with practiced ease, grabbing the weapon by the barrel and driving the butt right between his eyes.

It was a soft hit—or I thought it was, anyway. Just enough to stun him. But I must have been hyped up on adrenaline, and maybe a little pissed off, because Daryl's eyes rolled back in his head and he went lights out, dropping to the mud.

I stood over him, breathing hard, rain beating down on my head. I was freezing cold again, but this time I didn't notice. My heart thundered and I looked across the bank at the wreckage of bodies splayed around me.

Four guys. Maybe sixty seconds of action.

Man, they sucked at this.

I dropped the Beretta and checked the load. Of the fifteen-round capacity, only five rounds remained, and they were all full metal jackets—not the right kind of ammunition for anything save target shooting. But that was good news for Daryl's knee.

I disassembled the Beretta and slung it into the river, then retrieved Daryl's revolver and followed suit, once again missing my Smith. If these fools were going to keep taking passes at me, I'd want a gun.

A clean one.

Kneeling next to Daryl's inert frame, I pulled his belt off and used it to fashion a tourniquet over his knee. It wasn't perfect, but it would stop the blood flow long enough to keep him alive, which was more than he deserved. Then I started back up the bank, stopping at the first guy I knocked out with the wrench. I guessed him to the boss, based on the way he shouted at Daryl. Sifting through his pockets, I quickly located a cell phone and a wallet.

I helped myself to the eighty-four dollars in the wallet, figuring it a down payment on my pain and suffering settlement, then dug out the ID.

Floyd Crosby, of Corkville, North Carolina.

I didn't know where that was, but guessed it didn't matter. He was forty-two, and the little red label beneath his picture marked him as a sex offender. I regarded his unconscious body with disgust, then dropped the ID and started up the bank again.

The keys hung in the Bronco's ignition, and the big motor started right up. I took my time adjusting the seat and the mirrors, then inspected the rear for the presence of anything I might want to dump before leaving. There was nothing save a couple jackets and empty fast-food wrappers.

I dug Mia's photograph out and inspected it for damage. It was a little creased and still damp, but the photo paper was quality stuff. The image hadn't smudged, and her beautiful smile still shone at me like the sunrise. I replaced it in my pocket, then I spun the big Ford back onto the highway, taking note of the sign next to the bridge as I passed. It was the Cape Fear River—only about thirty yards wide here, but the same river that eventually washed past Eastport.

Once I was half a mile down the road I hit the power button on Crosby's phone. It was locked, but still allowed for emergency calls. I dialed 911 and waited.

"What is your emergency?"

"I just passed over the Cape Fear River bridge on highway eleven," I said. "There's a couple guys laid out on the bank. Looks like they may have fallen."

"We'll dispatch an ambulance. What's your name, sir?"

I hung up and opened my door long enough to fling the phone into the ditch. Then I settled back into the seat, and headed toward Eastport with more questions than I had left with.

21

I decided to visit Trudy first. I wanted to see what she had to say about the life policy, and while I didn't have her address, I figured Marley might know where she lived.

The rain had slackened by the time I rumbled past the Walmart on the outskirts of town, but the sky was still gray, and the air outside biting cold. The Bronco ran like a dream, obviously well maintained and prized by whoever owned it—Daryl, I guessed. He'd done some work to the engine, adding a little extra horsepower and torque, which accounted for how easily he had run me down on the highway.

I liked it. It reminded me of my old K10, but ran smoother, and had a nice sound. Maybe I would keep it. A ride like this might be recognized around town, but that could be useful. And, anyway, I considered it the remainder of my settlement for the pain and suffering of being needlessly attacked on two separate occasions, not to mention the loss of Mia's Corolla.

As I approached downtown Eastport, I knew something was wrong. I smelled the smoke before I saw it, but as I looked over the top of the trees the gray covering the sky was darker than the clouds behind it. I stepped on the accelerator, winding through streets toward the sound of fire engines.

Flashing red lights caught my eye as I turned a corner, then I stepped on the brakes as a burning house filled my view. It was a single-story, ranch-style home. Or, it had been. The roof had already caved in, despite the efforts of the two Eastport City fire engines dumping water on it.

Firefighters rushed around the scene, and several of the EPD's police Explorers blocked off a security perimeter.

I cut the engine and watched the house burn for a while, suddenly wondering if it was Trudy's. There was no reason to assume so, even in a town this small, but in my experience bad things come in pairs, or sometimes trios. If somebody was willing to kill me over my investigation into Daniel's death, would they be willing to set fire to Trudy's house to run her off?

The long wooden ramp leading up to the front door wasn't a good sign. A child with cerebral palsy would need a ramp like that.

I climbed out, my shoes squishing on the pavement. I was still soaked, but the Bronco's heavy heater had done wonders for my chilled body. I ignored the biting wind and approached the nearest Explorer.

A cop stood with his back to me, calling to a firefighter over the rumble of the fire engines. He turned as I neared, and my shoulders dropped.

It was Witmore. Just my luck.

He looked confused when he saw me, glancing to the Bronco and frowning. Then he turned that frown on me.

"What happened?" I said, lifting my chin toward the fire.

Witmore glared. "Didn't Chief tell you to get out of town?"

I shrugged. "Free country. Folks around here to seem to be confused by that concept."

Witmore breathed a curse and answered his radio as

somebody called to him. I recognized the police codes he growled as *suspicious person* and *stolen vehicle*.

Is that right? I thought.

I kept my hands in my pockets and remained relaxed. Witmore placed his hand on his gun and kept the nose of the Explorer between us.

"Take your hands out of your pockets," he ordered.

"Is that Trudy Porter's house?" I asked.

He did the goldfish thing with his lips again. It made me want to punch him in the mouth.

"I *said* take your *hands* out of your *pockets!*"

"I heard what you said, dimwit. I just don't care."

Witmore thumbed the retention strap on his holster. He drew breath to shout another warning, but then Chief Lowe appeared behind him, red faced and dressed in a rain jacket.

"Stand down, Sergeant!"

Witmore flushed. "He's resisting arrest, Chief. Won't show his hands."

Lowe ran a hand through his sodden hair and looked to me.

Then to the Bronco.

I saw something change in his face when he saw it, but he quickly looked away. Back to me.

"I thought I asked you to leave town," he said.

"You did."

"Why are you here?"

"Because I didn't leave town."

Lowe clenched his jaw, showing the first flash of irritation I'd seen since meeting him. I didn't give him a chance to take charge of the conversation.

"That Trudy Porter's house?" I motioned with a tilt of my head.

Lowe looked over his shoulder, as if he needed to clarify

which home was burning to ash. When he turned back he looked reserved, but he nodded.

"Yeah."

"What happened?"

"Electrical fire," he said, a little too quickly.

I raised both eyebrows. He realized his mistake, and swallowed.

"Least ways, that's what they think. Of course we won't know till the fire marshal can investigate."

"Where's Trudy?"

He licked his lips, hesitating again. Then shrugged. "With family. She's fine."

"That's nice."

"Where'd you get the Bronco?" Witmore spluttered, one hand still resting on his .357.

I looked over my shoulder, as though the street was full of Broncos and I needed to clarify. Then I shrugged.

"I borrowed it."

"You borrowed it?" Witmore said, his lips working again.

The Chief cleared his throat, subtly stepping far enough in front of Witmore to cut him off.

"Why don't you give us some space to clean this up? Come by the station this afternoon and I'll have your gun ready. Okay? Then you can *go*."

I stood, hands still in my pockets, evaluating him. Thinking about the last conversation we'd had, and how he'd refused to release the Smith.

"Funny," I said.

"What's funny?"

"I was just thinking. You asked me to leave before, but you wouldn't give me my gun."

"So?"

"So that's odd, don't you think? I mean, if you wanted me

to leave, you should have surrendered my property. Since that's what's kept me around."

Lowe didn't say anything. I smirked.

"It's almost like you didn't want me armed. You know. Just in case I was jumped."

I saw something turn cold behind Lowe's eyes—the facade of fake southern hospitality freezing over as his jaw locked.

I held his gaze, long enough for him to know I was onto him. Witmore blustered, but Lowe just stood there. His face red.

Then I turned back to the Bronco and started the engine without so much as a glance toward the two cops. They watched me as I completed a U-turn and drove to the end of the street, reaching the stop sign and breezing through without pause.

22

I returned to Marley's, mostly because I was hungry and I thought she might have put the burger on the menu. I could do with a hot shower, too, to ease the throbbing ache in my left shoulder and clean away the mud. I thought irritably about the new clothes I'd purchased in Wilmington, now washing somewhere down the Cape Fear River.

More justification for keeping Daryl's Bronco. I figured he and his buddies were at a hospital right now, taking questions from local cops about the bullet wound in his knee and the welts on their heads.

But they wouldn't talk. No, they had too much to hide. Too much explaining to do. And they probably had criminal records on file, which meant the officers who responded to the hospital's GSW alert wouldn't be predisposed to view them as victims.

Daryl and his goons wouldn't be a problem. At least, not before I was finished in Eastport.

The pub was occupied by a smattering of locals when I entered. I checked the darkened corners but didn't see

Cassandra. Maybe she was actually doing some photography, for a change.

I took a seat at the bar and nodded to Marley as she waved a greeting. She brought me a beer without asking, which made me feel a little like a local, but I would rather have had hot coffee. My damp clothes stuck to my body and reinforced the chill in my bones.

"Lunch?" Marley asked, surveying my muddy shirt but not asking questions.

"Burger," I said, pleased to find that it had returned to the chalkboard menu. "And fries."

"Coming right up."

She bustled off, and I sipped the beer, spinning around to survey the room again. I thought about Cassandra, and the strange conversation we shared at the diner. I hadn't devoted much brain power to the subject, but it didn't require a genius to feel out the cracks in her story.

Like why would a photographer from Philly drive all the way to Eastport just to shoot sunrises?

And why was she in my *room*? That was the big one. The one that stuck in the back of my mind like gum on the bottom of a table. In the face of Daryl trying to kill me, and the local cops trying to run me out of town, Cassandra's offenses felt relatively minor.

But still a problem.

"Hey, Marley! Can I use the phone?"

Marley looked up from the register, raising both eyebrows.

"What's with you and my phone? You ain't got a cell?"

I shrugged. She pointed to the cordless phone, and I leaned over to scoop it up. I punched a number in from memory, then retreated to a quieter corner of the pub. The person I was dialing would answer even when she didn't recognize the number.

Because she was a good cop.

"Detective Richardson, Phoenix Police Department."

"Jacquie...it's me."

Dead silence. I heard papers shuffling and a car door closed. "Mason?"

"Yeah."

"Oh my God...are you okay? Where are you? Why haven't you answered the phone? I've been calling all week!"

I expected the deluge of questions, but I still didn't know where to start. Knots returned to my stomach as Jacquie's familiar voice brought back a wave of memories.

Memories of Phoenix. And Mia.

"I'm in North Carolina," I said, picking an answer that I figured would be most likely to shut down further inquiries.

Jacquie was quiet a long time, and I figured she understood. When she spoke next her voice had softened. "Are you okay?"

I swapped the phone to my other ear. "Yeah. I'm good."

"If you wanted space you could have said so. You didn't have to ghost your best friend."

A weak smile pulled at my lips. It was exactly the sort of complaint I expected from Jacquie, but she was blind to her own hypocrisy. If I had told her where I was going she would have called the local cops to check up on me.

Because she was a good partner.

"I need a favor," I said.

"What's up?"

"I need you to run a plate for me. Virginia."

I rattled off Cassandra's plate number from memory, and heard Jacquie making a note.

"What are you up to, Sharpe?"

"It's a long story," I said. "Don't worry about it. Just run that plate and let me know what you find. Call this number and leave a message, if you have to."

"What happened to your phone?"

"I lost it," I said. The answer was a little true.

Long pause. "Okay. I'll run it. Anything else?"

I hesitated, knowing what I wanted to ask. Not sure if I wanted to dive headfirst into the possible answer.

"Did they...are there any updates on the shooters?"

Jacquie sighed. "Closed the case last week. Ruled an act of insanity. Couple of trailer trash guys living in the county. We searched their computers and found all kinds of conspiracy nonsense about teachers brainwashing the next generation to trigger the Armageddon. You know the type, Mason. Off their meds. Too much meth, and not enough therapy."

My eyes blurred as I stared across the bar, thinking again about those final moments. I shot the first guy in the side of the head. The second guy took two rounds to his chest and one to this throat.

Great shots, under pressure. Skills I learned in the Army, not the PPD.

But in the end, what did it matter? They were dead. That couldn't change what they did.

"I'm so sorry, Mason," Jacquie said.

I swallowed. "Thanks for letting me know. Call when you run that plate, okay?"

I hung up before she could ask another question, then returned to the bar and drained my beer. Marley came by, setting down the burger. She saw the look on my face and paused.

"You all right, buddy?"

I looked away, sliding the empty bottle toward her. "Sure. Just tired."

She replaced the bottle with a full one, but didn't leave. The other patrons in the pub seemed to be well cared for, and she leaned against the back counter, a rag wrapped around her hand.

I dug into the burger, eager to distract myself. It was juicy and cooked to perfection, just as before. I was becoming addicted.

"I'm closing early today," she said. "Gonna drive home to see some friends."

I poured ketchup on my plate, and mopped the burger through it.

"You don't live here?" I asked, more to make polite conversation than anything.

"Sure, but my family lives out in Evergreen County, near Corkville. It's a little ways inland."

I looked up, remembered Crosby's driver's license. "Corkville?"

"Little community about forty miles inland. Dot on the map, really. You know, kinda place where everybody knows everybody."

"You know a guy named Crosby?"

She squinted. "Mack Crosby?"

I tried to remember Crosby's first name. My mind blanked, but I knew it wasn't Mack.

"There's a lot of Crosbys out that way," Marley said. "Heck, they'll probably turn out for the fire tonight."

"What fire?"

"Bonfire. Kinda a winter tradition. The community gets together and builds a big fire, and sets up some tables. Good food, good music, plenty of beer. It's a great time."

I wiped my mouth, thinking again about Daryl tracking me down. Not once, but twice. And not just in Eastport. He'd driven all the way to Wilmington to run me off.

Why? What was I sniffing around that was so important as to gather up three buddies to deal with me?

Daniel's death had something to do with it. It had to. But even after visiting the social security office and talking to Sherman, I was at a loss.

I needed a break.

"Hey, you should come with me," Marley said, cracking open another beer, this one for herself.

I looked up. "Yeah?"

"Sure. You look like a guy who could use some fun. The rain is supposed to quit tonight. You could ride out with me and turn up a little, redneck style."

She winked and grinned.

I shared the laugh, but I wasn't thinking about good food and cold drinks. I was thinking about Crosby. I hadn't gotten anything from the four guys by the river—I hadn't had the chance.

But I might get something from some loose-lipped locals, half-drunk locals. Given a conversation piece, they might open right up.

"Sounds great," I said, draining my beer. "Let's take my Bronco."

23

I drove to Walmart for yet another change of cheap clothes, then spent the rest of the afternoon napping. Marley met me out by the Bronco just after sunset, dressed in skinny jeans, a tank top, and a black leather jacket.

She looked good. Exactly the kind of woman I would have chatted up at an Army bar, back in the day. Back before Mia.

Now I just smiled and held her door, because it seemed like the polite thing to do. She surveyed the Bronco and squinted.

"I feel like one of the Crosby guys drove a truck like this."

So Daryl was a Crosby, too. Figures.

"He did," I said. "Traded him for it yesterday."

"Weren't you driving some little import?"

I shrugged. "You know how it is. People trying to save money on gas."

She climbed into the passenger seat without further debate, but I noted a suspicious glance around the cabin. I shut her door and found my way to the driver's seat, firing up the modified motor while Marley fiddled with the radio. She found a country station and cranked the volume up. I found the highway and cranked the power up, cruising at seventy through tall groves of trees on either side.

Marley shuffled through her purse and dug out a pack of cigarettes. "You mind?"

"Free country."

She wound the passenger window down a couple inches before lighting up, and offering me a drag. I waved her off. I quit smoking right around the time I met Mia. She didn't like the taste of tobacco on my tongue, and worried about my health.

I'd never worried about my health. But her lips on mine tasted a lot better than cigarettes.

"Kind of a sucky weekend for a party," I commented, just to say something.

Marley shrugged, blowing smoke through the side of her mouth. "It usually is. But you get the fire hot enough, nobody cares."

"So you know a lot of Crosbys?"

"I mean, sure. I know of them. It's that kind of place, you know? Everybody kinda knows about everybody else, but not really. Not personally."

I didn't know. Growing up in one of America's largest cities and then transferring directly into the largest branch of the military, the closest things I ever saw to small towns were Afghani villages and military outposts. But I'd seen enough movies to guess about small-town life. I thought I saw the appeal.

"Is that why you joined the Marines?" I asked.

She squinted. "Huh?"

"Because it's smaller. Small-town life."

She sucked on the cigarette. "Nah, I joined the Corps because my daddy was a Marine. Fought in Desert Storm. Got blown away by an IED."

"I'm sorry."

She grinned, dryly. There was no humor in her eyes. "So are they."

"Why'd you get out?"

"Eh. I don't know. Gets old, after a while. Always on the grind. My uncle passed away and left me the bar. Felt like a good time to come home, you know? Set up shop. Pour drinks for rednecks."

"A nice life."

She nodded, looking out the window. "Yeah...a nice life."

I eased off the speed as we crossed into progressively more rural county roads. Marley had set her phone up on the dash with a GPS map leading me to the party, making it easy for me to find my way while appreciating the passing landscape.

North Carolina was beautiful. I tried to imagine it in summer, with leafy green trees and wildflowers littering the ditches. It was easy to understand why Mia loved it so much.

"What about you?" Marley asked.

"What about me?"

"Why did you get out?"

My hand tightened around the wheel, and I saw the bus again. The flash of fire. People shouting. The field of small bodies, strewn across the road.

A bad strike, they called it. An accident. A clerical error.

"I guess I stopped believing," I said, quietly.

Marley watched me out of the corner of her eye, the cigarette dangling from two fingers. Then she looked away and took another puff.

A fellow soldier. Smart enough to understand when to stop asking questions.

"You gonna get drunk tonight?" she asked.

I scratched my cheek, thinking I should have bought a razor at Walmart. "Probably not."

"Perfect. I'll need a driver."

WE REACHED the party half an hour later, and it was nothing like I expected. A wide gravel road led through twin cattle gates and down a tree-lined corridor. In the distance I saw an orange glow, and I smelled smoke. Then the Bronco's headlights flashed down a row of parked trucks and SUVs, reflecting off their taillights, and I saw the field.

It was maybe fifteen or twenty acres in size, encircled by trees. A giant metal barn sat to one side, illuminated by white light and packed with people. I heard country music blaring, and saw tables stacked with food and cases of beer.

Outside the barn was the largest bonfire I had ever seen. It blazed like a pit of hell, forty feet across and piled high with shipping pallets for fuel. A tractor with a loading fork dumped more pallets onto the fire while people stood back and drank beer.

They were all adults. No kids. And everybody already looked about half-lit.

"All right!" Marley grinned. "Gonna be a good one tonight."

I drove down the length of cars and navigated to the very front of the parking area, stopping the Bronco only fifty yards from the barn.

Right where everybody could see it.

Then I piled out, and we joined the party.

I'd never attended anything like this before. In my day we hit the clubs and the grimy little bars just off base. Rap music and hard rock were the anthems of choice, and we more often drank alongside motorcycle gangs than cowboys.

This was not that kind of party. Everybody wore boots and jeans, and quite a few wore cowboy hats. I made note of handguns worn openly on hips, like this was the old west or something, and there were no cops in sight.

A completely unregulated event, it seemed. Lubricated by a *ton* of alcohol.

Somebody shoved a beer in my hand without even asking my name, and Marley disappeared into the barn. I stood forty feet back from the fire, admiring the inferno and quickly understanding why nobody cared about the wet and cold weather. The ground around the fire was already dry, and standing any closer than I already was would have roasted me alive.

It was like midday in Iraq, all over again.

Some guy climbed out of the tractor and held up a bullhorn. He let out a loud *yippee* sound, which was apparently enough to arrest everybody's attention.

"Aw hell yeah! I'm sure glad y'all made it out tonight. Everybody got a beer handy?"

A chorus of cheers answered in the affirmative. He grinned wider.

"All right, then. Let's get this shindig started!"

I thought the shindig *was* started. I was wrong. The music cranked up, a wide circle marked by orange paint was designated a dance floor, and everybody got busy dancing. I stood back and watched, noting the bright eyes of young women dancing with guys in western belt buckles and button-down shirts. Old timers sat in camping chairs around the perimeter, knocking back beers and swapping jokes, while a constant train of hungry mouths passed through the barn, loading up plates.

Maybe everybody knew everybody, or maybe they just pretended to. At least twice, a passerby slapped my shoulder and said it was good to see me, but when I saw the gleam of intoxication in their eyes I didn't bother to correct them.

Why spoil the fun?

"Hey!"

I was enjoying my second beer when the voice growled at

me from behind. I had been expecting it—even hoping for it. But I didn't turn. I took another casual sip as a big man closed behind me, then shoved my back.

"Hey, I'm talking to you."

I looked up. He was taller than me by a couple inches, and broad. A little overweight, but still heavily muscled. Maybe forty years old, with a missing tooth and a short, groomed beard.

Like a slightly upgraded version of Daryl. Still backwoods, but cultured enough to untangle his facial hair.

"Yeah?" I said.

The guy pointed toward the parking lot. "You drive that Bronco?"

I didn't bother to look. "The blue one? That's me."

"Whar'd you get it?" he growled. I could tell by a slight slur in his voice that he was a little drunk, but probably not enough to alter his judgment.

"A buddy lent it to me." I took another sip. "Actually, he said his friends might be here tonight. You know a guy named Crosby?"

Something flashed across his eyes. Recognition, but also uncertainty. Maybe he hadn't expected me to be so relaxed.

"I know a guy in the hospital," he snarled. "My cousin. He's banged up pretty good. Said somebody took his truck!"

"Wait, for real?" I feigned shock. "Is he okay? He was fine when I saw him this morning."

Again, momentary confusion. Like his simple mind couldn't keep pace with my situational math.

"Who are you?" he demanded.

"Mason," I said, extending a hand. "And you?"

He looked at my hand but didn't shake it.

"I was wondering," I said. "What kind of work does Daryl do? I don't think he ever mentioned it."

The guy spat, then held out an open palm. "Gimme the keys."

"Huh?"

"I said, gimme the keys."

"Chill, dude. I'm just making friends. Let's get you a beer."

His right hand moved like a striking snake, knocking the bottle out of my fist as he closed the distance between us in one long step. I didn't move, remaining relaxed and tilting my head back to face him.

His breath smelled stale, tinged with beer.

"I don't know who the hell you are, but you're gonna gimme those damn keys, or I'm gonna beat your ass until you're pissin' out your nose."

I didn't move. Didn't so much as blink. I just stared him down, hands loose at my sides.

I hadn't expected a fight with so many people around. I thought the alcohol would work in my favor.

My mistake. But I wasn't backing down, either.

"I think you better have a seat, buddy," I said.

Our confrontation had garnered notice, now. The semi-inebriated partygoers immediately around us had fallen quiet, and were now watching the spectacle, a little breathless.

I figured that cut in my favor. Again, I miscalculated.

"Give me the keys," he snarled one last time.

"Screw off," I said, not breaking eye contact. Daring him to show his ass in front of two hundred people, and get the piss beat out of him.

He took the dare, but not like I expected. Instead of taking a swing at me, he took a step back then spat on the ground, and addressed the crowd.

"Ya'll clear that dance ring! We got beef to settle."

The music cut off, and he glared back down at me. A slow smile crept across his lips.

"You sure you wanna go this route?"

I didn't answer.

"All right, then. We gonna duke it out! Carolina style."

The dance circle began to clear, but the people didn't leave. They gathered around the painted line, leaving a corridor between us and an entrance. Forming a fighting ring, like a bunch of villagers ready to see a show. I could feel the anticipation in the air, broken only by the crackle of the fire.

None of the men wearing guns stepped in to stop it. Nobody objected.

This was how it was gonna be.

I scooped my beer bottle off the ground and tipped it back, finishing the last swallow. Then I gestured to the ring. "After you."

24

There's a principal in warfare—a savage sort of primal tactic used to overwhelm your enemy and bring them to a quick defeat.

William Sherman called it "total war," and he burned Atlanta to the ground.

The Nazis called it "blitzkrieg," and they ravished the whole of Poland in thirty-five days.

But the U.S. Army calls it *violence of action*—hitting your enemy quickly, with an overwhelming amount of force. Obliterating them with an unexpected and unreasonable intensity, all at once.

I'm a big believer in the strategy. Always have been. It worked for me in middle school with the bully who wanted my lunch money. It worked again in Ranger school with the worst the Army could throw at me.

And it worked in Iraq, battling ISIL.

I figured it would work in North Carolina, also.

As I passed down the corridor of onlookers, I saw the greedy anticipation in their eyes. A sort of strange, breathless calm had fallen over the gathered locals, punctuated here and there by drunk hiccups and drawled whispers.

A show was about to start. Something more interesting than the bonfire burning in the background, or the trays of barbecue in the barn. Some out-of-towner was about to have his ass kicked.

Except I wasn't in the mood to take a beating. And I've never had a problem fighting dirty.

The big guy stepped into the ring and grinned at the onlookers, popping his knuckles and then peeling his shirt off. I heard my name called and saw Marley push her way into the ring, panic overwhelming her semi-inebriated face.

"What's goin' on?"

I motioned her back, then handed off my empty beer bottle to an onlooker. Normally, I'd be more than happy to weaponize that bottle, breaking it over the guy's head then slashing his stomach open with the shattered neck. But there were a lot of guns around, and clearly this guy was a local favorite.

Any semblance of cheating might land me in a fight I couldn't win.

"Last chance," the big guy drawled. "Toss me those keys and we'll send ya off with a plate of ribs."

"What are you driving?" I asked.

He frowned.

"Your wheels," I clarified. "What do you drive?"

"Why?"

I shrugged. "I might like it better than the Bronco."

His eyes hardened, and he took a step toward the middle. I didn't bother peeling my shirt off. It was cold, and this wasn't gonna take that long.

I approached the middle, and he stuck his chest out, raring back like a UFC fighter facing off before the match. I guessed he was mimicking what he saw on TV, but it was a stupid look, and a stupid move. I walked right up to him, shoulders loose, hands down, moving like I was about to check the mail. Keeping him thinking we were going to face off for a moment before getting the show rolling.

Then I faked a right hook, watched him panic and lean away, then caught him with a left-handed uppercut sharp enough to shatter teeth. He grunted and fell back, scrambling for footing, and I stayed on him. A chop to his throat was followed by another left hook, this one to his ribs, then I stomped his left knee.

They weren't pretty moves. Not the stuff of *The Karate Kid* or the Olympics, but they were damn effective. In three seconds he was falling back, almost completely immobilized, and gasping for air.

A unified gasp rang from the crowd, but I still didn't let up. He swung a wild and miscalculated right jab toward my face, and I ducked it with ease, delivering a combo to his stomach followed by another brutal uppercut to the jaw.

Fast, harsh, nasty moves. All hurled at him in a blur.

And that did it. His eyes rolled back in his head and he just stood there for a moment, like a tree right before it falls. And then he did fall, slamming into the dirt with a meaty thud.

I wiped my lip, only a little winded, then walked to the edge of the circle and swiped the first beer I saw from a slack-jawed guy in a cowboy hat. I drained it, enjoying the harsh carbonation and cheap flavor, and still nobody spoke.

Then the crowd parted and three big guys rolled out, all gawking at the unconscious man in the dirt. For a moment they seemed incapable of comprehending what they were looking at—as though water were burning, or the sky had turned green.

Then the biggest guy—a shirtless blob in overalls and yet another trucker hat—pointed a meaty finger at me.

"Get 'im!"

All three of them rushed me at once, and this time I kept the beer bottle. Flipping it around and grabbing it by the neck, I broke it right across the face of the first guy, stunning him before slashing the broken edge of the neck across his gut.

It sliced right through his shirt and cut his stomach—not bad, but enough to draw blood and send him into a panic.

Another gasp from the crowd, followed by a couple horrified shouts. I heard a siren nearby, and blue lights flashed against my face, but I ignored them. The other two guys were on me now, and one of them scored a strike to my already wounded shoulder hard enough to send me stumbling back. I regained my footing as a shotgun blasted through the air.

Another slash with my improvised weapon laid the shirtless dude's arm open, then I went for his face.

I wasn't actually going to put his eye out, but he didn't know that, and he folded like a cheap jackknife, hitting the dirt.

Then I felt strong hands on my arms, hefting me back. The twin prongs of a stun gun poked me in the lower back, and I went automatically limp, dropping the bottle neck.

They hit me anyway, and pain raced through my body. I went rigid as my hands were wrenched behind my back and cuffs closed around them. The crowd had now fallen back and watched the spectacle like a bull fight—full of anticipation and a little in awe. I saw Marley rushing out of the lineup, shouting at the cops and pointing to the unconscious guy who started the fight.

It didn't matter. They shoved me in the back of a cruiser, still shaking from the blast of the stun gun, and slammed the door.

25

I t took me a few minutes to regain focus. The inside of
the cruiser was dark, and smelled of sour fast food. Two
guys rode up front, both dressed in the subdued tans
and browns of a sheriff's department. County deputies, I
figured, deployed to break up the fight.

They must have been stationed nearby, to arrive so
quickly. Or else they had some advance notice, which made
this whole thing a setup. My destination would expose the
truth.

I spit onto the floorboard, my head a little fuzzy and my
lower back still burning. But overall, in pretty good shape for
having fought four big rednecks, and three all at once.

I would take it.

The cruiser found the end of the gravel drive and turned
onto the county road. The cops didn't talk. They sat slouched
back, chewing tobacco like this was yet another midnight
shift, and they were hoping somebody would speed, just so
they'd have something to do.

It wasn't a good sign. It wasn't the body language of two

honest deputies who'd just arrested an out-of-towner for brawling. I'd done plenty of that, during my time as a beat cop. I always had questions. I always wanted to talk to witnesses, even if the truth was pretty evident.

"You guys know a fellow named Crosby?" I asked.

No answer. I scratched my chin with one shoulder, my hands still cuffed behind my back.

"So I guess we're going downtown."

Still no answer. One of the cops opened a packet of peanuts and crunched them right along with his tobacco. I settled into my seat and resigned myself to just ride. These guys weren't gonna talk, no matter what I said.

We drove down long and winding county roads for twenty minutes. They all looked the same to me, surrounded by alternating forests and fields. I saw very few houses, and most of what I did see were trailer homes parked a little ways off the road, usually with a couple old trucks sitting out front, and maybe a Rottweiler chained to a tree.

The stuff of movies, I thought. Not all Hollywood is fiction.

At last the cruiser pulled to the side of the road at a quiet intersection, and the driver cut off the headlights. But neither cop reached for their door, and the engine continued to rumble.

I looked out my window, surveying a rolling field, barren and muddy this time of year, with some kind of farm processing facility on the far side. I saw a couple silos, two barns, and a tractor.

But no people.

Not a good sign.

"I think you forgot something," I said.

No answer.

"If I'm under arrest you should have read me my rights."

The driver spat tobacco juice into an old coffee cup. His partner chewed peanuts.

"Come on. I know you guys watch cop shows. Or do you not get TV out here?"

The driver smiled. A brief flash of genuine humor across his scraggly face. But he still didn't answer.

Three minutes later a pickup pulled in next to the cruiser. It was some jacked up thing on mud tires, and two big guys spilled out—both wearing overalls. One of them approached the driver's side of the cruiser, and the cop lowered his window. The guy passed him what looked like a folded hundred-dollar bill while his companion circled to my side of the car and opened the door.

Grimy hands closed around my arm and dragged me out. I went without a fuss, watching the cruiser complete a U-turn. The driver flashed me a wink as he passed, then the cops were gone, back the way they came.

So much for that.

"All right, you," one of the guys growled. "Get in!"

They dropped the tailgate, then hauled me up and hurled me into the bed of the truck. It was cold and rusty, with empty beer bottles lying around. They slammed the gate and I rolled onto my back, fighting into a sitting position. I never got the chance. They laid on the gas and an obnoxious muffler barked like a crackhead dog. Then we were off, rushing down the highways again.

I didn't even bother trying to weaponize a beer bottle. With my hands cuffed, it was a worthless endeavor. I couldn't jump, either. The redneck behind the wheel drove hard, with a lot of accelerator and brakes. I tumbled against the side-walls and knocked my head against one wheel well, momentarily stunning myself.

The truck left the county road and hit a dirt track,

bouncing over potholes and ruts. Mud sprayed up against the underside of the bed, and the darkened limbs of leafless trees passed overhead. I was cold now, my skin numb from the blast of wind and icy metal. But the temperature was the least of my worries.

These guys were clearly connected to the army of rednecks I had been slowly disabling over the past three days. And, clearly, they had a score to settle.

Handcuffed and lost somewhere in Evergreen County, the odds were against me. I was starting to think the bonfire idea had been a really bad one.

The truck finally stopped, and the guys jumped out. They dropped the tailgate and dragged me out without ceremony, then grabbed me under my cuffed arms and frog-marched me across a muddy yard toward a small house. It was wooden and white, with a wraparound porch and a couple lights glowing in upstairs windows.

A nice looking place, but poorly maintained. Piles of junk littered the yard, and paint peeled off the siding. Behind the house I saw the edge of a barn, and on all sides trees wrapped around the property, obscuring it from view of any passing highway.

Not that I expected there to *be* a passing highway. Wherever we were, it was well off the beaten path.

Not good.

The frog-marching continued, all the way around behind the house and up the back steps onto the porch, where a shirtless fat guy sat in a battered cloth recliner, a beer in one hand and a cigarette dangling from his lips. He looked to be about sixty, with a scraggly gray beard and a bald spot encroaching over the top of his scalp. Despite the cold, a little sweat ran down his chest, maybe because of the electric heater pumping warmth from a card table a few feet away.

The two goons kicked the backside of my knees in unison,

and I hit the porch as they dropped me. The fat guy said nothing, taking a slow drag from his cigarette as I regained my balance and knelt on the porch.

I smelled cat piss, and unwashed bodies. Nearby, a dog slept, snoring and drooling.

All else was quiet.

I spat and held my head up, facing the guy. He blew smoke slowly between his teeth, then lowered the cigarette.

"Good evening," he drawled.

I nodded once, but didn't answer.

"Know who I am?"

I shrugged, my hands still cuffed behind my back. I didn't really care who he was, and figured he was about to tell me, anyway.

"Name's Mack Crosby," he said, then took a long pull of beer. "I'm sort of a...proprietor, 'round here."

Mack Crosby.

I remembered the name. Marley had mentioned it. I had to admit, I expected a *proprietor* to dress a little better. Maybe paint his house more than once every century.

Maybe I expected too much.

"I'm Mason," I said.

He grinned. "I know you are. Mason Sharpe...homicide detective for the Phoenix Police Department."

So word gets around.

"Why are you here, Detective Sharpe?"

I shrugged again. "Just passing through."

"Huh. Passing through. And beating the hell out of quite a few of my kin, aren't you?"

I didn't bother denying it. Whatever this guy wanted, he was going to get it. No use provoking him.

"Your kin seems to have an issue with personal liberty," I said. "They keep trying to run me off."

Crosby ran a thick finger under one lip, prying out a bit of compacted food and spitting it onto the porch. He grunted.

"I got lots of kin, son. Crosbys been farming this land since before the war. Back when we had help."

He laughed cheekily. I didn't get the joke.

"I don't think your kin spends a lot of time farming, anymore."

"Nope." He shook his head. "Most of 'em don't. Most of 'em are deadbeats, honestly. Pot slingers, or meth cookers." He sipped beer again. "Some of them take jobs from rich folk around here. Private security work. You know...runnin' folk out of town."

"Is that what Daryl does?"

A cloud passed across Mack's face, as if I'd just said an ugly word. He grimaced a little. "I ain't gonna lie to you, Detective. Daryl's a real piece of work. He wouldn't know a good thang if it slapped him in the face. I guess he caused you some trouble?"

"Not really. But I caused him some."

"Kinda like you caused Floyd."

Floyd. That was the name of the guy whose wallet I checked, back at the bridge.

"Is Floyd one of your people?"

Crosby shrugged. "He's one of *our* people. One of the family. You know how that is—or maybe you don't. I don't reckon folk from out west appreciate family heritage quite like we do here in the south."

"I appreciate organized crime," I said, pushing my luck. "I appreciate a bunch of hicks trying to mug me, twice in one weekend."

Crosby tilted his head apologetically. "I am sorry for that, Detective. Fact is, I don't rightly approve of everything my nephews and cousins get up to. Lots of them associate with rough characters."

"Like who?" I asked. "Who does Daryl work for?"

Crosby grinned. It was a slow, cunning smile. "Aw now, Detective. Just coz I don't approve of it don't mean I'm gonna rat on my kin. Them boys may be idiots, but they're still family."

I sighed. "Okay. So take me back to my Bronco, and let's call it a night."

"You mean Daryl's Bronco."

"Well, he ran my car into a river, and tried to shoot me. I'd say the Bronco is fair compensation."

Crosby laughed—hard. Like it was the funniest joke he'd heard all week. He scratched the back of his head, exposing a gnarled mass of sweaty armpit hair.

"Fair compensation? Well, son, you might just be right. And I might be inclined to let you have it. But the thing is—" he leaned forward, lowering his voice a little "—we got rules 'round here. You understand? A code. A set of values. And, like it or not, them values say that if some outsider rolls into my county and starts banging up my blood, I gots to deal with it. Set the karma straight. Balance the scales. You understand?"

I really didn't like where this was headed. I said nothing.

Crosby finished his beer. "So, I tell you what, Detective. You didn't kill none of my kin, so I won't kill you. I'll let you go. But first...I gotta balance the scales."

He tilted his head toward the two guys standing beside me, and I felt their strong arms dragging me back. I kicked and tried to break free, but they slung me in the mud behind the house, and a couple well-aimed boots crashed into my sides.

I gasped for air and rolled face-up, fighting to my knees. One of them shoved me back down again, hard into the dirt.

Then I heard an electric popping sound—harsh and loud, not far away. I lifted my head to see one of the guys approaching me, a cattle prod held in one hand, blue lightning sparking between the prongs.

I closed my eyes and gritted my teeth, bracing for the pain. As the first wave of electricity surged through my body, I knew I would have been better off letting the big guy at the bonfire knock me out cold.

26

I awoke sometime the next morning, sprawled out in a ditch next to a county road. My pants were wet—from a mud puddle, I hoped—and I was coated in drying dirt. I hurt all over—from my shoulders down to my ankles, burn marks like bee stings sent continual waves of pain racing through my nervous system.

My face was a little battered, also. One eye was swollen, and my nose hurt, but it wasn't broken and the handcuffs were gone. I scrambled to my feet and leaned against a speed limit sign, my stomach convulsing as I sprayed puke over the ground.

Everything felt blurry and out of focus. But I remembered the night before. I remembered old man Crosby on the back porch, and the two goons who hauled me off to "balance the scales." I remembered the cattle prod, and a few hefty kicks to my stomach and ribs. It felt like it would last forever, but in the end it all blurred together, and at some point they had mercifully knocked me unconscious.

My fingers traced the welt on the back of my skull, and I

figured that was responsible for me blacking out. Some kind of blow from a club, probably. Or a bat.

I puked again, and leaned against the signpost, wondering where I was and how I was going to find my way back to civilization. A quick inspection of my pockets turned out my wallet and my Swiss army knife. Crosby's goons had taken what remained of the cash I took from Floyd, but they had left my credit card and driver's license.

How considerate.

I peered up at the sun and noted that it was not yet high noon. Probably around ten o'clock, giving me a general bearing of which way was east. I knew we had driven inland —west—to get to the bonfire party. That meant that if I walked east, I would be headed in the general direction of the coast, and Eastport.

It wasn't a great plan, but I was short on options.

Staggering into the oncoming lane where I could see cars headed toward me and maybe flag one down, I set off. My feet ached and my head pounded like a drum, but I managed to stay upright. Overall, save for the cattle prod welts covering my body, I felt kind of like I had a bad hangover. Hopefully a gallon of water, a good meal, and some clean clothes would set me straight again.

I wouldn't say no to four or five Tylenol tablets, either.

I walked maybe a mile before the first car passed—a minivan, headed west. The woman steered well into the oncoming lane to avoid me, and kept driving. The next vehicle was a FedEx truck, headed east, but he also kept driving.

At last a rusted old pickup truck, rattling along the road toward Eastport, rose over the horizon behind me. I held my hand over my eyes to block out the sun, struggling to make out the driver behind dusty glass.

I didn't have a lot of experience hitchhiking. In the Army I used to bum rides from buddies when I didn't have access to a car, or simply call a cab. As a cop, hitchhiking was something I not only avoided, but actively discouraged. It was dangerous.

But as a beat up, dehydrated pedestrian desperately in need of a meal and some painkillers, petty concerns like personal safety took a back seat.

I extended one arm, and held up my thumb.

The truck squeaked and rumbled as it approached, not doing more than forty miles per hour. It was another old Dodge, similar to Sherman's, but in much worse condition. The windshield was cracked and the tailgate was missing. The front bumper was held up on one side by bailing twine, and the right-hand mirror was gone altogether.

It still looked like the best thing I'd seen all day.

The Dodge squealed to a stop near me, and an old codger with three teeth in his mouth leaned out the open window. He grinned, wisps of white hair tugged by gentle wind.

"You lost, sonny?"

I offered a friendly smile and pocketed my hands, trying to look casual and unthreatening.

"I'm afraid so. Trying to make it to Eastport."

"Eastport? Whall, yer a good twenty miles from Eastport. What happened to your face?"

I shrugged, thinking I could make up a lie, then decided to go with the blunt truth.

"I offended a local guy. My mistake."

The old codger laughed. "I'd say so! You want a ride? I'm headed down the coast for a little handyman work, but I don't mind swinging through Eastport."

"I'd be very grateful."

He tilted his head toward the passenger door, and I climbed in. Despite the exhausted appearance of the outside of the truck, the cabin was relatively clutter free. The seat had a tear in it, and there was a hole in the foot well. But I fit in nicely, shutting the door as the old man took his foot off the brake and we rattled ahead.

"I'm Bernard. Folk 'round here call me Bernie. And you?"

"Mason. A pleasure to meet you."

"Likewise." He leaned back in his seat, one hand on the bottom of the wheel, driving like he'd probably driven this same truck since it was new.

"Where you from, Mason?"

"Arizona."

"No kidding? What brings you all the way to Eastport?"

I shrugged, still unwilling to broach that topic. It seemed easier to be vague.

"I wanted to see the island. I heard it was beautiful."

"Saint Ellen? It certainly is. I remember when that island weren't nothing but trees and scrub brush!" He laughed, shaking his head. "All the Yankees like it now. Folk from New York and Boston and them such places."

"They build homes on the island?"

He nodded. "Oh yeah. Snow birds, we call them. Not as warm as Florida, but a bit cheaper. Or it used to be, anyway. I reckon it's pretty packed out, now."

He dangled one arm out of the window, the speedometer hoping around thirty-five or forty. Maybe that was as fast as the old truck was capable of. I wasn't in the mood to criticize.

"I hear Eastport has grown a lot, too," I said.

Bernie nodded. "Oh, for sure. A lot recently, actually. All them jewelry stores and fancy shops near the water."

I tilted my head, remembering the shops. Remembering what Marley had said about the non-profit that opened them.

"They're new, huh?"

"Oh yeah. Back like three, four years ago, weren't none of that down there. Just a couple restaurants and the trinket shops. You know, for the tourists."

"But not jewelry stores?"

"Nope. Not a one. They all got built together, over like six months. I remember, coz I helped with the electrical."

"You're an electrician?"

He beamed. "No, sonny. I'm *the* electrician. Been wiring homes and businesses round these parts for fifty-five years. Since I was a young sprout!"

I laughed, noting the proud smile that hung over his toothless mouth. He leaned back and scratched his chin.

"Yep. Back in the day, you didn't need all these permits and whatnot. I was wiring up stuff barefoot, working with my old man. Barely old enough to drive!"

"I'm sure you've seen some changes."

His eyes grew distant, and he nodded slowly. "Yeah, son. Lots of changes. But you know what never changes?"

"What's that?"

Bernie tilted his face toward the roof of the truck. "Christ Jesus, son. All these years, all this hustle and bustle. Wars and recessions and me being in and out of work...but He's always looked after me. Always kept me going."

I fell silent, watching him slouched with one arm out the window. There was a quiet peace in his face that I hadn't seen in more than a few people in my lifetime. A sort of confidence—not a brash thing. But certainly a resolved thing.

I thought of Mia's worn Bible, still in my hotel room, and looked out the windshield again, suddenly tired of talking. Bernie took the hint, and for the last fifteen miles we rode in silence.

He dropped me right in front of Marley's, shooting me a wink and a wave as I piled out.

"God bless ya, Mason! Stay out of trouble, you hear?"

I waved and watched him rattle off, one arm still hanging out the truck. As he went, I drew a long breath, strangely calmed by my interaction with him. It was nice to talk to somebody so at ease with themselves.

A rare thing.

Back inside the pub, I found Marley gearing up for lunch, serving a couple tables and two guys at the bar. I conducted a quick sweep of the occupants, but didn't see any Crosbys.

That was good. I'd had my fill of them.

Marley saw me and her eyes went wide. She hurried to refill a round of beer glasses, and I helped myself to a stool at the quiet end of the bar. My back and legs protested as I settled in, but the smooth vinyl cushion felt good.

"Mason!" Marley snapped, keeping her voice low as she reached my spot. "What the hell happened?"

I looked up to the chalkboard menu, noting the burger again. "Mack Crosby happened. Apparently I stepped on the wrong toes."

"I'll say so. You wasted that guy."

I thought about the big dude in the dance ring—the one I had laid out in about five seconds. He wasn't the reason for Crosby's application of the cattle prod, but I didn't see a need to clarify.

"Are you okay?" Her voice dropped a little, carrying an edge of concern. I met her hazel eyes and saw the look of one soldier watching out for another. Not a personal concern, but not a professional concern, either. A brotherhood thing. Or, in this case, concern from a sister.

"Never better," I said with a forced grin. "How about a burger and fries? And beer, if you have it."

She rolled her eyes and went for the beer, then stopped by the phone.

"Oh, by the way. Somebody called asking for you. Jacquie somebody? She left a message."

Marley pointed to a folded scrap of paper next to the phone, and I helped myself to it while she went to the beer cooler.

Marley's handwriting was atrocious—barely legible. But

the message, written in a series of police codes, was legible, and I understood it immediately. I frowned at the paper, then heard the door swing open behind me. I glanced over one shoulder.

Cassandra stood in the doorway, a bag in one hand, staring right at me. We made eye contact as I fingered the paper, then she turned and hurried out.

I took a long pull from the beer Marley passed me, then canceled my lunch order.

"I'll be back," I said.

27

"Hey!"

Cassandra had made it to her car by the time I exited the pub. She stood with one hand on the door handle, and surveyed my face. For a moment I thought she would open the door and drive right off.

Instead she just waited while I approached, self-consciously brushing dirt off my arms.

"Where you headed?" I asked, pocketing my hands.

"I'm going home."

I tilted my head toward the sun. "Just now? The sun's out."

I let a hint of sarcasm slip into my tone. Enough so that she would know her cover was blown.

She impulsively glanced toward the street, but nobody was passing nearby. I decided to press ahead.

"Why don't you let me buy you a coffee?"

"Why would I do that?"

"Because I think we should have a chat."

She hesitated again, still studying my busted face. I must really look special, I thought.

"What happened to you?"

"Cattle prod."

She flinched. "Seriously?"

"Not the kind of thing I'd lie about."

"Why?"

"I crossed the wrong people."

"Locals?"

"Yep."

"Why?"

"I've been poking around. They don't like that."

She chewed her lip. I rocked my head toward the row of cutie boutiques across the street, with a coffee shop on one end.

"Let's get coffee."

CASSANDRA FINALLY AGREED, and I thought I knew why, but I didn't vocalize the guess. She left her bag in the car and we ordered cappuccinos. I also ordered a Danish, because I was hungry. Then we walked down the main drag, all the way to the boardwalk where Main Street terminated at the Cape Fear River.

I took a seat on a park bench, enjoying the sun on my skin. It wasn't quite warm yet, but after days of icy cold wind and rain, the bright sky felt like paradise. Cassandra sat at the far end of the bench, crossing her legs and holding her coffee without drinking it.

I tore into the Danish, my stomach growling. What I really wanted was the burger I'd ordered at Marley's.

"Who are you?" Cassandra asked.

"I told you. My name is Mason."

"Yeah, you said that. But why are you here?"

I sipped the coffee and took my time answering. "I came

here for personal reasons. Then I got caught up with the Daniel Porter murder. I've been poking around."

"What happened to your face?"

"Like I said, I crossed some locals."

"Not the black eye. I'm asking about the burn mark on your cheek. It was there when we spoke at the diner."

I finished the Danish, wadding up the paper wrapper and taking my time again. Then I decided to tell the truth.

"Handgun," I said. "Burn scar."

Cassandra nodded slowly, and I thought she understood. But she didn't comment.

"Let's talk about you," I said. "And why you're really here."

"I told you why I'm here."

"You did, and you lied."

"Did I?"

"Yep. Probably not about being from Philly. You sound like you're from Philly. But you lied about the photography, that's for sure."

"How do you know?"

"Because that car you're driving isn't a rental. It's a government vehicle, leased to the FBI."

I faced her as I finished the sentence, a little confrontation in my tone. She didn't move. Didn't blink.

"How would you know that?" she asked calmly.

"Because I'm a cop. Phoenix Police Department. After you searched my room the other night, and then lied about it, I had a buddy run your plates."

Cassandra picked at the edge of her coffee cup lid, not breaking eye contact. And also not speaking.

"I don't know why you're here," I said. "But you're doing a lousy job at staying undercover. You stick out like a tourist."

"Maybe I am a tourist."

"Nope. Not this time of year. You and I are the only two

outsiders in town. And you know that, which is why you went snooping."

"I told you. I stumbled into the wrong room."

"After you lock-picked it, you mean."

She flinched, just a little. I grinned and slurped coffee.

"One professional to another. Can we just tell the truth?"

A gentle wind rippled off the river, blowing against my battered face. It felt good. Cassandra made a small, noncommittal shrug.

"Okay. You're right. I'm not a photographer."

"And your name isn't Cassandra."

"My name isn't important."

"Why are you here?"

"Why do you think?"

"I'd assume you're investigating something."

"You'd be right."

"What?"

"I can't say."

I grunted and looked out over the water. Seagulls bobbed and swept across the dock, fighting over bits of trash. In the distance I could see the edge of Saint Ellen Island, and imagined I could make out the crest of the old lighthouse poking out from the trees.

"You should leave town," Cassandra said.

"Why?"

"Because you're not helping. And because if you keep blundering around, you're gonna get hurt."

I shrugged. "I'm three-and-one, thus far. I like those odds."

"Well, I don't. People like you, playing hero and crashing into things, make my job a lot harder."

"I'm sorry about that."

"Then leave. Before you make things worse."

I twisted to face her. "You gonna tell me what you're looking into?"

She didn't answer.

"Daniel Porter?"

"No."

"Related?"

"I highly doubt it."

"So why not share? One professional to another."

"Because you're not a professional. You have no jurisdiction here. And I don't like your approach—not even a little. You're a bull in a china shop, and that's not how the bureau functions."

I stood up. I still felt stiff. I still needed a shower.

And, most importantly, I still needed a burger.

"Well, I wish we could have helped each other. Good luck with whatever you're working on."

She rose, cradling the untouched coffee. "You're not leaving, are you?"

"Nope." I started toward Marley's.

"Why not?"

I paused, running my tongue along the inside of a busted cheek. Feeling all the little wounds inflicted on me by the cattle prod, the boots, and the two guys' fists. They had really worked me over. Really done their best to run me out of town.

I looked over one shoulder.

"Because this is personal now."

28

I returned to my hotel room and showered, then changed into my now dry clothes from the boat trip with Sherman. My legs, back, and stomach were pock-marked with burns from the cattle prod that, for all I knew, were permanent. My face looked like something out of a bizarre art piece, with the left side scalded by my revolver and blackened by fists, but the right side pretty much untouched.

All in all, I felt good about myself. If Mack Crosby had been actively engaged in whatever conspiracy Daryl and Floyd were wrapped up in, he probably would have killed me. As it was, I could deal with the fading soreness and ache in my bones.

I had work to do.

After stopping by the bar for a burger and a couple of beers, I proceeded to the road leading out of Eastport and pocketed my hands, settling in for a long walk. I recalled Trudy telling me that she had left her son with family in a town called Lowberg, and I also recalled seeing signs pointing toward such a town during my drive out to the bonfire the night before. Now that Trudy was homeless, I figured she had probably assumed semi-permanent residence with the aforementioned family, and I wanted to talk to her.

I had more questions about Daniel.

The sun was out and warm on my face, doing a nice job at loosening my muscles. After a weekend of freezing rain and clouds, the warmth and vitamin D felt like heaven itself, and I didn't even mind walking. But I held my thumb out to every passing car anyway, because it was over twenty miles to Lowberg.

The first vehicle to stop was a utility van owned by some carpet company. He took me as far as the intersection of the highway leading into Lowberg, where I hopped out and turned west. The next ride came from a passerby in a pickup, who took me the remaining seven miles to my destination. I borrowed his phone to call Trudy. Her number was smudged on the scrap of paper she'd given me, forcing me to guess the last digit and dial three times before she answered. Trudy seemed a little surprised to hear from me, but when I told her I was still looking into Daniel's death she was willing to talk, and gave me her address.

The guy in the pickup was familiar with the street name and offered to drop me off right at her house. We drove through the heart of Lowberg, which looked a lot more like a traditional American city than Eastport. Fast food, grocery stores, gas stations, and small businesses lined the main drag, where a surge of cars rushed by and nobody waved. Everything felt a little grimy and aged, and the houses we passed were all constructed in a distinct 1970s style. It reminded me of a lot of expansion neighborhoods built around Phoenix during that era, back when everybody wanted to be in Los Angeles, but only about half of them made it that far.

I climbed out of the truck in front of a split-level home sitting on a hill, with green gunk growing up the north face, and a litter of sticks and leaves carpeting the yard beneath a giant oak tree. Trudy's modified minivan sat alone in the driveway, and the mailbox leaned a little.

I thanked the driver, then walked right to the door and hit the bell. It took Trudy a moment to answer, and when she did the emotions playing across her face were as distinct as a flashing digital billboard. Momentary uncertainty, instantly replaced by shock. Probably at the sight of my face.

"Hey, Trudy," I said, hands in my pockets. "Mind if I come in?"

She glanced around the street, maybe looking for the person responsible for my black eye. Then she nodded a couple times and pushed the glass door back.

Trudy didn't have a black eye, but all things considered, she didn't look a lot better than me. Crow's feet crinkled around her eyes, and her hair was tangled into a messy bun. Sweatpants and a sweatshirt were matched to house slippers, and the deep pain I saw in her eyes was almost too visceral to look into.

Not just visceral. Familiar.

"Thanks for coming by," she said, leading me down a narrow hall and straight into a kitchen. Dirty dishes lined the counters, and a half-made sandwich lay on a paper plate. Trudy wrung her hands absently, turning from one counter to the next as if she didn't know what to do with herself.

"I'm sorry about the mess. There's been so much going on. This is my sister's place—she's at work. Do you want a sandwich? I was just about to eat. Timmy's sleeping."

She spoke at ninety miles an hour, slopping mayonnaise over bread and spreading it with a spoon. I accepted a bologna sandwich with a gentle smile, then followed her through a living room scattered with books and board games and onto a screened-in back porch.

Trudy pulled back a chair next to a picnic table and invited me to sit. I laid the plate down and looked over the backyard.

It was covered in oak trees, much like the front, stretching down to a privacy fence now weathered by time. There was a doghouse, but I didn't see a dog. Everything was very quiet.

Trudy took a seat across from me, rubbing her palms over the legs of her sweatpants and avoiding my gaze. She picked at her nails, and I took a bite of the sandwich to give her time to relax.

It was good. Far too much mayonnaise, but I could live with that. My gaze drifted around the porch and I noticed two cardboard boxes laden with picture frames, dirty clothes, and a few china plates. Everything looked smoky, with a dusting of soot gathered on the glass surface of the pictures.

Relics from the house fire, I figured. So Trudy was there. Or maybe the firemen saved the things for her.

I put the sandwich down. "I'm sorry about your home."

Trudy's eyes rimmed red. She nodded a couple times and her lips twisted. I thought she was about to cry.

"Do they know what happened?" I figured it was better to lead with mechanical questions about the house, versus diving straight into conversation about Daniel. The home was by far the lesser loss.

"They say electrical," Trudy said. "I guess that's possible. It was an old home."

"Well, it takes time to investigate."

"Did you ever do that? As a cop?"

I shook my head. "No. The fire marshal does that. They're really good at it, too. You'd be surprised what they can find."

Trudy picked at her nails again.

"I've been looking around," I said.

"About Daniel?"

"Yes."

She hesitated. "Have you...found anything?"

"I'm not sure. I've hit some...resistance."

"Is that what happened to your face?"

I offered a sheepish smile. "Well. You know. Not everybody likes cops."

My gaze drifted back to the boxes in the corner. I thought I saw something poking from one side, beneath a folded pile of clothes. It was wooden, and looked a little glossy, with curvature that made me think of scrollwork. I wiped my mouth and walked to the box, kneeling quietly and lifting away the clothes.

A violin lay inside, leaned against the cardboard with soot staining the smooth amber face of the bout. Worn strings and a gently marred fingerboard indicated extensive but loving use, and as I traced the F-holes I felt the familiar touch of quality rosewood.

A beautiful instrument. A Cecilio, I thought. Exactly the kind of mid-grade violin a practiced amateur might select.

I looked over my shoulder. "Did Daniel play?"

Trudy stood behind me, tears bubbling in her eyes as she looked down at the box. She wiped her nose and nodded.

I ran my fingers behind the elegant neck, brushing away soot from the fire. "May I?"

Trudy hesitated a moment, then nodded again. I found the bow deeper in the box, a little battered by the hasty recovery from the house fire, but still in operational shape. Retreating to the table I laid the instrument in my lap and used my napkin to gently clean it, clearing away ash and dust and adjusting the strings by feel. Daniel had kept them loose, which meant he knew something about storing a violin, and maybe hadn't played in a while. Back home I always kept mine tight.

Because Mia wanted me to play every night.

The thought put knots into my stomach, but touching the worn instrument felt like home. I adjusted the bow, then gently glided it across the strings, twisting the pegs until the tune sounded right to my practiced ears.

Then I laid the violin on my shoulder, and tucked it under my chin. For a moment I let the bow rest over the strings, thoughts of Trudy and the unfamiliar house around me fading away. Leaving me alone, imagining my couch back home. Imagining Mia sitting there, smiling up at me while I sat on a stool and leaned against the wall, my own violin pressed against my cheek.

The bow resting on the strings. Perfect stillness in the moment between deciding to play, then deciding what to play.

I closed my eyes and moved the bow, choosing the first piece that came to mind. It was one of Mia's favorites, a somewhat unknown song written by an American folk artist named Jay Ungar. Entitled "Ashokan Farewell," it was used as the title track for a documentary series about the American Civil War that Mia and I had watched one weekend while she was sick, and she fell in love with the melancholy melody.

As the bow glided across the strings and my fingers worked the neck, I forgot altogether about Trudy. My eyes remained closed, and I saw Mia on the couch, her head tilted to one side, her eyes rimmed red. The whine and resonance of the violin filled the air, and I leaned back in my chair as though I were leaning back against the wall.

The world no longer existed. Dead bodies and rednecks with baseball bats faded away. Only the haunting, soothing sound of the music mattered.

And, for just a moment, I pretended she was with me.

I stretched the piece into a full five minutes, and when I opened my eyes again they were blurry. Trudy shamelessly sobbed across from me. She clutched a cloth to her face and bent over, embracing the grief, and for a few minutes I joined her.

They say there are stages of grief. I've never found that to be true. As both a soldier and a cop, I've seen a lot of people lose a lot of things, and to me the emotional fallout that results looks more like a bomb blast than a road map. Denial, anger, bargaining, depression, and acceptance all merge together, some dominating others for a short period, before fading and blending into the background.

Nothing is linear. Nothing is final.

Listening to myself play, and picturing Mia so clearly as she had sat on the couch, all curled up, I felt them all at once. The rage at her pointless loss. The denial that it could even be real. An acceptance that yes, it was real. It would always be real. And a depression that clouded my mind the moment I admitted that.

The only thing I didn't feel was any desire to bargain with God. Because I'd bargained with Him before, and it never brought people back from the dead.

Trudy mopped her eyes, sniffing and breaking me out of my silent stupor. She stared at the violin and swallowed. "That was beautiful."

I forced a smile, even though I didn't feel it. "It was my fiancée's favorite piece."

"Was?"

I met her gaze. "I lost her in November. School shooter."

The pain in Trudy's gaze matched my own in a deep and resonate way. And then she said the only words she could say. The only words I needed to hear.

"I'm sorry."

"Me too," I whispered.

She dropped her face and I laid the violin on the table,

brushing the back of my hand across my eyes and thinking about Daniel again.

Thinking about the lacerations on his wrists, and the thugs who seemed so interested in derailing my investigations.

"I want to talk about your husband," I said. "I've got some questions."

29

T rudy fixed us both hot tea before she would talk, and we spent a few minutes sipping in silence. Then she simply nodded to me.

"How long did Daniel work for the social security office?" It was a question I already knew the answer to, but it felt like a safe place to start.

"Seven years. He used to be a trucker, believe it or not. But after we had Timmy he wanted to be close to home. Especially with Timmy's health, and all."

"Did he enjoy the work?"

Trudy shrugged. "I think it was pretty boring. I mean, it was a government job. But the health insurance was good, and we needed that."

"I understand cerebral palsy can be very expensive."

"Enormously. I mean, you hit your deductibles and healthcare kicks in. But you'd be amazed how much insurance won't cover. Not just travel expenses, but certain procedures and therapies. Anything they deem to be 'experimental.'"

She made air quotes with her hands, and I thought I knew what she meant. I had a buddy who lost his leg in Iraq, and needed a lot of physical therapy and prosthetic specialists. Despite being wounded in combat and being awarded disability pay from the Department of Defense, the mountain of bills that piled up was stupendous.

"Did you guys struggle with money?" I asked.

"Always. We did the best we could. Daniel had actually been working overtime a lot. The social security office paid him to manage excess paperwork on the weekends."

I frowned. "What do you mean, *manage excess paperwork*?"

She sighed. "I don't know the details. Apparently they were short on processors, or whatever. It was menial work, but the money was actually pretty good. He made an extra forty grand in about ten months."

A dull tingle ran up my spine. It was an instinctual feeling I had learned to trust—a subconscious alert that I had just stumbled onto something important.

I had never heard of a government institution such as a social security office working weekends, or offering overtime. In my experience, such offices were more than content to let the paperwork backlog, and simply get to it when they got to it. But the far bigger red flag was the money. A thousand bucks for a weekend's worth of work? No way. Not from a government job.

"Did Daniel work every weekend?"

"All day Saturdays. Occasionally on Sunday afternoons."

The time periods sounded familiar, and I knew why. They were the same weekly slots Sherman said Daniel used to come fishing with him.

So Daniel was lying about the overtime, and Trudy had bought it. That much was clear. But that didn't explain the influx of cash. If he was actually fishing with Sherman, he hadn't indulged in any illicit weekend activity she didn't know about, so where did the money come from?

"Did he ever work late during the week?" I asked. "Or go in early?"

Trudy shook her head. "No. Pretty normal hours...eight to five, plus an hour commute each way."

Those hours corresponded perfectly to his legitimate schedule at the social security office, and Gerry had made no mention of missed work during the week.

Daniel hadn't been up to anything sketchy Monday through Friday, either. Had he borrowed the money?

I decided to switch gears. Come at this from another angle.

"I stopped by his office...I hope you don't mind. I just wanted to talk to his coworkers."

She kept picking at her fingernails.

"His boss said Daniel had a large life insurance policy... did you know about that?"

Trudy snorted and looked through the screen at the back-yard. It was a derisive sound. Almost disgusted.

Not the reaction I expected.

"It's a government program," she said. "Supposedly Daniel got better rates on life insurance if he bought it through payroll deductions. But, like anything the govern-ment does, the paperwork took forever. He just completed the medical exam a couple weeks ago. The policy was due to kick in thirty days later."

I felt the defeat in her words, and my shoulders slumped.

"Maybe you can fight that," I said. "If he passed the medical and signed all the paperwork...maybe they'll work with you."

Trudy rolled her eyes. "You don't know much about the government, do you?"

I did. In fact, government work was pretty much the *only* thing I knew about. And I knew I was blowing smoke at her. There was no chance anybody was writing a million-dollar check unless they absolutely had to.

"Gerry said Daniel applied for the policy recently?"

Trudy nodded. "Couple months ago."

"Why? Was it a new program?"

"No. Not new. He just...came home one day and said we should look into it. I guess he was thinking about all the bills."

Her eyes watered, and she looked away. I thought again about the bump on Daniel's head. If he really had a life policy this large on hand, the Eastport Police Department's explanation of his death might make sense. The policy wouldn't pay out for suicide, but it might pay out for what appeared to be an accidental death.

Would Daniel have staged a suicide that didn't look like a suicide, just to ensure his family's financial security?

No. It didn't make sense. If Trudy knew the policy wasn't yet in effect, Daniel should have known that also. And life policies usually don't pay out if the policy holder dies while conducting illegal activity, anyway. Stealing a boat would void the policy.

Plus there were the lacerations on his wrists. They still bothered me.

"Have you talked to the police?" I asked.

"They called to update me on the fire investigation. They said they should have final results tomorrow."

Tomorrow.

That didn't sit right with me. In a big city like Phoenix, flush with resources and fancy equipment, it might take days or even weeks to identify the source of a fire. The thought of a backwater fire department completing an investigation in under forty-eight hours was suspect at best.

But I didn't say so. No reason to further distress her.

"What about Daniel? Have they said anything more about him?"

She began to sob again. I gave her time to wipe her eyes with the cloth and regain a little of her composure.

"They still say it was an accident. That he stole a boat and went out too far..." She swallowed hard. "I just don't understand it. He used to fish with Sherman sometimes, in the summer after work, or on Sundays. But not lately. Not with all the overtime. And he would *never* steal a thing. It just wasn't like him."

I said nothing, sorting through the pieces in my mind and wondering exactly how much I could trust Trudy's judgment. I would never say so, not to her face. But, in my experience, any husband who is willing to lie to his wife about the source of forty grand might very well be the sort to steal a friend's boat.

But for what purpose? That was the question. Why would a guy take a boat that small so far off the coast, in the middle of the night, when he had fished those waters long enough to know how dangerous they were?

What was he looking for?

Or had he not stolen it at all? Had somebody tied him up, hit him over the head, drowned him, then cut the ties and dumped his body in the water?

That still didn't explain where Sherman's second boat was, and it still left the ultimate question: *why?*

Again, I thought about the money. Forty grand was a lot of cash. If Daniel had borrowed it from the wrong people, then failed to pay up...

That might be the beginning and end of the story. Regardless, I wasn't going to let it rest until I knew for sure, and I knew who was responsible.

It wouldn't bring Daniel or Mia back from the grave, but it

would give me peace of mind. It would resolve something in place of the death I couldn't resolve.

"I'm going to find the truth," I said. "You can bet on that."

Trudy's lip quivered.

"I...I can't pay you."

"I don't want you to pay me. I'm doing this for myself."

Her eyes watered and she looked down. "Thank you," she whispered.

"It's my pleasure."

I loosened the violin strings, then the bow. I wiped them both down one more time with the napkin, then gently laid them in front of her.

"Keep this someplace dry, and don't leave the strings tight for too long. It's a beautiful instrument."

She cradled the violin almost like a baby. I thought I understood why.

"Daniel wasn't very good," she said. "Not like you. But...he loved it a lot. I loved it a lot."

"That's all that matters."

"Is there any way I can help?" She looked up.

"Focus on your family. Look after yourself. I'll call you when I know."

Trudy gave me a hug as I left, offering another sandwich. I politely declined, then started off down the street again. I had thought about asking her for a ride back to Eastport, but she had her son to look after, and besides, I was growing to like hitchhiking. It was like Forrest Gump and his box of chocolates. You held your thumb out, never knowing what you were gonna get.

It took me two hours to travel twenty miles, eventually catching a ride with the same carpet van who'd drove me out to the highway. When I finally arrived back at Marley's, I was a little tired, and thinking about another burger.

But, more than that, I was thinking about the coming night, and what I was going to do next. Because I now believed more than ever that Daniel's death was a matter of foul play.

It was time to find his killer.

30

I ate a hot meal at Marley's and asked her for a map of the Cape Fear River. She gave me a strange look, like when I had asked to borrow her phone, but after digging through drawers a minute she resorted to surrendering her personal iPad, cheekily instructing me not to look at her browsing history.

I chugged my beer and navigated to the map application, switching to satellite mode and slowly scanning up and down the coast. The Cape Fear River was wide at Eastport, but not very far to the north it narrowed considerably. With the satellite image it wasn't difficult for me to find what I was looking for, and after zooming in to inspect the spot I made a note of nearby landmarks, then returned the iPad.

"Any place around here where I can rent a boat?"

"What kind of boat?" she asked, wiping down whiskey glasses with the sort of absent-minded obsession only bartenders ever master.

"Any kind, I guess. Fishing boat."

She frowned. "Why?"

"I want to go fishing."

The rag stopped over a glass, and she shot me a sideways look. "*For what?*"

A perceptive question, I thought. But not something I wanted to get into.

"Trout, I suppose."

I wasn't actually sure if saltwater trout were a thing around the North Carolina coast, but it felt like a safer bet than catfish or tuna—the only other two kinds of fish I knew anything about.

"I've got a boat," Marley said cautiously. "Flat bottom, fourteen-footer with an outboard."

I perked up. "Sounds great. How much?"

She rubbed the glass slowly, still looking suspicious. "Where's your fishing rod?"

"Gotta buy one."

"Uh-huh." She sounded very unconvinced, but she had mentioned the boat, which I took to mean she was open to doing business.

"Hundred bucks?" I said.

She pursed her lips, pouring herself a double shot of whiskey into the freshly cleaned glass. She took a long sip, then inspected me over the rim.

"You're looking into the Daniel Porter thing, aren't you?"

I didn't answer, focusing on my beer.

"You know what, I don't want to know. Boat's around back. Don't wreck it."

I left her a hundred dollar tip on my credit card receipt anyway, then found my way outside the pub, pausing at the old pickup on my way to find the boat. It sat on rotten tires, and a long crack ran across the windshield, but overall the truck was in far better condition than I expected. The interior was pretty clean, with a fully restored seat and a graduation tassel hanging from the rearview mirror. It was a GMC C15, probably a '67 or '68. Two tone, green and white, with dual headlights and a long bed.

A nice truck. It reminded me a lot of my old K10, and made me miss it.

I patted the hood and passed around to the back of the pub, where a mess of beer kegs, rotting cardboard boxes, and pallets leaned against the wall. Next to them an aluminum trailer sat with a flat-bottomed metal boat resting on it. It was old, but looked to be in good shape, with a twenty-five-horse Johnson hanging off the back.

Perfect.

I walked down Main Street until I located a small general store, where I purchased the best flashlight they offered, and a coat that was a little too small, but would be better than nothing. As the sun set the cold was returning, and I didn't want to face the night with nothing better than a T-shirt.

Then I returned to Marley's and asked her about towing the boat to the water. She wanted to know when, and squinted at me when I said after dark.

"Trout bite better at night," I said with a shrug. It was probably complete nonsense, I really had no idea. But I figured she already knew I was up to something off the books, and wouldn't question me.

She didn't, and I returned to my room for another shower and a long nap to finish out the afternoon.

I would need to be alert tonight. On my A-game. Because if I found what I expected to find, a fight was coming.

And this time, somebody wouldn't walk away.

31

I met Marley outside just after ten PM. The pub was bumping for a Monday night, but she didn't seem bothered to leave it for a minute. She backed a newish Jeep Wrangler to the nose of the boat trailer, and I hooked it up. Then we rode in silence the one mile through downtown to the public boat ramp, where I waded right into the water and guided the vessel against the pier.

Marley parked the Jeep, then wandered down the pier to watch me fiddling with the Johnson. It was a tiller-controlled motor, meaning that I would sit in the stern of the boat and manage speed via a simple twist throttle, like the grip on a motorcycle.

I'd used small boats like this before, and while I don't fancy myself any sort of sailor, I felt comfortable with the system.

"You got enough gas?" she asked, hands in her pockets.

I had walked to the gas station down the street from the pub earlier that day, carrying the Johnson's detachable five-gallon tank with me. I wasn't really sure how long five gallons would last, but figured it was enough.

"Sure," I said.

"And you know about the primer?" She pointed to the little rubber bulb mounted beneath the Johnson's pull cord. I pumped it a couple times, priming the motor with fresh fuel. Marley didn't comment further, but when I looked up she appeared disgruntled. As though she were second-guessing her decision to loan me the boat in the first place.

I settled into the stern, laying my flashlight next to my feet and suddenly realizing I had forgotten to bring a fishing pole. I had only planned to do so to reinforce my ruse, but if Marley didn't know I had zero interest in angling by now she was a lot dumber than I thought.

"You're not going out front, are you?"

I shook my head. "Just upriver a ways."

"Okay..."

She shivered under a breath of salty wind, pulling her coat tighter around her chest. I was cold also, and the ill-fitting jacket wasn't helping. But there was nothing to do about that now.

"Well. Good luck, I guess," she said. "I hope you find what you're looking for."

"Me too," I said. Then I squeezed the throttle, and pulled the starter cord. The Johnson turned over a few times before finally coughing to life, but ran smoothly once started. Marley reached out with her foot and pushed the nose of the boat away from the pier, helping me to swing out to sea. I shot her a two-finger salute, then gunned the motor and rumbled into the river.

I TURNED DIRECTLY UPSTREAM, keeping not more than fifty yards offshore with Eastport passing to my left. Overhead the sky had cleared of the clouds that had infested it for so many days, exposing a field of stars and a half moon. The light over the dark water reflected in my eyes, with nothing other than the rumble of the Johnson to break the calm.

It was peaceful, reminding me of two nights previously when Sherman and I went looking for his missing boat. For the first time in a while I thought about Daryl and his friends dumping the bag of credit card and paper shreds into the water, and wondered how in the world that fit into all this mess.

Whatever the reason behind Daniel's death and the persistent campaign to have me run out of town, I knew Daryl wasn't calling the shots, and neither was Floyd or any of the other guys I had broken down like Lego men. They weren't smart enough for anything more complex than basic dirty work, but more than that, it was the work itself that convinced me of a darker mastermind behind it all.

Daryl was *paid* to run me off. And unless he spent his evenings shredding stuff for the heck of it, somebody must have paid him to dump that trash, too.

For some reason.

I pulled the jacket tighter around my chest and focused on the here and now, sidelining the questions. Ever since talking to Trudy earlier that day, I'd been working on a theory. It was rudimentary at best, and might well be wrong. But it wasn't illogical.

Assuming Daniel had been killed, and wasn't simply the victim of a bizarre accident, that still left the question of Sherman's missing boat. Of course, it could have been stolen by somebody else, completely unrelated to Daniel and his untimely demise. A sort of tragic coincidence.

But I didn't think so. The far more logical option was that somebody had stolen it as a *part* of Daniel's demise, setting the stage for the entire boating mishap theory that Chief Lowe and the rest of his department were so convinced of.

After all, assuming Daniel's death was meant to look like an accident, the killer would have needed a plausible explanation for how Daniel ended up out to sea by himself.

The missing boat was in fact the missing piece. But Sherman and I hadn't found it offshore, despite Sherman's thorough knowledge of the undersea topography and where it may have sunk. Maybe whoever had killed Daniel took it farther off the coast before sinking it, but I didn't think so.

Because, as Sherman described it, it was a nice boat. Why not keep it? Scrub the serial numbers, repaint the hull, then flip it like a stolen car. There had to be a thriving boat market around Eastport. Sure, this particular vessel had been employed in a murder, but somebody as dumb as Daryl probably didn't care about that. He was probably just seeing dollar signs. Why waste an asset?

Selling it would take time, though. In the interim the thief would need to hide it. Someplace along the river, probably. Inland, amid the trees and little inlets, north of Sherman's house.

My inspection of the map on Marley's iPad had revealed only one such possible hiding place—a smaller river or maybe a creek a few miles upriver, sheltered by trees. If I was hiding a boat, and couldn't risk trailering it, that was where I'd park it. Up that creek, under the trees. Out of sight.

Tonight's mission was all about testing that theory by investigating the creek.

I hadn't bothered to measure the distance from Eastport to my destination, and shortly after leaving the pier I regretted that. Even with a relatively light load the Johnson struggled against the current of the Cape Fear River, and sucked greedily on my meager gas supply. I kept the motor on half throttle to conserve fuel and keep the noise down, but at that speed the coast dragged by in slow motion.

To keep myself awake I used the flashlight to scan the

coast, just in case I had miscalculated and Daryl had parked the boat closer to Eastport. Twice I saw nocturnal life, wandering amid the dark and rural stretches of coastline devoid of development or humanity. But I saw no center console boat.

The fuel tank drifted down to a quarter, and what gas remained sloshed around every time I steered too harshly. I knew I was now well past the point of no return, and wouldn't be able to make it back with what I had. If nothing else, I would steer into the edge of the river and use the motor as a sort of rudder while the current drove me downstream to Eastport.

Right now I wanted to keep going, as long as I could.

I was maybe ten miles upriver when I finally reached the inlet. I recognized it by the landmarks I had selected on Marley's iPad—a low sandbar off to my right, and a giant oak tree rising out of the bank.

The creek was about fifty yards wide, and sheltered on both sides by dense groves of trees, their limbs leaning over the water and blocking out the bulk of the moon. I didn't see any houses, or lights. The coastline both north and south of the creek was dark and desolate, with only the continued burble of the Johnson to join the breath of wind overhead.

I steered gently into the creek, twisting the throttle just enough to overcome the flood of water dumping into the Cape Fear River. The flat-bottomed boat glided upstream with ease, deep shadows passing on either side.

I saw more wildlife in the darkness, yellow eyes staring at me with curious intensity, but still no humans.

All was still.

A hundred yards upstream, the creek narrowed to barely twenty yards wide, but it was still deep. I shone the light into the water next to me and couldn't see the bottom. Around every gentle curve I swept the flashlight into shadowy recesses beneath tree limbs, but saw nothing save more forest, and occasional animal eyes.

After another hundred yards I was almost ready to give up. The gasoline in the bottom of the tank was about to run dry, and I didn't trust the weaker current of the creek to drive me back into the river without power.

I decided to give it one more turn in the waterway, and twisted the tiller to the right. The nose of Marley's boat edged around a last curve, swinging wide to avoid the draping fingers of a willow tree leaning down close to the water. I eased off the throttle, and cut the engine. Quiet engulfed me as my own momentum carried me through the bend and to the other side. I swept left with the flashlight, searching through the trees, driving back the dark.

Then I saw it.

32

The boat matched Sherman's description of his missing center console—eighteen foot long, with a single outboard motor and a sort of roof overhanging the controls. It was half-beached against the muddy bank, with a dirty rope lashing it off to a nearby tree.

And it wasn't alone. I recognized the larger, twin-engined craft tied off next to it as the boat I'd seen Daryl dump the presumed body bag from two nights previously. Both vessels lay encrusted in shadow, completely invisible to a casual passerby who wasn't searching for them.

I pushed the tiller hard left, and glided into the bank, only ten yards down from the makeshift marina. For a moment I just sat there, sweeping my light down the length of Sherman's boat, and trying to put the pieces together.

Then I heard voices. They came from deep within the trees, and I snapped the flashlight off. For a moment I sat frozen, just listening for approaching footsteps, but the muted sounds I heard only a moment before grew no louder. As the wind changed and blew against my back, they faded altogether.

I moved quickly to the nose of Marley's boat, using a short length of rope in the bow to tie it off before I crept down the bank. Sherman's center console was rammed far enough against the shore for me to lift a tree limb and expose the interior. I swept the light across the front deck, and immediately noticed two things: snapped wire ties, about twelve inches in length, and faint traces of blood.

My heart rate quickened and I debated hauling myself aboard for a more thorough inspection. Then I decided against it. My investigative training wouldn't allow me to risk contaminating evidence.

I crept to the second, larger craft instead, and repeated a quick search over the bow. Credit card fragments and scraps of paper littered the floor, along with empty beer cans. No blood or wire ties, though.

I swept the light to the ground at my feet and quickly identified packed earth, marred by heavy boot prints. The track led clearly between the trees, up the bank, and deeper into the forest.

I flipped the light off and followed the trail on the balls of my feet, my detective instincts now taking backstage to the years of intensive army training. Moving through woods like these, silent and stealthy, was second nature to me. In a strange way, it felt like home.

I just lacked the rifle.

Keeping my head low, I made quick progress toward a growing orange light. I heard the voices again, also. Still muted, but becoming louder. Through the fading trees I thought I made out the hulking shadow of a structure. A house, maybe. Or a barn.

And a fire. The light grew brighter, and I smelled smoke on the air. Stopping fifty yards out, I bent over almost double and moved from one tree to the next, closing in on the spot.

I could now make out individual words, slurred by alcohol. Three figures surrounded the fire, two slouched back in camping chairs while the third dug through an ice chest. The structure beyond the fire was some sort of lodge, or cabin. Not very large, but topped in a gunky metal roof and covered in bare cedar siding. An ATV and a jacked up pickup truck sat next to the cabin, both covered in mud. The ATV I didn't recognize, but the truck was very familiar.

It had served as my unwelcome taxi to Mack Crosby's house, and the two guys slouched in camping chairs were my tormentors with the cattle prod.

The third guy, the one digging beer out of the ice chest, was Floyd Crosby. I recognized his ugly face and noted the lump on the back of his head, highlighted by the dancing glow of the fire.

The handiwork of Mia's lug wrench.

Floyd staggered to a chair, but didn't sit down. He knocked back a full can of beer while swaying on his feet, then tore his fly open and proceeded to piss straight into the fire. The other two guys shouted curses, rushing from their chairs to avoid the cloud of urine steam. Floyd just chuckled, spraying piss everywhere.

Idiots.

I dropped to my stomach and eased forward, army crawling another ten yards until only the deep shadows and scraggly brush of the tree line sheltered my position. Floyd finished his piss and zipped the fly, then looked to the ice chest as though he were contemplating another beer.

Instead he collapsed into his chair, and promptly passed out.

"Stupid fool," one guy drawled. "If he weren't the old man's nephew I'd bury his ass in the mud."

The second guy toed Floyd's chair, hard enough to send the unconscious drunk's head rolling. Floyd didn't wake.

"Don't worry about it," the second guy said. "He'll get what's comin' to him."

"He better. You know Bill said Floyd's responsible for what happened to Daryl. Said Floyd let that damn cop get the jump on them."

"That so?"

"It's what Bill said."

The second guy snorted. "Bill's no less busted up than Daryl. You ask me, they're all to blame. I mean, who loses a fight, four-to-one?"

"We shoulda kilt that guy. Dumped his body in the river."

"Nah, man. The boss is right about that. I mean, how many bodies before the feds come sniffing around again?"

I squinted as the disgruntled conversation faded into another round of beers and extended silence. Part of me wanted to take the guys out now. Storm out of the trees and go to work on them, right there next to the fire. I had my Victorinox with its three-inch stainless-steel blade. More than enough edged real estate to eliminate two of them, then carve the truth out of the survivor.

I'd done it before.

But something in the back of my mind told me to wait, and I didn't have to wait long.

Headlights flashed through the trees, up a narrow road behind the parked pickup. Neither guy seemed surprised, abandoning their chairs and leaving Floyd snoring as they moved to meet the newcomer.

I shielded my face from the blast of the high beams as the vehicle stopped, its nose pointed right at me. I thought it was an SUV of some kind, probably black, but in the glare of the lights it was impossible to be sure.

The two rednecks approached and held a conference with the driver. I couldn't make out the words over the rumble of the SUV's engine and the continued crackle of the fire. The driver was obscured by shadow, but I saw him raise one hand and jab a thumb toward the rear of the vehicle.

Both guys moved around back, and the rear hatch rose above the roofline. A moment later they returned, each dragging a long black bag, identical to the one I'd found at the bottom of the bay while diving off Sherman's trawler.

I watched in focused silence as both bags were dragged across the clearing and dumped near the fire. I guessed by their floppy consistency that they were loaded with more of the same from the previous night—paper, and maybe more shredded credit cards.

The bags hit the dirt, and the two rednecks shuffled back to the SUV. But then the headlights flashed from low to high beams, and I ducked my head to avoid the glare. The driver's door popped open, and boots hit the dirt.

"Hey!"

I froze. Not daring to move, hardly daring to breathe. Wondering if my scant cover had been defeated by the headlights.

"What's that?" It was a new voice—one I didn't recognize. A faint New York accent accentuated the angry demand.

"Huh? What?"

"Is that Sherman's boat?"

I risked a peek above the leaves, and my heart skipped. The driver stood next to the fire, pointing angrily over my head toward the riverbank, forty yards away. He was tall, dressed in black slacks and a black overcoat, with slicked-back hair.

And I recognized him. He was the guy I had seen the previous weekend while exploring Eastport—the man with the duffel bag, walking in and out of the jewelry stores.

"Hey!" The New Yorker backhanded one of the rednecks across the shoulder. "I'm *talking to you*. Is that Sherman's boat?"

The rednecks peered through the trees as if they required visual confirmation of the vessel's presence. The New Yorker cursed.

"I *told you* to scuttle it!"

"Yeah, yeah. We heard you. But we ain't scuttlin' no perfectly good boat! You know how much that thing's worth?"

"You know how much prison time *you'll* be worth if the cops find it?"

"You said you paid them off!"

The New Yorker's hand struck like a snake, cracking the guy right across the face. He stumbled back, holding his nose. But to my surprise he didn't fight back. Instead he cowered a little next to the fire, and his buddy made no move to defend him.

"You *listen to me*," the New Yorker snarled. "You get your grungy, inbred ass in that boat and you *scuttle it*. Right now! You hear me? I better never see it again!"

The New Yorker kicked at the cowering guy, and both men scrambled toward their truck—to retrieve the boat keys, I figured. I didn't wait for them to head for the river. Moving quickly to my feet, I leveraged the confusion to circle left around the clearing, jogging between the trees as the New Yorker stopped to berate the rednecks a little longer.

By the time he turned for his vehicle, I had already circled behind it. By the time he reached the driver's door, I had slipped into the back.

And, by the time he reached for the switch to close the automatic tailgate, I was already nestled safely inside, hidden only a few feet behind him.

My suspicions about Daniel's death had been confirmed by the bloody wire ties I'd seen in the bottom of Sherman's boat. But I still didn't know why—*why* they had killed him.

It was time to find out. I was tired of playing it safe.

33

The New Yorker drove silently for a long while, the SUV bumping over ruts and potholes on its way back to the blacktop. By now I'd determined the vehicle to be the black Escalade I'd seen before, but connecting the duffel bag guy at the jewelry stores to Daniel's death brought me no closer to understanding his motivation.

Or what he was up to.

The rear of the Escalade was expansive, and empty, leaving me plenty of room to stretch out comfortably behind the back seats and to sneak occasional glimpses through the tinted glass. The driver eventually flicked on the radio, tuning in to a jazz station and providing a mask to obscure any soft noises I made.

It was almost too easy.

As we turned onto a blacktopped road, I saw trees passing on either side, and thought we might be heading north, but there was really no way to be sure. Occasional passing cars blazed light across the sides of the Escalade, but it was a long time before I noticed any houses or developments. I saw a sign in the opposing lane, indicating Eastport and Lowberg ahead, and concluded we must be on the road north to Wilmington.

Did the guy live up there? If we ended up at his house, what happened next? I could stay in the shadows, observing and waiting for something to happen.

Or I could resort to the knife in my pocket, and *make* something happen. I wasn't enthusiastic about that option, but I reminded myself that this guy had killed Daniel. Or had Daniel killed.

Either way, he had it coming.

A buzzing sound rang from the dash, cutting off the music. A button clicked, then the New Yorker spoke. His accent was just as heavy as before, but his tone had changed from the barking command he used against the rednecks. Now his words were slow and cunning. I had the immediate image of a snake charming its prey.

"Sylvia! Well, aren't you up late."

The woman who replied sounded young, maybe late twenties, and southern. I could hear her voice clearly over the Escalade's Bluetooth system.

"They moved my shift. I just got off work."

The New Yorker leaned back in his seat. "Well, I hate to disappoint, darling, but I'm out of town this evening. I'll have to see you tomorrow."

"That's fine. I wasn't calling about that."

"Oh?" His voice dropped a notch. I couldn't tell if it was curiosity or irritation.

"I...it's about the school. They sent me a bill. For field trips and things. Apparently it's outside of regular tuition."

"And you want me to pay it." Now I was sure he was irritated. His voice had dropped to a low growl.

"Yes." The woman snapped back quickly, blustering with mustered courage. "I do. That's the deal, Lewis."

"The deal? You want to remind me of the deal? Because

the deal was for me not to evict your broke ass. Paying for your retarded son's education is called generosity."

The woman snorted. It was an angry sound. "A gift isn't a gift if you expect payment."

I peered through the crack in the back seat and watched the New Yorker sit up, one fist clenched over the console. I thought he might be about to explode, but instead he drew a long breath, then a toothy grin crept across his face. I could see it, barely visible in the rearview mirror.

"How much is the bill?"

The woman paused. Maybe she wasn't expecting him to acquiesce. Or maybe she was on guard.

"Four hundred."

"I'll make the transfer tonight. A thousand. Use the rest to buy that phone you wanted."

Another long pause.

"Thank you," she said. Her voice was soft now, but not sweet. More demure. Almost broken.

The New Yorker leaned back in his seat, his big arms twisting as he turned the Escalade off the highway. I felt us bouncing into a parking lot, but I didn't risk a look. He was talking again.

"Like I said, Sylvia. I'm a generous man. I like making you happy. Do you know why?"

"Because I make you happy."

Her voice had the robotic characteristic of a person regurgitating a party line. The New Yorker didn't seem to mind.

"Absolutely. So very happy. Now, I ordered you something. It'll be there tomorrow. I want you to wear it when I come over."

"I...I won't be available tomorrow night. I have to work."

The Escalade stopped and he shifted into park. Risking a glance out the back window I swept my gaze across an empty parking lot, with a brick building facing us. It was a post office, now closed for business without a person in sight.

What?

My attention was arrested as the New Yorker spoke again. "Now, Sylvia. You know I get irritable when you're unavailable. That's not part of the deal, is it?"

"I told you, they moved my shift!" the woman protested. "I can't help—"

"Well, you better help it!" His voice snapped like a gunshot. "Or I'll cancel those tuition checks faster than you can drop your pants. You hear me?"

Dead silence. My fingers curled into an involuntary fist. I wanted to throat punch him.

"Please...Lewis..."

Her voice gurgled with suppressed tears.

"Save it," the New Yorker barked. "Call your boss. Tell him you're sick. Get the schedule changed. I'll be there at nine. Am I clear?"

"Yes." Another broken answer.

"Great!" The anger evaporated like vapor in the desert, his snake-like charm returning. "So I'll see you tomorrow, then. And, Sylvia?"

"Yes?"

"Don't forget my gift. I'd like you to wear it. Only it."

He hung up before she could reply, and I sat a little stunned as he climbed out and slammed the door. I watched him through the back glass, marching into the post office and disappearing behind tinted windowpanes. He was gone about three minutes, then returned with a wad of envelopes clutched under one arm.

He dumped the mail onto the front passenger seat, then we were off again. I grew bolder in the back of the SUV, peering through the glass to watch Wilmington roll by. We stopped at another post office on the far side of town, where the New Yorker repeated the procedure. Then we were on the highway, with signs flashing by advertising Raleigh, one hundred and thirty miles away.

I settled in, listening as he took three more phone calls. I could tell by his tone of voice when he answered what kind of person was calling. The first two were business associates, and they received the same brash, Long Island tone he used with the rednecks. The third was another woman, equally as broken as the first, subjecting herself to a lengthy and graphic session of phone sex while the New Yorker continued his snake-charming manipulation.

I learned nothing from the business calls, and the sex call made me sick. I blocked out most of it, watching the signs flash by on the highway, but I gathered that the woman was being blackmailed in some way similar to Sylvia.

It made me think of Daniel, and Trudy, and the mountain of medical bills streaming into their mailbox.

Did the New Yorker hold something over them, as well? What had he demanded from Daniel in return?

In Raleigh we stopped at one post office, then immediately hit the highway before I could consider whether to abandon ship. The phone calls ceased, leaving the vehicle in alternating periods of jazz music or silence.

It was well past midnight, now. We crossed north of the Virginia state line and I noted signs advertising the state capital—Richmond. I began to think it was a mistake not leaving the Escalade in Wilmington, and was relieved to hear the New Yorker flick the turn signal on.

We took a ramp off the highway, and not to my surprise, found our way to yet another post office. He parked out front and I waited for him to walk inside. Then I slipped over the back seat and exited through a rear door, jogging to the edge of the brick building.

I peered around a corner, squinting through the glass,

and saw the New Yorker making his way down a row of post office boxes with a fist full of keys in one hand. He opened a door, slid a wad of mail out, then locked it and moved across the room to another. After four separate boxes he dumped the pile on a table next to a trash can and quickly sorted through it, tossing about half the envelopes into the trash before retaining the rest and moving to the door.

I slid into the shadows, watching as he boarded the SUV and started the engine. I made note of the Escalade's license plate number as he navigated out of the parking lot, and then he was gone. Headed back toward the highway.

I hurried through the exterior doors and into the twenty-four hour PO Box room of the post office.

The wad of envelopes and colorful mailers resting in the trash matched those I'd seen him discard. I sorted through them quickly, checking the names and addresses on each, and searching for any sort of cohesion in subject matter.

It was classic junk mail, all of it. The kind of crap I disposed of three or four times a week whenever I remembered to check the mailbox. Grocery store coupons, cruise advertisements, vehicle warranty alerts, and an absolute slew of credit card offers. Dozens of them.

The names printed on the envelopes weren't names I recognized, but I found it odd how many names shared the same PO Box.

Dorothy Hutchins
Matthew Webber
Clair Ramirez
Chauncy Kincaid

I've used PO Boxes before, all around the country. It wasn't unusual for me to lease a new box and wind up collecting a smattering of mail for the previous tenant. But I never remembered finding *this* many unrecognized names in a single box. And not with so much volume, either.

It made me think all these people shared the same box. And that was strange.

I dumped the lot of it back into the trash, then returned outside and sank my hands in my pockets. The Richmond skyline gleamed on the horizon, not far away. I figured there was probably a bus station nearby, and with luck there would be a route back to Wilmington in the next few hours.

From there I could hitchhike to Eastport.

And then what?

I stood, just staring at the skyline, arranging each piece of the puzzle in my mind. Everything from Daniel's body washing ashore, to Sherman's missing boat, to the credit card shreds at the bottom of the bay. I thought about the rednecks running me out of town, and the New Yorker with his unexplained operation.

Whatever he was up to, it was clearly illicit. Sordid, even. Enough so to get Daniel killed.

But not before he'd paid Daniel for something. Forty grand over ten months, Trudy had said. Money trickling in, like a regular salary. A recurring payment for an ongoing service.

I closed my eyes. Thought about Trudy. Thought about her disabled son, struggling with a life-threatening, incredibly expensive illness.

Thought about what a parent would do to provide for their child. Like what Sylvia was willing to do to put her kid in a good school.

What had Daniel been willing to do?

My eyes opened, and I saw it. Not quite a complete picture—there were still some holes in my mental image.

But I saw the gist of it. I knew what the New Yorker was

doing. I knew what he paid Daniel to do, and I knew why Daniel kept it a secret.

I knew what this whole nasty operation was about, and I also knew that *somebody* had lied to me.

Turning down the sidewalk, I started toward the heart of town. Bus stations are always located downtown, for easy access to other forms of public transportation. With luck I could be back in Eastport by noon.

And then it would be time to deal with this thing. Once and for all.

34

I made it back to Eastport nine hours later. The Greyhound from Richmond to Wilmington was only fifty bucks, and departed shortly after I bought my ticket, but it took a nerve-grinding seven hours to travel less than three hundred miles.

After arriving in downtown Wilmington, I made a half-hearted attempt at hitchhiking, then resorted to hailing cabs and bribing them to take me on a one-way trip into the middle of nowhere. The third guy agreed to do it for a hundred bucks, and we were off.

It was just past noon when I stepped into Marley's, a little haggard, but not sopping wet for a change. She stood behind the bar, wiping down the counter in the midst of the midday lunch rush, and the look she flashed me said she was glad to see me.

Maybe because I still had her boat.

I walked to the end of the counter and raised my voice to be heard over the commotion of a dozen hungry patrons.

"Where's the photographer?"

Marley squinted, annoyed. "Where's my *boat*?"

I waved the question off, tilting my head in the general direction of the river. "It's fine. Upriver. Have you seen her?"

"Who?"

"The photographer. The woman with the backpack. She was staying here."

"Oh. Cassandra? She checked out this morning. Left half an hour ago."

Dammit.

I hurried back outside, ignoring Marley's shouted questions about where I had been—and where her boat was.

Cassandra's government sedan was gone from the parking lot, and even as I stepped into the street I didn't see it. In fact, I didn't see anything. The city was quiet for a Wednesday afternoon, with only a few cars parked along the curb, a warm sun beating down from overhead.

I stopped, forcing myself into Cassandra's shoes. If she had abandoned her mission—whatever that mission was—she may have left town. By now she could be halfway to Virginia, probably headed to Washington.

But the determination I'd seen in her face only the previous afternoon made me think otherwise. She didn't look like a woman who was ready to quit. Maybe she had checked out of Marley's to change scenery, or avoid being noticed by staying in one place longer than a photographer might.

But she wasn't quitting. She would still be searching, probably turning up the heat a little.

Kicking it up a notch.

What would that mean?

A car topped the rise, four blocks away, headed toward me. Sun glinted off the hood, but I recognized the blue and gray paint of an Eastport police Explorer. As the vehicle drew closer, I thought I recognized the cop behind the wheel—one of the guys who'd hauled me in for questioning after I found Daniel's body.

The cops.

The thought clicked in my mind and I broke into a jog. It might be a long shot, but if Cassandra was who I thought she was, she wouldn't leave town without confronting the police. If she'd only left Marley's half an hour ago, she might still be at the station.

I completed the one mile stretch between Marley's and the two-story, mint green police station in under twelve minutes without breaking a sweat. The parking lot lay on the sheltered side of the station, but long before I reached it I heard a woman's voice, sharp and angry, and I knew my bet had paid off.

I rounded the corner and saw Cassandra standing just outside the main entrance, one hand on her hip, the other jabbing a finger at Witmore. The cop was doing the goldfish thing with his lips, and Cassandra looked ready to knock his head off. Chief Lowe was there, also, and he was red faced.

Cassandra finished her tirade, calling Witmore an "incompetent slob," then stomped toward her government car. Witmore spluttered and clenched his fist, but Lowe propelled him back into the station before he could explode further.

"You said you paid them off."

The redneck's protests from the night before, referring to the local cops, echoed in my mind. I had suspected Chief Lowe, Witmore, and perhaps the entire department might be dirty ever since they rushed Daniel's autopsy, but now I had proof.

It was something to be dealt with, but not right now.

Right now I needed the truth.

I jogged to Cassandra's car just as she slammed the door. The engine started, but she didn't drive away. Her head slumped against the wheel, and her shoulders shook just a little.

I rapped on the window with my knuckles.

Cassandra sat bolt upright, her face snapping toward me. Her eyes were red-rimmed and laced with anger, but her countenance changed when she saw my face.

Probably not the face she was expecting.

I motioned for her to roll down the window. She hesitated, then hit the switch.

"You won't get anywhere with them," I said, tilting my head toward the station. "They're in on it."

She squinted, wrinkling her nose in an obvious attempt to not sniff.

"In on what?"

"On what got Daniel Porter killed."

Another hesitation.

"I know why you're here," I said. "You work for the financial crimes division, right? Money laundering."

She didn't answer.

"You're in the right place, investigating the wrong crime," I said. "They aren't laundering money. Or, maybe they are, but only as a byproduct."

Again, no answer. She seemed to be wrestling with something. I was getting impatient.

"Look, I've spent the last four days looking into this, and I've got it mapped out. But I don't travel on one-way streets. If you want my help, you're gonna have to let me in on what you know."

She stared at me, her hair disheveled, chewing her bottom lip. I gave her a few seconds, then grunted in disgust.

"All right. Have it your way." I smacked the hood of her car and turned away, pocketing my hands. I gave it five steps before she changed her mind.

I made it only three.

"Wait."

I looked over one shoulder.

"You're a cop for real, aren't you?"

"You already know I am."

She licked her lips, then cut the motor and stepped out of the car. She played with the keys a moment, and I noticed the busted fingernails on her right hand where she had played with those keys for a few hours over the past week.

A strained woman. Ready to make a deal.

"I...I can take a two-way street."

"Great," I said. "Let's get coffee."

35

We returned to the coffee shop for refreshments. I ordered mine black this time, to help with the sleepiness, and doubled up on the Danishes. Then we walked to the same bench overlooking the Cape Fear River, and took our seats facing the water.

I liked the spot. It was far enough in the open for me to be sure nobody could be hiding nearby, listening. And now that the clouds had rolled back, the view was amazing.

I started on my first Danish.

"Name," I said.

Cassandra folded her arms. "I told you my name."

"No. You told me your cover. If we're gonna do this, we're gonna do it honestly."

"And why should I blow my cover?" she demanded.

"Because you've already blown it. You blew it with me after that nonsense spiel about photography. And you blew it with the bad guys just now, talking to Lowe and Witmore."

She thought about that a moment, evaluating me. Probably evaluating what harm, if any, could arise from admitting her true identity.

Then she shrugged. "I'm Paulette. Paulette Sherman."

I glanced sideways at her. "Sherman? Like Pat Sherman?"

"Who?"

"Never mind. Why are you here, Paulette?"

She tilted her head. "I'm not sure I'm ready to divulge that information."

"Cool." I moved to stand up. She raised a hand.

"Okay! Geez, man."

I sipped my coffee. Stared at her.

"All of this is...strictly confidential. Okay? Can we agree on that?"

"Sure."

She looked out to the river, her coffee once again abandoned. I saw her struggling with the reality of divulging her mission, then she seemed to reach a *screw it* moment, and the gates opened.

"You're right, I work for financial crimes. Analyst. Seven years with the bureau."

Analyst. Not a field agent. Well, that explained her sloppy cover and inexperience at lying to people. She wasn't used to this kind of work—probably had no business being here at all.

"What the hell is an analyst doing in the field, searching people's hotel rooms?"

She didn't answer right away, and I got the feeling she was trying to decide whether to lie. Instead she said: "It's a long story."

I grunted, willing to accept that punt for now. "Okay. Why Eastport, then?"

"We got some tips about some funny business, down here. I'm sure you've noticed all the jewelry shops."

"I have."

"They were all opened at once, about four years ago. A lot of other places have opened around here, also. Gift shops.

Convenience stores. The town's economy is outstripping its population average by a ratio of four to one."

"What does that mean?"

She shrugged. "Well, you know what GDP is?"

"Gross domestic product. Like, the total value of an economy."

"Right. Every municipality has a GDP, even if they don't usually call it that. The census bureau has calculated a formula by which we are able to estimate the economy of a region based on the number of people who live there, and whatever primary industries are at play. Obviously, a place like Silicone Valley has a much higher GDP per person than, say, Topeka Kansas."

"But there's an average."

"Exactly. On average, adjusted for region and industry, the formula indicates how much income a municipality should generate, based on the number of inhabitants. So, if we say there are four thousand people living in Eastport, give or take, there's a GDP range we'd expect to see for this region."

"And the GDP you're seeing is four times higher than it should be," I said. "That's what you meant by four-to-one."

"Exactly."

"But it's a tourist town. In the summer this place is popping. All the locals say so."

"Sure, but remember, our calculations include regional industries. We're already assuming a GDP influx during the warmer months. Eastport's economy is still much larger than it should be."

I looked across the water, processing the new information, and quickly deciding that it fit perfectly with the theories I had already formulated.

"So you measure an economy based on recorded financials?" I said.

"Right. Stuff the treasury department has. Tax returns. Non-profit reports. All that."

"And you're seeing an influx of cash."

"A *significant* influx."

"Which set off money laundering alarms."

"Exactly."

I sipped my coffee, taking time to formulate my response. Checking and double-checking my logic. I didn't want to be wrong.

"They're not laundering money," I said. "They're running an identity theft scheme. A *massive* one."

"Say what?"

I twisted toward her. "Daniel Porter worked for the social security department in their new files division."

"Daniel who?"

"Porter. The dead guy who washed ashore last Friday. I found his body and I've been poking around ever since. Like I said, he worked for the social security department up in Wilmington, managing new files. Like, when a baby is born, or somebody emigrates. They're assigned a new social security number. He managed that paperwork."

"Okay…"

"Porter has a kid with a major medical condition. Bills through the roof. But his wife told me he's been working overtime and earned an extra forty grand in the past ten months."

"Geez…"

"My thoughts exactly. I visited his office, and his boss confirmed he's only worked regular hours. I also visited his fishing buddy, who gave me an explanation for where Daniel was when his wife thought he was working overtime."

"He was fishing?"

"Right. He netted an extra forty grand, but he wasn't

working overtime, and he wasn't working elsewhere. So what was he up to?"

She played with her car keys for a minute, thinking it through. Then she snapped her fingers. "He was selling social security numbers."

"Exactly. A lot of them. New social security numbers, issued to recently born children—victims who have no way of knowing they are being victimized."

"Which would enable somebody to commit mass identity theft without being caught."

"Yep. Probably by grooming the numbers. A churn and dump racket," I told her.

"Huh?" She raised her eyebrows at me.

"It's a financial scheme. You take a social security number assigned to a child, with no credit history, and you match it with a false date of birth, then open a credit card. You pay it on time, keep the balance low. Let the credit score grow for six, twelve, or eighteen months."

"Then take on a crap ton of debt," she finished. "Cash out and abandon the number."

"Bingo. Churn and dump. I saw it on a small scale in Phoenix. Something the guys in financial crimes were working on. I thought it was crazy, but I'd bet money that's happening here. Last night I followed a guy through Wilmington, Raleigh, and Richmond. He was checking PO Boxes and collecting mail for all these people—identities he was grooming, I'd guess."

"Richmond *Virginia*?"

"Right."

"That's almost three hundred miles."

"Sure. But think about it. If you're grooming a couple hundred fake identities attached to real social security numbers, you can't have all those people linked to the same address. It would be a massive red flag for people like you—

analysts evaluating identity theft. Spreading the names around a couple dozen PO Boxes would help minimize risk."

"Damn…" she breathed, running her tongue over her lips. I could see the wheels spinning behind her eyes, calculating and evaluating. The investigator in her kicking in. Thrilled by the chase. "But what about all the jewelry stores? Are they unrelated?"

"Actually, I think they're right at the core of this thing. Cash is king, right? But the only way to convert credit cards into cash is to run them through legitimate processors. Make a large charge to a credit card, then have the business that processed the charge kick back the majority of cash to you, without actually selling you any merchandise."

"And that's why they're using jewelry stores," she said, raising a finger. "Because single large purchases make sense at jewelry stores."

"Exactly. And you know how you can make a purchase online, and your credit card statement reads some random address across the country?"

She nodded.

"That's because the business is headquartered there—it's the address their credit card portal is linked to. I'll bet these stores—" I motioned with my thumb back toward town "—are linking their card processing accounts to false addresses all around the country. So it never looks like a large volume of transactions linked to default accounts are being processed in one place. It looks random. Small peanuts, for massive credit card companies. But it could be hundreds of thousands for these people."

Paulette's fingers worked the keys, her coffee still untouched. For a while she sat in wonderment, the excitement growing on her face. Then her features fell.

"But…this is just a theory? You don't have proof."

"Not hard proof, no. But I've watched these people. The

guy I rode with last night...I first saw him here in town, ducking in and out of jewelry stores with a duffel bag. Collecting cash from his collaborators, probably. I also saw him handing off bags of shredded documents and credit cards to the thugs who keep trying to run me out of town, and I saw those thugs dumping the same material offshore. Hiding evidence."

I swallowed black coffee. The bitter burn tasted good. "Something else. Marley mentioned an investment firm that rolled into town a few years back to build these jewelry stores. She said it was from New York, or Boston. The guy I trailed had a heavy New York accent."

"So you think he was behind the investment firm, also?"

"Why not? He comes down here and opens all these high-end jewelry stores in the name of building the next Panama City. Then he uses those stores to launder the money from his identity theft scheme. It's the full circle. Keeping everything in-house, for extra security."

"Wow..." she breathed. "How did you come up with all this?"

I shrugged. "It's just how my mind works."

"But is it airtight? Can we prove it?"

"It's not airtight. There's still some big questions on the table. For instance, if this thing was chugging on so smoothly, why did they kill Daniel? Also, we still haven't found the heart of this thing. An operation this size will need some kind of headquarter. A discrete place with internet and heavy-duty computers where smart people can groom credit profiles and apply for credit without their IP addresses being traced."

"An office, maybe? An abandoned commercial space?"

I shook my head. "No. More discrete than that. Probably something out of town. Close enough to be shielded by the local cops, but not close enough to be noticed by people like us. Some place where the actual grooming takes place—

where all the computers are. You find that, and you find your proof."

"Okay...so how do we find it?"

"You're gonna run the plate number of the Escalade I hitched a ride on last night. Get the name and address of the owner. We'll start at his place, and have ourselves an old-fashioned stakeout. But first, there's one more thing we need to discuss."

She stiffened, just a little. As if she knew what was coming. "What?"

"You," I said. "Because you're still not being honest with me."

36

Paulette looked away, her brown hair snapping across her face in a fresh gust of river breeze. She sipped the coffee for the first time, and for a moment I thought she might walk. Take what I had told her and try to run it to ground on her own.

But I hadn't given her anything concrete yet. I still hadn't told her the Escalade's license plate number. And, in her defense, she wasn't that kind of analyst. She didn't want to backstab the person who was quickly becoming her new partner.

"You're not being honest with me either," she said at last.

I felt a twist in my stomach, knowing she was right. I set my coffee cup down and folded my arms.

"Okay. One for one, then. Ladies first."

"Why are you here? Really."

Good question.

I inhaled deeply, and wanted to lie. But I knew my eye was still black and my left cheek was still scarred by the blast of my Smith. Not the face of a convincing liar.

"Last November my fiancée was killed in a school shooting," I said, my voice softening. The words hurt, but I rushed ahead with them before I could overthink it. "We were going to honeymoon here. Stay on the island. After she died...I came by myself. To..."

I swallowed hard, my eyes stinging. Looking back toward the island, I thought about sitting in the sand. One hand on the gun. One finger on the trigger.

So close.

"To find her again," I finished, my voice dry. I wasn't sure if Paulette connected the dots or not, but it was as much as I was willing to say about my moments on the beach.

As much as I would ever say.

"I was on the island when Daniel's body washed ashore," I continued. "I reported it to the cops, but something felt fishy. I felt like they were lying to me. Then I met Trudy—Daniel's wife—and I guess...I knew how she felt. Losing somebody. So I started digging."

I finished, staring at my shoes. Eager to move on without further questions.

"I'm sorry," Paulette said. I nodded my thanks, then took my turn.

"Why is an analyst down here, investigating alone?"

She brushed hair out of her eyes, then let out a sigh, as if to say, *where to begin?*

"Short answer? I suck at my job."

It wasn't the answer I expected.

"I never wanted to be in law enforcement. I wanted to be a concert pianist, believe it or not. But my father was with the FBI, and he was killed investigating organized crime in Detroit. I was headed to college at the time and I guess...I don't know. It got to me. I felt like I owed him something."

"So you signed up."

"Yeah. Finished school. Got parked behind a desk. Always

trying to get that field job. Always trying to...make his death right, somehow. Bust some criminals. Make him proud."

She looked away suddenly, as if she had said more than she meant to. I gave her time, knowing what that pain felt like. Losing a father might not be the same as losing a fiancée. Truth be told, I wouldn't know. My mother died when I was fifteen of a drug overdose. I never knew my father.

But, on some level, loss is loss. And I knew she was telling the truth.

"So why are you still riding a desk?" I asked.

She snorted a little laugh. "Like I said. I suck at my job. I'm not good at police work—not good at puzzles. I want to quit."

"But you can't," I guessed. "Because it feels like failing your father."

She didn't answer. She didn't need to.

I knew what it felt like to fail somebody.

"They don't know you're here, do they?" I asked.

She shook her head. "I'm supposed to be on vacation."

"In their car?"

She shrugged. "For the last couple months I've been digging into this GDP thing. Trying to explain why a town of four thousand people is producing the economy of a town five times that size. We do this all the time—check up on cash flows, review reports from treasury, all that. Hunting drug activity, usually. My bosses think Eastport is a wild goose chase. No drug gangs here."

"But not you?"

"I guess I had a feeling. Like something was here. But without something tangible, nobody would take me seriously. So I emailed the local sheriff's office and spoke to state law enforcement. Just fishing for enough evidence to get a field agent involved. After I came up empty-handed, I decided to take some vacation and drive down. Figured I would poke around myself. Try to make something happen."

I watched her fidget with the cup and avoid my gaze. A person far out of her depth, treading water and begging for something to be true.

It explained the sloppy photography cover story, anyway. It explained why an undercover investigator would be stupid enough to use a government car. But Paulette was being too hard on herself. The lock-picking of my hotel room was quality work—work I'd only noticed because I've spent years studying the little things.

And, more importantly, her instincts were sharp—sharper than her boss's. Because there *was* something going on down here. Something ugly.

"If I find you solid evidence, do you have the pull to get people down here? Actual field agents?"

She nodded eagerly. "Absolutely. No problem."

"Okay. I can make that happen. But only under one condition."

She gave me a blank stare, as though she were half expecting a sexual solicitation.

That wasn't close to what I had in mind.

"When the cavalry shows up, and you write your reports, I'm nowhere on them. I never existed."

Paulette frowned. "Huh?"

I faced her. "I don't want to be caught up in this mess. I promised Trudy I would find the truth, and I will. But then I'm on my way. You take the credit, and I take the sunset."

Again with the blank stare. Maybe she didn't understand, or maybe she questioned the integrity of a man who didn't want to be involved in an investigation.

Fair enough. But that was the deal.

I held out my hand, and Paulette took it. We shook once, and I drained the coffee. I could feel the excitement in her posture—the promise of an impossible win, just around the corner.

It was rookie energy. The stuff stakeouts are made of.

"Where do we start?" she asked.

I dumped my cup in the nearby trash can. "Marley's. You're gonna run that plate on one of your computers, and I'm gonna eat a burger."

"A burger? Seriously?"

I started down Main Street. "Field work 101, Paulette. You never hunt bad guys on an empty stomach."

arley's burger was as delicious as ever. We sat in the corner and I sipped beer and packed away the food while Paulette used the pub's Wi-Fi to log into some kind of federal database and run a search on the plate. I gave her the digits from memory, and observed the clumsy way she wrote them down on a cluttered sketchpad, then bumbled through the software.

She wasn't good at this. It wasn't her natural bent, like it had always been mine. But I'll take a clueless partner with effort over an experienced partner with apathy any day.

Marley watched us from the bar between tending to the lunch crowd. I could see the curiosity on her face. Possibly even mild suspicion. But she didn't ask questions—not yet, anyway.

"This guy?"

Paulette rotated the laptop, and I squinted at a digital image of a driver's license.

Lewis Frederick Carrol, Eastport, North Carolina.

"That's him," I said, recognizing the smug smile and heavy eyes. He was a big dude. Six foot two, according to the ID, born in 1972. Black hair, brown eyes. A little Italian looking, but with a name like Carrol, who knew.

"He's a pimp," I said.

"Huh?"

"Two of the calls he made last night were to women he has his thumb on. He's blackmailing them for sexual favors."

"Are you serious?"

"He had phone sex while driving. To completion."

Her face twisted into a sickened grimace. "That's..."

"Obscene," I finished. "Does the address on his ID match his vehicle registration?"

"Why?"

"Because driver's licenses are only updated every four to six years. Twelve years, in Arizona. But vehicle registration updates every twelve months. It's more likely to be accurate."

"Oh..."

Paulette did some clicking, eventually producing the North Carolina tag receipt issued by the county.

"Different address," she said.

"Told you. Where?"

"Some street in Highland Bay."

I took control of the laptop, scanning the vehicle registration for the Escalade. In addition to the address, there was a phone number with a local 910 area code. I scrawled them both on a napkin, then opened Google Maps and punched in the address. Highland Bay was a bedroom community about five miles outside of Eastport. A quick survey of online maps told me what I already suspected—it was an affluent area, stocked with multiple six-figure homes on lush green lawns.

No actual highlands. No actual bay. Exactly the kind of place a guy who drove an Escalade would live.

"This is it," I said, finishing my beer. "Let's roll."

LEWIS FREDERICK CARROL'S house was opulent compared to the humble abodes populating the remainder of the county. Built in an adobe style that reminded me of Arizona, it looked bizarre this near the coast. It sat on a small green hill fifty yards off the street, with a winding driveway, two stone gateposts, and a three-car garage. I couldn't see it, but I would have bet money a nice-sized pool sat out back. A giant front door guarded the two-story home's facade, and gentle sprinklers watered a lush lawn.

A nice place. Paulette looked up the home on Zillow and put the price tag at around four hundred thousand. Dirt cheap, compared to Phoenix prices. But still far north of the national average.

This guy made good money.

"What did you do before you were a cop?" Paulette asked suddenly.

We were parked down the street, next to a carpet cleaning van. It was the kind of neighborhood where people only parked in garages, so we wouldn't last long, but I wasn't worried about other people seeing us. Only Carrol.

"Why?" I asked.

Paulette hesitated. "You don't...feel like a cop."

"What does a cop feel like?"

I knew what she was driving at. I'd heard it all before, from pretty much any cop without a military background. But I wasn't in the mood to cater to her nosiness.

"You're aggressive," she said. "Almost...forceful. Most cops aren't like that. They play it safe. Take it slow. Call for backup."

"That's how they stay alive."

"So why are you different?"

I watched the house and suddenly wished I had a packet

of peanuts, or some potato chips. People make fun of cops for always eating. What they don't understand is that it isn't about hunger. It's about boredom. You sit in a car staring at nothing long enough, and you'll eat just about anything simply to break the monotony.

"I was a Ranger," I said.

"Army?"

"Right."

"How long?"

"Long enough to build aggressive habits, apparently."

She didn't seem to know what to say to that. I hoped she would take the hint and lapse into silence—my preferred environment for a stakeout. But, much like Jacquie, Paulette wasn't that type.

"How do we even know he's here?"

I tilted my chin toward the back corner of the house, where a barely visible cloud of steam rose into the air.

"See that?"

"Yeah..."

"Clothes dryer vent. He's been washing laundry."

"Maybe he started the dryer, then left."

I shook my head. "Dryer vents only dump that much moisture right after you start them. He's in there."

"Could be a maid."

"A maid would park in the driveway. We'd see her car."

Paulette twisted toward me. "You're pretty good at this, aren't you?"

I shrugged. "Depends on who you ask."

"What does that mean?"

I sighed. For somebody who, only hours ago, was lying to me about her real name, Paulette had become comfortable with personal conversation quickly. It made me wish I was listening to Jacquie whine about her Suns instead—something I never imagined wishing for.

"I'm good at solving puzzles," I said. "I'm good at thinking like other people, and predicting what they're gonna do, and why. But, like you said, I'm also aggressive. Some people don't like that."

"Some people as in your bosses."

I laughed. "You're not so bad at this yourself."

"It's a logical answer. When I joined the FBI I thought they would appreciate aggression. Being a go-getter. But..."

"But it's way more political than it looks on TV," I finished.

"Exactly."

We lapsed into silence for a change, and I enjoyed it. From my position in the passenger seat of Paulette's government car, I could make out the front door and part of the garage. The steam from the dryer was fading, but I had noticed a couple dim lights glinting between the blinds of second-story windows.

Somebody was in there, all right. Maybe not Carrol. But this was as safe a bet as any.

"Will you go back to being a cop?" Paulette asked.

I drew an irritated breath to brush the question away. But then I stopped. The question hit harder than I expected, and I knew why.

I thought again about the beach. Again about my handgun, and the plans I had kept in the back of my mind for what would happen after I finished dealing with Carrol.

I hadn't even considered my abandoned job in Phoenix because it wasn't something I intended to return to.

But I couldn't tell Paulette about the gun, or the beach. And as I pictured it now...I felt doubt wiggle into my mind. Maybe it was watching the pain in Trudy's eyes or listening to Sylvia plead on the phone the night before.

It made me think I wasn't the only one hurting in life. It made the idea of checking out feel suddenly...very selfish.

"I don't know," I said softly, letting honesty slip out. I was conscious of Paulette watching me out of the corner of my eye, but I looked away. A glint of light caught my attention from the garage, and I saw one of the doors shift, then begin to wind up.

Saved by the bell.

"Here we go."

The door opened, exposing the jet-black tail of the Escalade. I recognized the plate number as the vehicle backed slowly out, brake lights reflecting the sun.

Then I saw Carrol, sitting behind the wheel, his eyes sheltered by dark sunglasses, his smug face illuminated as his mouth moved with animation.

On another phone call, I figured.

Manipulating yet another victim.

Paulette shifted into gear, and as soon as the Escalade disappeared around the corner, we slid into pursuit.

38

C arrol drove into downtown Eastport, first. He parked on the street near the rows of jewelry stores, and got out with his black duffel bag.

We parked a hundred yards away and watched him complete the same routine I'd observed the first time I saw him. He moved from store to store, the bag looking a little more bloated each time.

"How are the prices?" I asked.

"High," Paulette said. "I didn't buy anything. Most of what they have is kinda junky."

"Figures. Why invest in expensive inventory if you aren't actually trying to sell anything?"

After completing a pickup at the fourth shop, Carrol returned to the Escalade and turned down the main drag, headed out of town. I coached Paulette on how to remain far enough behind him to avoid drawing attention, while not losing him. She seemed a little nervous, licking her lips a lot and adjusting her position in the seat.

But she also looked excited. I saw the gleam in her eyes

and knew that, even if she wasn't really cut out to be an FBI agent, she was still feeling the rush.

Carrol drove to the outskirts of town and swung into a Burger King drive-thru. We waited him out in the adjacent grocery store parking lot, then followed him out of town. The countryside became increasingly rural, with tall trees crowding the road and only sparse traffic.

It was peaceful. But I felt that we were close.

Carrol turned abruptly down a dirt road connecting to the two-lane highway, almost as if the turn had snuck up on him, and I waved Paulette ahead. Maybe he'd almost missed his turn, or maybe he was suspecting us. Rushing on by would set his mind at ease.

We passed another mile down the road, then pulled to the shoulder and waited four minutes for the Escalade to catch up. It never did, and I directed Paulette to pull a U-turn and head back.

The black SUV was gone, leaving fresh tire tracks in the loose mud. We passed slowly by and I looked into the trees, pondering the possibility of taking the government sedan off the asphalt. I couldn't discern whether the dirt road was in fact a road, maintained in some way by the county, or simply a wide driveway.

I decided to play it safe and had Paulette park two hundred yards away, pointed back toward Eastport. Then I had her pop the hood, and I got out and propped it open with the hood support. It wasn't a perfect disguise, but it looked less suspicious than a car sitting next to the road for no apparent reason. A kind-hearted local might stop to offer help, but hopefully they would move along when they found the car abandoned.

"Do you have a service pistol?"

Paulette shook her head. "They don't give guns to analysts."

I hadn't thought they did, and I was okay with that. I just wanted to make sure she wasn't going to take me off guard and open fire on somebody.

"Okay, then. Time to get muddy."

We crossed through a mucky ditch and into the pine trees beyond, working our way at an angle for a few hundred yards until we intersected with the dirt road. The grove we crossed through seemed to be planted pines—an organized field of neat rows, with only light brush scattered among them. Easy enough to walk through, save for the endless cloud of spider webs woven among the trees.

It didn't take long following next to the road for me to make out the house on the other side of the pines. It was tall, white, and old. Very old. Probably pre-Civil War, with four massive columns lining a two-level front porch that slouched to one side. An aged roof was heaped with pine straw and caked with mildew, and the windows were gunky, or boarded up altogether.

We crouched behind a cluster of brush and surveyed the property from fifty yards. The Escalade was parked to the left side next to a couple smaller SUVs and a Chevy Avalanche. Enough transportation for anywhere between four and twelve people, I figured, depending on carpooling.

Trailing through the trees, strung along a row of poles leading back to the highway, I noticed a heavy electrical cable feeding power to the house, and tacked beneath it was a lighter black phone cable.

Or an internet cable. Just as I predicted.

There was only one person visible outside the house, and he sat so still on the second level of the front porch that I almost missed him. But as I squinted through the shaded darkness I noted the rifle leaned against his lawn chair, and the faint cloud of cigarette smoke gathered around his head.

The lookout, I figured. Watching for intruders headed up the driveway.

The entire picture of the place, so rural and disheveled, with so many cars outside and the armed lookout on the second level, all reinforced everything I'd already assumed about Carrol's operation. But I still needed hard proof—something tangible Paulette could take back to her bosses.

I saw a flash of light near a ground-level window, and then a hint of movement from the wing of the house nearest the cars. A guy stepped out, dressed in sweatpants and a sweatshirt, a cigarette dangling from his lips. He was small and pale, like he rarely saw the light of day.

Carrol followed just behind him, and they held a conference. I couldn't hear the words, but Carrol seemed to be doing most of the talking. The guy nodded and rocked his head like he'd heard it all before.

Some kind of executive check-in, I figured. Something he was used to, and bored with.

I held my finger to my lips, then crept forward to the very edge of the pines, cutting the distance between myself and the house in half. Paulette followed, crawling from one clump of brush to the next, and keeping her head down.

She wasn't half bad at sneaking. She learned quickly.

Dropping to my stomach behind the last tree, I rocked my head to one side and listened carefully. The executive check-in was winding down. Carrol looked ready to leave. Sweatpants had lit a fresh cigarette, and was still nodding along in impatient boredom.

"...and finish out the week," Carrol said. "Okay?"

Sweatpants nodded, flicking cigarette ash across the mud. Carrol seemed irritated.

"Hey. This is the big haul, right? We push it through, then we pull up stakes. You'll be in Miami next week!"

He slapped the guy on the shoulder with a confident

laugh. The guy nodded and said, "Yeah, yeah." Then Carrol turned for the Escalade.

"All right, then. Call me if you have issues. I'll be back later—I've got some rat killing to do."

The SUV's big motor roared to life, and Sweatpants watched Carrol rumble off, a look of semi-disgust on his face.

I couldn't blame him.

He dropped the smoke and stomped it out, then returned to the house. I dusted pine needles off my knees and checked my pocket for the Victorinox—my only weapon, at this point.

"I'm going in," I whispered. "Stay here and keep a lookout."

A lookout wouldn't do me much good without communication, but the truth was I didn't want her slowing me down. Paulette shook her head.

"I'm going with you. I want to see this."

"It's a one-man job. Stay here."

"*No*," she snapped. "I've sat back my whole life. If this is my moment, I want it."

I saw sudden resolve in her eyes, and wondered if she was tangling past losses with current struggles, the same way I was. It was easier to pick out her logical fallacies than my own, but they were no less understandable.

"Fine," I said. "But do exactly what I say. No exceptions."

Her head bobbed, and I glanced back to the lookout on the upper level of the porch. He might be asleep, for all I knew, but we couldn't take the chance.

We'd circle around to the back. Look for an unguarded entrance.

And then we'd infiltrate.

39

The pine straw was still matted and damp from the deluge of the past few days. Creeping along between the trees was easy enough, hugging close to the ground and sticking behind the brush. We passed the right end of the house, noting more dirty windows and what appeared to be the original kitchen.

Behind the house, across an overgrown clearing, I noted a number of outbuildings. A barn, and a couple small cabins—slave quarters, back in the day, now long empty and abandoned.

As we reached the back corner, I first noticed the basement. It was a modern addition, maybe converted from an old root cellar, with narrow windows framed in concrete overlooking the backyard at the very base of the house. There was a sprawling back porch, too, laden with old appliances and other household junk, but no people.

No lookout.

I knelt at the tree line and inspected the open yard, knowing we'd have to cross the clearing in full view of the second-story windows before reaching the back porch. From there, our best bet would be one of the basement windows, giving us access to the house without needing a door.

I selected a window and pointed. "Stay low and don't stop once we leave the trees. We'll breach a window. Got it?"

Another bob of Paulette's head. I patted her shoulder, then swept the backyard one more time for sentries or possible onlookers before breaking into a sprint. I covered the fifty yards to the back wall in a few seconds, Paulette right behind me. By the time I reached the window I was already reaching for the Victorinox, ready to strip away aged caulk and lift the windowpane out. I needn't have bothered. The window was hinged at the top and unlocked at the bottom, swinging open with only a soft groan and exposing a gap just tall enough to slide through.

I rolled onto my shoulder and peered inside, surveying a dank and dusty basement, almost pitch black with puddles of water gathered on the floor.

"Hold the window," I whispered.

Paulette held it up, casting a nervous glance around the yard, and I rolled though.

I was right about one thing—the basement was a converted root cellar. The floor was dirt and the walls brick, with gunky water rising almost to my ankles as I slipped in. Overhead, a mess of air conditioning ducts, water pipes, and copper gas lines snaked back and forth, and even in the dim light I could make out the outline of a stairway leading upward across the room.

I pocketed the Victorinox, and helped Paulette through the window. She was far from athletic, but made it inside with only a soft splash of water, wrinkling her nose at the smell. I held a finger to my lips, then tilted my head toward the stairwell.

We crept across the dank cellar floor slowly, noting a couple of oversized rats rustling among the shadows. Paulette jumped a little and hugged my side as we reached the stairs, but she didn't make a sound.

At the foot of the steps, I looked up to see a crack of light spilling beneath the door. We waited a few moments, listening for the creak of floorboards or the dull thump of footsteps. I thought I heard muted voices from the front side of the house, but directly overhead all was silent.

I waved ahead with two fingers, and we started slowly up the steps. They were made of block, and grimy like everything else, but didn't squeak. At the top I put my hand on the knob, and waited again.

Still no sound.

As I eased the door open, I smelled sour fast food and cigarette smoke—two smells that can tell you a lot about a place. Dirty wood floors, aged and abused, covered what appeared to be a mud room, with shoes strewn against the walls. There was nobody in sight.

Paulette followed me out of the cellar, and I pivoted to the left through an open doorway, moving on the balls of my feet. I heard voices now, from someplace across the house, mixed with the click of computer keyboards.

But I saw no one.

The next room was a kitchen. Not the original kitchen, which would have been detached from the main house, but a makeshift room equipped with a couple counters, a microwave, a stove and oven combo, and a mini fridge. There was a card table laden with stacks of abandoned pizza boxes and McDonald's bags. Crushed beer cans littered the floor alongside wadded up burger wrappers.

Behind me, Paulette moved stealthily across the room, drawing her phone to snap pictures. I left her to it, slipping up to the next door, which was closed. I could hear voices and the click of those computer keyboards, but couldn't discern any specific words.

I twisted the knob and pushed the door open, just a little. Light slipped through the crack, and I peered into a wide room hung with outdated wallpaper, and lined with wooden file cabinets. Dozens of them, packed against the walls with little white labels marking each drawer. A single light bulb glowed overhead to offer illumination, and beyond the room I looked through another open doorway to see the edge of a desk poking into view. Wires trailed the floor, and the keyboard clicking continued.

I eased back from the door and held my finger across my lips, then motioned for Paulette to stand back. For a change she didn't argue, instead slipping behind the counter and kneeling.

I crept through the door. The floorboards were rough under my feet, but they didn't creak. They were nailed tightly together, craftsmanship of a bygone era when this house was constructed for some ultra-rich landowner, who demanded flawless floors.

As I moved around the corner of the first row of filing cabinets, the clack of the keyboards grew louder. I fell into a low crouch, easing toward the next door, and listening for footsteps. The voices I had heard before were loud enough to discern individual words, but they weren't worth listening to. It wasn't the occupants speaking; it was a television playing some kind of sitcom. Every few seconds a crowd laughed on cue, matched on occasion by amused grunts from somewhere in the next room.

I dropped to my hands and knees, keeping my breaths soft as I eased slowly to the open door. Inches from the opening I descended to my stomach, worming my way forward until my face crossed the threshold, and I finally gained a glimpse of the next room.

40

It wasn't a room, really. It was the entire front side of the house, with walls that formerly separated bedrooms now torn down to expose a wide open space. A train of plastic tables ran wall to wall, fully thirty foot across with cheap computer chairs parked in front of them. Those tables were *stacked* with electronics—laptops, computers, keyboards, wireless modems, and a *ton* of credit card processing machines. Maybe twenty of them, all blinking soft green lights, all plugged into a tangled web of black cables.

Half a dozen people sat slouched in their cheap computer chairs, working a sort of assembly line from the right-hand side to the left, their backs turned to me. The first sifted through a mountain of envelopes, prying out glossy new credit cards and working a telephone to dial the numbers on the back and activate them. I knew he was activating them because he input each credit card number using the phone's keypad, following prompts with a bored and sleepy look on his face, his attention half fixed on the TV.

The next guy in line sat in front of a computer, and seemed to be indexing the numbers and expiration dates of each card into some kind of spreadsheet, after which the card was slid to the last guy in the lineup, who filed it into a massive credit card folio.

Meanwhile, on the far side of the table, three more workers busied themselves processing charges, selecting cards from another stack of folios and marking something off on a clipboard before swiping each one.

The machines beeped at random, and spat out receipts. Everybody worked in relative silence, their unwashed hair gleaming in the nasty fluorescent glow of the overhead lights.

All men, all grungy, and all about half awake.

I tilted my head around the corner, looking down the lineup toward a melon-sized hole in the wall where a mess of cable stretched into a darkened room. A computer center of some kind, I figured. The operational heart of the tech laid out around me.

It was an impressive operation. Elegantly simple in execution, yet complex enough to require a mastermind behind it. Exactly the kind of scheme that white collar crime thrived upon.

Carrol might be a conniving SOB, manipulating single mothers into sexual favors, but he wasn't stupid. A long way from it.

I thought about worming my way backward, back into the kitchen. But just then wood groaned and footsteps thumped from my left, and I pivoted to look up the shadowy mouth of the stairwell leading to the second floor. It lay at the far side of the open space, and I watched the sweatsuit guy I had seen before appear from the darkness, carrying two duffel bags bulging with unidentifiable contents. He tossed them irritably on the end of the row of tables, then unceremoniously unzipped the first and dumped a *mountain* of cash across the plastic.

A hundred grand, easily. Wads of tens, twenties, and

fifties, some rolled, some bundled. It spilled across the edges of the table amid curses from Sweatsuit, while the remainder of the workers lining the table barely gave it a second glance.

Sweatsuit snapped at the nearest guy to help him, then they went to work sorting it, snapping off rubber bands and feeding loose cash through a currency counter.

I lay in stunned silence, feeling as though I were peering into the midst of a drug operation. But there were no drugs present. Only loads of cash, *stacks* of credit cards, and an operation smooth and oiled enough to run until the end of time.

I eased my way back, still on my stomach. I'd seen enough. With a federal warrant, the FBI could bypass any corrupt local judges. A week from now this place would be a crime scene, slowly disassembled by the meticulous efforts of two dozen field agents and financial crimes specialists.

It would make headlines. Carrol would go to prison. My work here was done.

I took my time retreating into the file room before easing up onto my knees and crawling to the door. Then I was back in the kitchen, slipping the door shut and chewing my lip.

I'd been right about the credit card scheme. That much was clear. I'd been right about the jewelry stores, and the PO Boxes, and probably Daniel Porter's involvement, also. Those filing cabinets were likely chock-full of social security files—numbers to be groomed into profitable credit scores, just waiting to be exploited.

But something was still missing. One question unanswered.

"Mason!" Paulette hissed. I pivoted to see her kneeling next to the stove, the door half-open, pointing inside. Lying on the top rack of the oven was another stack of cash—maybe twenty grand, all in twenties, neatly banded and arranged as though it would make a delicious dinner after baking at 350 for eighteen to twenty minutes, or until golden brown.

I saw the cash, and the victorious grin on her face, but my mind was a thousand miles away. Still wrestling with that last question. The second half of the puzzle that had started my investigation in the first place.

"Come on," I said, tilting my head toward the mud room. "We have what we need. Let's go."

She closed the oven and crept to follow me. We skipped the cellar this time, opting for the side door instead. The rows of cars lining the small dirt parking lot were dusty and still. We slid between them and hurried into the trees, keeping the corner of the house between our backs and the lookout until we were sheltered in the pine grove. Then I navigated by instinct back to the road, and the abandoned government sedan resting next to it.

Paulette was ecstatic. As soon as we were safely buried in the trees she peppered me with questions, and I filled her in on what I had seen in the front room. By the time we slid into the car she was so excited she indulged in a happy squeal, pounding her open palm against the wheel.

"This is it! Mason, we've got them. I'll call my boss, tell him he's got to get down here. We'll think of a reason for a warrant. Then it's over!"

I stared out the windows, still chewing my lip. Not answering. Still thinking.

"Mason?"

I looked into the shadows between the planted pines, noting the tangles of a spider web only a few feet outside the car. Tracing each translucent line from a pine limb, through the ornate pattern of the web, and right to the core where a large black arthropod waited for a passing insect to become its next victim.

Every strand had a point of origin, and it led someplace.

Every one of them *meant* something. Had a logical explanation for its existence.

But one strand of the bizarre web I had been tracing ever since Daniel Porter's body washed ashore *didn't* have a logical explanation.

"Mason?" Paulette said again, her tone dropping with concern.

"Why?" I asked, still watching the spider web.

"Why what?"

I turned to her. "Why did they kill Daniel Porter?"

She frowned, drew breath to answer, then hesitated.

"Think about it," I said. "It's a perfect operation. Daniel sells them new social security numbers, then they groom those identities into healthy credit reports before applying for credit cards, converting those cards into cash via a slew of fake retailers and jewelry stores, then abandoning those identities. Churn and burn. Keep it moving. A *very* profitable enterprise."

"Right..."

"So why pull the plug? Daniel was the key to the entire operation. Without new social security numbers, the party ends. We heard Carrol say so himself—they're pulling up stakes. They can't run without Daniel. So why did they kill him?"

"I guess...did he want out?"

I shook my head. "No. He was getting away with it. And he needed the money. Why quit?"

Paulette licked her lips, squinting at the dash a long time. Then she shrugged. "Maybe it just happened that way. They disagreed about something. Maybe he wanted more money."

I looked back to the spider web, and didn't say so, but I knew that wasn't it. I remembered Daniel Porter's simple house, simple family car, and humdrum existence at the social security office. He wasn't a greedy guy. He just wanted to care for his son.

Paulette started the car, still babbling on about FBI investigative protocols and obtaining federal warrants. I barely listened, watching the trees pass and thinking about that spider web.

Everything connected. Everything meant something.

Carrol was too smart a guy. If he killed Daniel, there was a reason.

As we neared Marley's, Paulette dialed her cell phone into some kind of automated FBI call system, trying to reach her boss. I heard the computer speaking through her phone, loud in the small car.

"Please enter your federal ID."

Paulette rattled off a number, followed by: "Sherman, Paulette, J."

The name cracked like a gunshot in my mind, and my head snapped up.

"What's your middle name?" I said.

Paulette turned into Marley's parking lot. "Huh?"

"Your middle name begins with a J?"

She shifted into park, confusion clouding her face. "Uh... yeah. It's Jules."

Paulette Jules Sherman.

P.J. Sherman.

It hit me like a ton of bricks in the face, and I remembered what Carrol said to Sweatsuit, only an hour previously.

I'll be back later. I've got some rat killing to do.

I bolted out of the car and hurried to the driver's side, motioning Paulette out.

"I need the car! Wait here."

She mumbled into her phone then hung up, panic creeping into her eyes when she saw the urgency on my face.

"What's going on?"

I ignored her, pushing by and ratcheting the seat back before I slid in. She blocked the door.

"Mason! What happened?"

"*Stay here*," I snapped. "Don't talk to anyone. I'll be back in an hour."

Then I shifted into reverse and slammed on the gas, spinning around in the narrow gravel lot. Marley was coming out of the front door and scurried to avoid the deluge of small stones. The driver's door slammed and I raced onto Main Street, turning upriver.

Toward the isolated house that sat by itself just above the water.

Because I now knew why Carrol killed Daniel Porter. And if I didn't hurry, he was going to kill again.

41

I pushed the government sedan well past eighty miles per hour, blazing through town like a bat out of hell. My heart pounded and I cursed myself for not seeing what lay right under my nose—what should have been brutally obvious from the first moment I met Paulette.

It was a rookie mistake. An oversight brought on by a fixation with unimportant details, and too little sleep. But there was no excuse. The final pieces to this bizarre puzzle had lain in my lap for almost two days, and I was only now putting them together.

Stupid.

I rocketed past the Saint Ellen Island ferry, rushing right by a sleepy EPD patrolman eating a burger in the parking lot, before I turned north and hit the rural road running just west of the Cape Fear River.

To P.J. Sherman's house.

The long gravel drive was damp, and rocks snapped under my tires as I screamed to the end. Sherman's old Dodge pickup sat next to the house, dusty and unused, but fresh tire tracks lay next to it.

Wide tracks, from a large and heavy vehicle.

I slid to a stop and hurtled out, not even bothering to cut the engine as I pulled my Victorinox and snapped the blade open. I took the front porch steps two at a time.

And then I stopped. The front door hung open on the other side of a screen door, a little mud on the wood floor beyond. I could see straight into Sherman's polished home, past the bright walls hung with picture frames and into the living room laden with knickknacks. I could see the back porch, stretching across the rear of the house and facing the river. I could see the edge of the kitchen, with a bottle of Jack resting on the counter, a small puddle of whiskey next to it.

But I didn't see the old man.

"Sherman?" I called, loud enough for my voice to echo through the house.

No answer.

I placed a hand on the screen door and eased it open. It groaned on a loose spring, and I called out again.

"Sherman? It's Sharpe!"

No answer.

I took a step inside, the knife held next to my hip. I noted faint footprints on the clean floors, outlined by a hint of mud. They may have been Sherman's. But they looked too large.

"Sherman!" I shouted this time, unconcerned about exposing myself to an intruder. My heart rate accelerated, and I hurried into the living room.

Empty.

I turned into the kitchen, sweeping my gaze across the counters. A half-consumed turkey sandwich lay on a plate next to an open bag of potato chips. A stack of mail was strewn across the counter.

But no Sherman.

Then my eye caught a flutter of motion to my left, and I pivoted, raising the knife.

The motion I had seen came from the back porch, barely visible at the edge of a window. It was gone now, but as a gust of wind blasted across the porch, it swung into view again, for just a moment.

The end of a sleeve.

I ran around the kitchen island, to the rolling back door, and hurled it open. The porch boards thundered beneath my feet as I rounded the corner and rushed onto the deck, already knowing what I would find. Already knowing I was much too late.

Sherman hung from the rafters of the porch roof, a thick rope knotted around his neck, his eyes bulging. His hands weren't tied, but I saw faint lacerations around his wrists where wire ties had restrained him, not long ago. A toppled chair lay on the deck beneath his feet, and as his body slowly turned in the wind, his lifeless eyes stared out over his beloved Cape Fear River.

42

I snatched the chair up, using it to reach the rope over his head. The Victorinox made short work of the thick cord, and Sherman toppled to the deck. I hurried to strip the noose from his throat, but it was much too late.

Sherman had been dead at least twenty minutes. Probably longer.

And it was my fault.

I knelt next to his body and stared into the weathered old Coastie's face. I thought about that night on the bay, smoking cigars in the back of his trawler. It had only been a couple of days ago, but it felt like weeks.

Just a few short hours together. A few short conversations. And yet I felt like I had known the old guy for years.

And now they had killed him.

My hands were ice cold as I closed the knife and looked to the table. A suicide note lay pinned beneath a half-empty glass of whiskey. It wasn't Sherman's handwriting—I felt sure of that. But it didn't matter. Chief Lowe and the rest of his corrupt department would rule it to be Sherman's handwriting.

They'd rule this a suicide. Or maybe even try to pin it on me.

Because this whole damn town was bought and paid for. A playground for Carrol and any scheme he could dream of.

"*I emailed the local sheriff's office.*"

Paulette's words echoed in my mind, and I wanted to scream. She didn't know it, but it was those emails that led to Daniel Porter's death.

Somebody in the local sheriff's department—somebody who was bought and paid for—let Carrol know that the FBI was sniffing around.

Who, specifically?

Some agent named P.J. Sherman. Paulette's email signature was probably just initials. Lots of women working in traditionally male-dominated fields pulled that trick to minimize discrimination. I'd seen it a few dozen times, both in the military and the PPD. There was no way for Carrol to know that P.J. stood for Paulette Jules.

But he had to take action. He would have done some research. He would have discovered that Daniel Porter frequently associated with an old man on the river, who claimed to be a retired Coastie.

A man by the name of P.J. Sherman.

A man who just might be an undercover FBI agent.

At that point, the next step was inevitable.

Daniel had to go.

He would have objected, of course. Insisted that he was innocent, and that old man Sherman had nothing to do with the FBI, even as Daryl and his goons wire-tied his hands, then dragged him out to sea on Sherman's stolen boat.

It wouldn't have mattered, in the end. They hit him over the head, drowned him, then cut the wire ties and dumped his body anyway. Because that's what Carrol had told them to do.

The worst of it was, the entire thing had been under my nose all along, and I'd only seen it half an hour too late. I pocketed the Victorinox and gently closed Sherman's eyes, working the noose over his head and tossing it aside. I embraced a moment of silence for the old salt, the cold wind blowing off the bay and tousling my hair.

Then I returned to the kitchen and snatched up the phone, calling directory assistance and asking for the number to Marley's pub. It rang five times, but I didn't hang up. All I saw was red.

"Hello?" It was Marley.

"Marley, put Paulette on the phone."

"Who?"

"Cassandra. The photographer."

"Mason...nobody's here. Everything's a mess. What the hell happened?"

I moved away from the counter, the phone's outdated wire trailing back to the wall. "What are you talking about? I left Cassandra at your place. What do you mean, it's a mess?"

"Everything's wrecked! The bar, the windows—they kicked down a door!"

Marley spoke in an endless stream, her words falling over themselves. I could barely follow, and I snapped my fingers even though I knew she couldn't hear.

"Marley! Stop. Start from the beginning. What happened? Where's Cassandra?"

Marley's teeth ground. "They *trashed* my place, Mason! I closed up for lunch. The power was out, so I went down to the diner to eat. When I got back, the whole place was a wreck. Windows busted, liquor everywhere. Cassandra is gone."

"*Gone?* What do you mean, she's gone?"

"She was here when the power went out! I offered her a

ride to the diner, but she said she'd wait in the pub. Now I can't find her!"

Marley's voice edged into panic as she finished the sentence, but I remained calm. Something instinctual clicked into place, deep in my gut. Or maybe it wasn't instinctual. Maybe it was just years of training for high-pressure situations, now taking control.

"Stay calm," I said. "Call the police and make sure they come. Have them search the place."

"What about Paulette?"

"I know where she is."

Before Marley could answer, I hung up, digging into my pocket for the napkin from the pub. The one I had scrawled Carrol's address and phone number on.

I jabbed the digits in, my finger making angry snaps with each press of a key. I knew it was a mistake. I knew solid tactics and good strategy would demand that I take my enemy by surprise.

But I didn't care. Because he'd hurt one too many people, and I wanted Carrol to see the axe as it swung for his neck.

"Is this Sharpe?" Carrol's voice was brash with his trademark Long Island accent.

"You better believe it is," I snarled. "Where is she?"

"The Fed is with me, and she won't be long for this world if you don't start cooperating."

"Cut her loose," I said. "Or you'll wish you had."

Carrol laughed. It was an angry, frustrated sound, devoid of any humor.

"You're a real piece of work, you know that? You've caused a lot of problems for me. I should have had Daryl shoot you from day one."

"And I should have busted your ugly face two nights ago, in Richmond."

Strained silence.

"That's right, *Carrol*. I know all about your little PO Box route. I was riding in the back the whole time. I know about your credit card operation, too. The jewelry stores. The house in the woods. The whole enchilada. So you better think long and hard before you hurt that woman, because there's only two ways for this to end: serving life, or losing it. You choose."

A long pause.

I wondered how much impact my bravado really carried, or if Carrol already knew I was onto him. At this point he had to know there were two P.J. Shermans. Paulette tipped her hand when she confronted Lowe and Witmore at the police station. They probably saw her and me talking on the bench at the boardwalk, not long after, and connected the dots.

When Carrol said he had some rat killing to do, he didn't just mean Sherman. He meant all three of us.

A complete clean-up job.

"Serving life or losing it, huh?" Carrol snarled, all humanity leaving his tone. "Well, aren't you witty. But we're gonna go with option C."

"Which is?"

"Which is you show up at the house in the woods—since you know the place. You come alone, and unarmed, within the hour. No cops!"

I snorted. "Cops are bought off anyway. And busy investigating Marley's ransacked pub."

"You know what I mean. No more *feds*."

"What if I refuse?"

"Then she dies, and I come after you anyway."

"I'm shaking in my boots."

Carrol shouted to somebody in the background. I heard a meaty thumping sound, followed by muted screams.

I recognized the voice. It was Paulette's.

"Sure you wanna play games with me?" Carrol growled.

My fingers closed around the phone's receiver, so tight it trembled against my face. But I kept my voice calm.

"House in the woods. One hour."

"*One hour*. Alone and unarmed. You better be there."

"She better be *alive*."

Carrol hung up, and I slammed the phone against the counter, hard enough to crack the plastic. Blood pounded in my ears and the red I had seen since arriving at Sherman's house turned a bloody crimson.

But now that crimson was focused. Honed in. I was angry about Sherman's death. Angry about Marley's smashed pub, and angry about Paulette's kidnapping.

But anger could wait. Right now I had a job to do.

Abandoning the phone on the counter, I rushed outside and conducted a sweep of the back porch. I didn't find what I was looking for, so I returned inside and searched the kitchen, then the first room down the hall—Sherman's home office. It was littered with stacks of mail, books, and the scattered fragments of a model sailing ship strewn across the desk. I ignored it all and opened the closet, digging past a row of coats until my fingers fell across cold steel in the back corner.

The weapon was a Marlin Model 60, one of the finest .22 long rifles ever made, with a polished walnut stock and a blued barrel. A quick inspection of the magazine tube confirmed that the rifle was unloaded, but after searching the drawers of the desk I found a box of copper-plated ammunition, and the original target of my search—Sherman's four-inch Colt Python, loaded with six rounds of .357 magnum hollow points.

Back in the kitchen, I deposited everything on the table, then turned to Sherman's liquor cabinet and shuffled past a row of dusty glass bottles before I found what I was looking for—Fireball whiskey, contained in a flat plastic bottle about an inch thick and four inches wide.

I dumped the contents into the sink, then reached for the roll of paper towels on the counter and tore off a series of small strips, stuffing them into the bottle. I kept going until the bottle was packed tight, then I slid the mouth over the muzzle of the Marlin, rotating it so that the flat side faced upward, leaving the rifle's sights fully visible.

I used duct tape from the kitchen drawer to secure it in place, and the reamer on the backside of my Victorinox to punch a series of pen-head-sized holes across the top and bottom of the bottle.

The entire process was complete in under three minutes, then I loaded the Marlin with fifteen rounds and ratcheted one into the chamber before pressing the muzzle through the back door and firing toward the river.

The first two rounds blasted a tunnel through the paper towel and punched through the bottle's bottom with dull snaps. The next three whistled through the makeshift silencer with muted pops, like champagne corks.

I reloaded the Marlin, then scooped up the Python and shot one last look over my shoulder to Sherman's lifeless form.

And I made a promise. Not just for Sherman, or Daniel, or Paulette.

For Sylvia, also. And her nameless fellow victim.

For Trudy, and her fatherless son.

For Mia.

Then I kicked past the screen door and returned to the government sedan, locked and loaded.

43

It was dusk by the time I reached the dirt road leading to the house, and I drove right by it. Fresh tire tracks marred the dirt—a lot of them, wide and heavy.

Carrol had called for reinforcements. He wasn't playing around anymore. He wanted my head.

Parking alongside the road a mile away, I double-checked each of my weapons, then tucked the Python into my pants and started into the trees.

Within seconds of leaving the blacktop, instincts from years gone by took over. It didn't matter that I was sneaking through a pine grove in North Carolina instead of mountain ridges in northern Iraq. It didn't matter that I was armed with a .22 rifle instead of an M4A1.

It didn't matter that I was hunting Americans instead of the Taliban. The soldier I had buried deep in my psyche, suppressing him under willpower and a desire to be an every-man, had returned. I couldn't stop what was about to happen any more than Carrol could.

I saw the headlights a hundred yards outside the house. They blazed between the trees, shooting out from a circle of pickup trucks and muddy SUVs, all pointed toward the forest. Between them I made out the shadows of pacing men, little more than silhouettes in the darkness, cradling shotguns and assault rifles.

It wasn't a half-bad strategy on Carrol's part. With the headlamps spotlighting the trees on all sides, I could hardly expect to slip in close without being detected, and even for a Ranger, shooting into the sun is never easy.

But he had also made a critical mistake. The army of rednecks assembled around the vehicles had left multiple motors running, and the soft burble of the heavy engines combined with my improvised silencer would completely mask my shots. They had no idea what was coming.

I sank to my knees, dipping my hands between the pine needles to scoop up soft dirt, still damp with the deluge of the past weekend. In seconds I covered my face and neck with the grime, obscuring pale skin with makeshift camouflage paint.

An old trick. But still an effective one.

Cradling the Marlin in both hands, I leaned low and crept around to the back corner of the house. Only an idiot would approach directly up the driveway, and I had spent the last five days proving to anybody watching that I wasn't an idiot.

But the rednecks were, because the bulk of their force was concentrated on securing the dirt road leading to the highway, leaving only a couple riflemen to worry about other angles of attack.

I made it to the south side of the house and moved at an angle toward a Chevrolet Tahoe parked with its high beams blazing toward me. An ugly guy with a tangled beard and a heavy cast around one knee stood smoking next to the vehicle, an AK-47 cradled in his arms. A pair of crutches rested next to him, and he leaned against the SUV's hood.

It was Daryl, back for more. Fool.

I descended to my stomach, worming the next forty yards between the brush. Headlight glare was lost on my dirty clothes and muddy face, and Daryl's darting eyes were fixed on the far reaches of the trees, his finger twitching over the trigger guard.

I closed to within fifty feet, then gently flicked the safety off and settled the stock into my shoulder. Daryl's ugly jaw ground in rhythmic circles as he chomped down on tobacco, and I worked my rifle sights up from his boots and across his stomach.

Straight to his face. Because I'd warned him twice. He'd failed to listen or learn either time, and more importantly than that, he'd killed Daniel.

There would be no third warning.

I pressed the trigger and heard another champagne cork pop. The bullet caught Daryl in the left eye and tore straight through his brain. He dropped like a log, and I was already on my feet, a whisper in the wind as I moved across the Tahoe's front bumper and circled in behind the line of vehicles guarding the drive.

I dropped into a crouch, now barely enclosed inside the tree line, and opened fire.

The next guy caught a bullet in the foot. The third took a slug right through his ass cheek, ripping and tearing like a bee from hell as he dropped his gun and broke into a shrill scream. Guy number four received one shot through the fleshy part of his left ear, and a second scraped his right thigh.

I wasn't shooting to kill anymore—I didn't know these guys, or what level of culpability they bore for Carrol's dirty work. But I had no problem shedding a little blood as complete chaos exploded among their ranks. Screams were joined by desperate, random gunfire, while most of Carrol's remaining thugs scrambled for cover behind trucks and trees.

Nothing induces panic quite like a sniper.

I lunged to my feet, rushing from the tree line to the bed of the nearest pickup and swapping the Marlin for an abandoned AR-15. It was some kind of box store model, with a junky red dot site fixed to the top. Redneck crap, but it didn't matter. I flicked the safety off, and opened fire.

Windshields, tires, and headlights all detonated in sprays of glass and rubber as I dumped the full magazine on the vehicles surrounding me. I could barely hear the screams now—they were lost amid my gunfire and the few scattered potshots that fired randomly into the trees around me.

Despite my muzzle flash, the thugs were already far too disoriented to have any idea where I was. They had no idea what to shoot at.

Total anarchy had consumed their ranks in under ten seconds.

The rifle locked back on empty, and I slid for cover behind another truck, breathing evenly and listening. The potshots and shouts continued, mixed with mournful cries of pain. Somebody cursed Carrol.

Somebody else called for their mother.

Nobody save Daryl was seriously injured. Everybody had taken cover.

I dropped the AR-15 and pulled Sherman's Python, impulsively checking the load again. Six rounds of hollow point .357 magnums. Killing rounds.

I snapped the cylinder shut and gauged the distance to the house. I would circle behind a Tahoe, next to the collapsed front porch, and then around to the north wall. Fifty yards, open dash.

I gripped the Python, finger just above the trigger guard. Then I was off, sprinting through the shadows and vanishing around the side of the house before anyone even knew I was there. In seconds I circled to the back, Python at the ready.

Carrol's reinforcements, if he had any, would flow through the front door, heavily armed and eager to confront the gunfight exploding at the mouth of the drive.

That would leave the back door exposed—an open path into the basement, where Paulette would be held, and Carrol would be waiting.

44

I reached the back door and pinned my shoulders against the house, just to one side. Then I made a fist and pounded the door, loud and urgent.

The first guy who poked his head out caught the butt of Sherman's Python, right across his skull. He collapsed, lights out, then a shotgun boomed. The screen door was obliterated by a blast of buckshot, and I kicked it open as the harsh *shlick-shlick* of a pump action shotgun rang down the hall, followed by another boom.

I cocked the Python and swung into the doorway, all in one fluid motion. The shooter stood five yards inside, frantically ratcheting another shell into the chamber. There was no time to consider a non-lethal option—I shot him twice, back to back. Once in the chest, once in the head, sending him flipping backward like a limp rag doll. Blood streamed across the aged hardwood, as I swept the Python across a dusty parlor where cobwebs covered outdated furniture. I moved to the kitchen.

Piles of pizza boxes and fast-food bags from the day before were strewn across the floor, and the table was now stacked with shotgun shells and AR-15 mags. Outside, a chorus of shouts around the vehicles had reached a crescendo as anarchy continued, but the rednecks couldn't locate the shooter. Random gunfire erupted toward the trees, and a horn blared.

Complete chaos. Idiots at work.

I turned to the basement door and kicked it open, leading with the Python and the three rounds that remained. A dim light glowed from below, and I smelled stagnant water on the air.

But I heard no voices. Not Carrol shouting for reinforcements. Not Paulette, gagged and grunting for help.

All was quiet.

I started down the stairs, turning sideways to give me a peripheral view of the kitchen, just in case somebody rushed in from behind.

I reached the bottom and quickly swept the basement. The damp floor was covered in puddles, as before, but this time I noticed a metal chair in one corner. Torn bits of duct tape stuck to the seat, and shoe marks rutted the dirt near the legs.

But Paulette wasn't there. And neither was Carrol.

I hesitated in the darkness, momentarily wondering if I had miscalculated. Maybe Carrol had taken her upstairs, sheltered behind a series of heavy doors and more gunmen.

Or maybe Paulette wasn't here at all. Maybe he'd taken her someplace else, or already killed her.

But then I heard a shrill scream, ripping across the yard outside the house. I rushed to the same narrow window Paulette and I had infiltrated through only hours before, and pushed it open as the panicked sound repeated.

I saw Paulette, bound hands and feet, kicking and screaming as she was dragged toward Carrol's black Escalade. The vehicle sat behind one of the abandoned cabins, barely visible in the darkness, and beyond it I noticed a second dirt road leading into the trees.

The man carrying Paulette was bulky but out of condition. Not Carrol—another one of his local thugs. But then I saw Carrol too, hurling himself into the driver's seat and waving for his man to hurry. Panic flooded his face, as he looked toward the house.

Willing me not to appear. Now convinced that he had drastically overplayed his hand.

I took in a long breath and started toward the stairs, ready to run him down. But then I thought about the army of thugs out front—another six or eight of them, still heavily armed. I didn't have the element of surprise, anymore. I wouldn't get the jump on them.

Not without a distraction.

Switching the Python to my left hand, I dug the Victorinox out of my pocket and deployed the three-inch metal saw. Selecting one of the heavy copper pipes funneling propane through the house, I went to work with a series of aggressive, tearing strokes. The saw broke through the outside of the pipe in only seconds, and ice-cold propane blasted into the basement. It stank, and I choked, but kept sawing until I cut all the way through and yanked the broken pipe down, pointed at the floor, as gas surged out in an endless stream.

Then I ran for the steps, reaching the kitchen and sweeping the Python across the room. Nobody waited for me, and I hurtled straight to the stove, heaping pizza boxes over the electric burner elements before flicking all four to full power. A wisp of smoke drifted between the boxes, and I ran.

45

Propane is heavier than air. It filled the basement first, then the crawl space beneath the house.

By the time it reached the kitchen and the pizza box bonfire burning on the stove, I had crossed the backyard and taken shelter behind a cabin, watching as Carrol's taillights disappeared down the second dirt road.

Then the ground itself convulsed, and the house detonated. Flames exploded out of every first-floor window, and shards of antebellum siding blasted across the yard. In an instant, the entire building was consumed in hot red flames as smoke gushed toward the sky, and the outraged screams I had heard from the front yard only minutes prior were replaced by cries of panic. Motors roared and tires spun, most of the vehicles rushing for the main drive.

Most. Not all.

There was a Tahoe parked twenty yards away from me, next to another of the old cabins. It was blocked from the front driveway by a row of oak trees, meaning that it must have entered the property via the same rear access road Carrol had just used to escape.

I wasn't sure if the keys would be in the ignition, but as the last of the propane blast shrapnel rained over the yard, I saw a tall guy with an AK-47 bounding through the smoke, headed for the Tahoe.

I didn't hesitate. Leaving the cover of my cabin, I sprinted to intercept him, moving around the rear of the Tahoe just as he circled the front and reached for the driver's door.

He was halfway inside before he noticed me. A frantic attempt to raise the AK-47 was thwarted by a swift kick to the knee, followed by a blow to the side of his head from the butt of Sherman's Python.

The guy crumpled, car keys spilling to the ground. And then I saw his face.

It was Floyd Crosby—the same guy I had belted over the back of the head with Mia's lug wrench after losing the Corolla.

Some people never learn.

I snatched up the keys and kicked his body aside, throwing myself into the Tahoe. The motor had barely started before I was slamming it into gear and hurling mud toward the house. The back end swung around, and then I was off, rocketing toward the road Carrol had escaped down. I passed fifty miles per hour as I hit the muddy surface of the dirt road with no clue what lay around the next corner, and hurtled on.

Carrol had a two-minute head start. He could be halfway back to Eastport by now.

But I didn't think so. Because he wasn't willing to drive like I would drive. He wasn't willing to go as far as I would go.

He wasn't nearly prepared for the violence of action I was about to rain on his head.

I ground around a corner in the road, almost sliding into the ditch. The Tahoe's tires caught, and I thought I saw tail-lights in the distance. I pressed harder, and the big engine thundered. The Python almost slid off the seat, but I caught it.

Then I saw the Escalade. Carrol had wrecked the tires, losing traction on the muddy road and slamming right into the ditch. Steam poured from the front end and the hood was buckled, sticking up over the roof. Glass was shattered. Oil drained into the ditch.

And then I saw Carrol. He and his bulky thug were fleeing down the road, Paulette in tow. They had cut the tape around her ankles and were forcing her to run now, her hands still tied off to a length of rope.

Carrol saw me coming and pointed frantically, screaming for his man to shoot.

The fat guy stepped to one side and raised a semi-automatic handgun, opening fire.

I dropped my head and slammed on the gas. The Tahoe fishtailed and bullets exploded through the windshield. Paulette screamed. I grabbed the wheel and snatched it left, lifting my head just far enough to see the guy standing fifty yards ahead of me just as my front left tire exploded.

The wheel jerked in my hand, and I knew I had lost control. I slammed on the brake and clung on, sending the Tahoe into a spin.

The fat guy saw what was coming. It was just far too late for him to do anything about it. The right side of the Tahoe struck him at forty miles per hour as the vehicle completed a full spin. Then he, I, and the SUV rocketed into the ditch. Mud exploded over the hood and the air bag detonated. My head slammed against the driver's window and glass cracked. The world spun and metal crunched. I imagined I heard the guy scream, but he was dead long before the vehicle jerked to a stop.

Everything blurred. I sat in the seat and looked dumbly down at my hands, noting the streaks of crimson coating my skin, but not really registering that the blood must be mine. My ears rang and I dumbly reached for the keys, shutting the ignition off even though the motor had stopped on impact.

My stomach tightened, and then I vomited. Fragments of my last burger sprayed across the dash, and I fumbled for the Python.

When I spilled into the ditch I saw the fat guy's legs sticking out from beneath the Tahoe. The vehicle had rolled him right into the ditch and landed on top of him, probably crushing his entire torso. A wisp of smoke rose from the engine bay, and one front tire whirled like a Ferris wheel.

I stumbled back and swayed on my feet, feeling ready to drop. The Python hung heavy in my right hand, and I almost fell.

But then I heard a scream. Long and shrill, it was coming from the trees on the far side of the road.

Paulette.

46

It wasn't difficult to follow Carrol's path. He'd dragged Paulette between the trees, kicking and screaming, leaving a torn trail of dirt and displaced pine needles the entire way. But, as I cleared the ditch, the screams ceased abruptly, and my heart skipped.

"Paulette?" I shouted through the trees, cradling the Python.

The trail led through another knot of pines, overgrown by heavy underbrush. Wind whispered through their limbs, carrying the scent of damp earth, and I noted blood on the ground.

Then I skidded around a corner and saw everything, all at once. Paulette swung from the rope, tied off to the gnarled limb of an oak tree. The noose closed around her neck was knotted behind her head, and she thrashed and fought with her bound hands, her face turning blue.

And, to my left, dashing between the trees, Carrol bolted for freedom.

I saw it all, I calculated the moments since Paulette had stopped screaming, and I made a split-second decision.

Stepping into the soft clearing beneath the canopy of the oak, I cocked the Python. Stood ten feet from Paulette and calmly lifted the revolver. Sighted down the barrel at Carrol's bolting form, now forty yards away.

Then fifty. He ran, ducking and weaving, thrashing through the brush. No longer the bold and brash commander of a multimillion-dollar fraud scheme.

No longer the blackmailing predator, exploiting broke single moms.

Now just a pathetic criminal, run into a corner. Desperate to preserve his own miserable life.

He looked over his shoulder, and our eyes locked, for just an instant. He saw the mouth of Sherman's revolver, and maybe he thought of the old man.

Or Daniel.

It didn't matter. I pulled the trigger.

The gun cracked and spat a .357 magnum slug across the clearing, between the pines, and right between his eyes. Carrol flipped backward into the mud like a bowling ball, dead before he even hit the ground.

I lowered the gun, conscious of Paulette still thrashing next to me. Then I walked calmly to the base of the oak where the end of the rope was tied off, flicked my Victorinox open, and cut it.

She hit the ground in a gasping mass, clawing the rope away from her throat as I knelt next to her. I cut her hands free and pulled the noose over her head. For a long while she just struggled for air. Harsh red marks decorated her neck where the rope had sunk in, and her face was still blue.

But she was alive.

I closed the Victorinox and pocketed it, then sat down next to her and gently opened the cylinder of the Python, spinning it and surveying the spent shells.

Three shots. Two kills. Plus Daryl, and the fat guy I'd flattened with the Tahoe.

A hard day's work, for any soldier. Something I would probably question, in weeks to come. But not right now.

Right now, I was just glad to be alive.

"What the hell was that?" Paulette gasped, her voice dry and raspy.

I looked up to see her glowering at me, rubbing her neck.

"What?" I asked.

"You couldn't be bothered to cut me down before shooting the guy? I could have broken my neck!"

I laughed dryly, then motioned to the rope. "You have to place the knot over a person's shoulder to break their neck. He knotted it off behind your head, so you'd strangle slowly. You were fine."

She studied the rope, momentarily perplexed by my logic, and then disgusted. "So you're saying I'm lucky?"

I shook my head. "Nah. He knew. He set the noose that way on purpose, to buy time. Trying to escape."

"Too bad you knew better," she scoffed, still rubbing her neck.

I looked down at the empty casings in my hand, rolling them around for a moment. Thinking about Daniel Porter, washing up on the beach. Ice cold and long dead.

Thinking about P.J. Sherman, choking to death on his own back porch. Alone. Forgotten, after so many years of public service.

And then thinking about Mia. Gunned down while shielding her students. Laying down her life in the face of pointless, maniacal hate.

Three deaths. Three good people...snuffed out. For no reason.

"Yeah," I said softly. "It's too bad."

47

Paulette and I walked back to the road where the two wrecked SUVs lay, leaving Carrol and his thugs right where they lay. I knew there would be a reckoning coming, for all the death. But just now I really couldn't care less.

After we eventually reached the government sedan, I drove her to Wilmington to get checked out by a local ER. She objected, but I knew how battlefield wounds could be. In the moment they might not seem so bad, while you were jacked up on adrenaline, or simply happy to be alive. But residual effects and long-term damage could be sneaky, deadly things. It was better to be cautious.

It took several hours for her to be seen, inspected, and cleared. The doctors had a lot of questions, probably assuming the rope burns on her neck to be the marks of an attempted suicide. I sat in the lobby and kept to myself, leaving the explaining to Paulette.

I didn't feel like lying. In fact, I didn't feel like talking at all. I kind of just wanted to be alone.

The sun was cresting the Atlantic by the time we finally

got free of the hospital. I drove to a burger place to order a milkshake for Paulette—something soft and easy on her throat—but they weren't serving milkshakes for breakfast, so she settled for an orange juice. Then we turned back south and headed to Eastport.

Ashes and charred timber were all that remained of the burned-out antebellum home by the time we returned. Smoke drifted up from the pile, and the bodies of the men I sniped with Sherman's Marlin lay right where they had fallen, next to a couple abandoned pickups. One of those pickups was parked too close to the house, and it had burned also.

All the grass and fallen pine needles around the property were charred, and the air hung thick with dust.

Everything felt very still, and surreal. Like the moment after an IED detonates, blasting a truck full of Army infantry across an Iraqi highway.

I stepped out of the sedan and pocketed my hands, wandering slowly toward the burned-out house. There was no sign of the surviving gunmen Carrol had hired to protect his empire. No sign of local cops or firefighters, either.

I wondered where Lowe was, just now. Where Witmore was, with his goldfish lips. If they were running for the hills, scared for their lives.

They ought to be. I was finished killing, but they had plenty more problems headed their way. The cat was out of the bag, now. There was no escaping what they had done.

I approached the north side of the house and squinted through the smoke to see a hulk of blackened metal rising out of the ashes of the primary structure. As I neared the edges of the foundations, I recognized the remains of the stove—the source of the entire fire, a lone survivor of the inferno.

Irony at its finest.

I stepped cautiously forward, sifting through ash and dirt with my toes, and dodging smoldering timbers. I knew embers could remain hot and deadly for days after a house fire, but the wood of the old home was so dry almost nothing was left. Just fine ash.

The stove sat near the perimeter, and I wadded up the tail of my shirt to open the oven door.

The stacks of cash lay inside, a little charred at the edges from the heat outside, but mostly untouched thanks to the oven's insulation.

I lifted the bundles out, counting each by the band wrapped around it before tucking them into my cargo pants pocket.

Twenty-four thousand dollars. Not a bad haul.

"Finder's fee?" Paulette croaked from the edge of the fire. I found my way out of the ashes, surveying the mess one more time. There was nothing left. No credit card machines, file cabinets, or duffel bags full of cash.

No evidence.

But that wasn't my problem.

"It's not for me," I said, referring to the cash. "Call your FBI people. Get them down here to investigate."

I started back toward the car, recovering Sherman's fallen Marlin on the way. Paulette followed.

"What about..." she hesitated. "What about the bodies?"

"What bodies?" I asked, opening the door. She motioned in the general direction of Daryl, the guy with the shotgun, Carrol and his driver. I surveyed the battlefield and shrugged.

"They're dead."

"*I know*," she rasped, hands on her hips. "I'm asking...I mean, the FBI will want to know—"

"Who killed them," I finished.

She nodded.

I looked at the ashes again. Then I shrugged.

"Gonna be hard to find the shooter. He didn't leave any evidence. And there weren't any witnesses...right?"

I shot her a sideways look. Paulette absently rubbed her neck, feeling the spot where the rope had burned her.

Maybe thinking about the long moments of oxygen slowly burning away in her body. Signaling the approaching end of her life.

Maybe thinking about Carrol, and Daniel Porter, and Sherman. I had told her about Sherman—how he died the same way Carrol intended her to die, at the end of a rope.

"You get the sunset?" she asked.

I nodded. "And you get the credit."

We made eye contact, then we both climbed into the sedan, and without another word we drove back to Eastport.

48

I burned the Tahoe I wrecked while chasing Carrol to ensure that none of my fingerprints survived, then I scrubbed away any prints on Sherman's firearms and returned them both to his house. Maybe they would be inherited by his next of kin. Maybe they would be seized as evidence. Either way, it seemed wrong to dump them in the river. I knew they meant a lot to Sherman.

After returning Marley's boat, I spend the next week lying low at the pub, sleeping a lot and eating one burger and one rib eye each day. I wanted to see Trudy, but I knew what to expect the moment Paulette made a phone call to Washington, and was smart enough not to associate myself too closely with a victim's wife in the midst of an explosive investigation.

The FBI descended on Eastport like a ravaging army. Maybe Paulette had more pull with the bureau than she gave herself credit for, or maybe the prospect of a mass shooting at the heart of an enormous fraud ring was simply too tasty a slice for the FBI to ignore.

Whatever the reason, the feds took Carrol's operation seriously. Within days they had the burned-out house in the woods taped off, the bodies collected, and both Daniel and Sherman's deaths relegated to homicide.

The Eastport Police Department, meanwhile, became the target of North Carolina's State Bureau of Investigation. SBI officers out of Raleigh came down to comb through the EPD's records, interview each member of the department, and have a long chat with Chief Lowe.

Lowe pointed them to me, much as I expected, and I was asked for an interview. They wanted to know why I was in town, and what I had been doing there. I kept my answers vague, knowing there was no physical evidence to tie me to Carrol's death, and that Lowe's credibility would soon be mired in the truth of his own corruption.

The agents moved to Marley next, inquiring about suspicious persons passing through town, but Marley couldn't recall any. Apparently, she had an unreliable memory. Something to do with an IED blast in Iraq. She was happy to tell the story in detail. It all began in middle school, when she first met a United States Marine on career day. He was a captain...or maybe a major.

There went that unreliable memory again.

The agents' eyes glazed over and they left an hour later, no wiser than when they arrived. Marley passed by the bar and slid me a fresh beer joined with a hard look. I took a sip and nodded once, and that was the only conversation we ever had about what happened at that house in the woods.

Maybe she already knew. Or maybe she didn't want to know. Maybe she simply understood...one soldier to another.

Four days later I hitched rides back into Lowberg, and showed up at Trudy's sister's house unannounced. I had shaved and bought yet another fresh change of clothes, but I couldn't hide the exhaustion in my eyes. When Trudy answered the door I saw the look of concern on her face, and she beckoned me in.

The house was much the same as it had been on my last visit—a little disorderly, with clothes and personal items strewn about the living room. Trudy's sister was at work again, and Trudy poured me a tall glass of sweet iced tea before she ushered me onto the porch.

We sat at the same table as before, and I sipped my tea as a soft breeze blew in from the trees. It had warmed considerably in the past week. I was beginning to see why people liked it here.

"They say Daniel was murdered," Trudy said after a protracted period of quiet.

"I heard," I said.

"Some FBI agents came by. They said he was involved in some kind of...credit card thing. I didn't really understand. I guess he was selling social security numbers."

She shifted in her chair, picking at the bottom seam of her blouse. Her face turned a little red, and I thought I noticed fresh crow's feet near her eyes.

"I really thought it was overtime," she said with a self-deprecating laugh.

I offered a gentle smile, twisting the glass in my hand. She looked out over the backyard, her lips trembling. A tear bubbled in her eye, and when she spoke her voice faltered.

"They said...the man who killed Daniel...he's dead." She faced me. "Somebody shot him. And three of his people."

"Really?" I kept my voice calm, and didn't break eye contact.

She nodded. "But they don't know who."

"Maybe it was internal," I said. "Maybe they killed each other."

"They think so. But I don't."

"Oh?"

"No."

I twisted the glass again, taking my time with a long sip. "What do you think, Trudy?"

She looked at her hands, rubbing her thumb over her fingers and taking her time answering.

"I think I'm grateful. And I think that's all that matters."

I set the glass down and nodded once. Grateful, also, to leave it there.

Trudy got up and walked into the house. She returned with Daniel's worn violin and held it out in trembling hands.

"Will you play again?"

I took the bow and gently adjusted the strings. Found my place at the start of Billy Joel, and played through Johnny Cash to George Straight. I ended with Leonard Cohen's "Hallelujah"...another one of Mia's favorites. Long and slow. Deep and sad. Speaking words that didn't need to be said. Maybe just needed to be felt.

Trudy sat and cried quietly, her hands in her lap, staring off into the trees. When I laid the violin down we sat in silence, and I felt my own eyes blur. I thought of Mia in the living room, her bare feet kicked up on the couch while she drew with charcoal and listened to the soft whine of the violin.

I thought of her smile. Her smell, fresh out of the shower on a Sunday morning. The care she invested into her job. The passion she shared with anyone who would listen.

An angel of a person. A treasure I would never forget.

Much as Daniel was for Trudy.

There weren't words to convey those feelings. But the music bridged the gap, at least for now.

I reached into my cargo pockets and pulled out a paper sack. I had wrapped the cash from the oven inside—barely a drop in the bucket, in the face of so many medical bills and the loss of the family breadwinner.

But something. A start.

I laid the package on the table and pushed it gently toward Trudy. I saw a question in her eyes.

"From Daniel," I said. Then I stood, hands in my pockets, and started toward the door.

"Wait," Trudy called. I looked over one shoulder.

"Will I see you again?"

"Probably not," I answered, honestly.

She nodded softly, working her fingers around the hem of her blouse. Then she scooped up the violin and held it out.

"Take this."

I looked at the worn instrument, well loved by a loving man. I smiled, but shook my head.

"I can't take that."

She took a step toward me. "Please. I don't want to look at it if I can't hear it. I'd be happy to know somebody loved it as much as Daniel."

She held it out again, and I felt the smooth wood between my battered fingers. It felt familiar. Like the old friend I didn't know I needed.

I gave Trudy another smile, tucking the violin under my arm. Then I walked back to the street, and started toward Eastport. One last time.

49

One of the state cops released my Smith & Wesson. I told him it was being illegally held without just cause, and after reviewing the paperwork, he could find nothing to state the contrary.

Maybe he was just eager to get me out of his face. He returned the revolver in a plastic evidence bag—complete with four hollow point loads of .357 magnum, and one empty casing.

I stepped outside and discarded the bag, then rolled the bullets in my hand. For a while I stared at their gleaming tips.

Then I slowly loaded four of the five cartridges, pocketed the gun, and started toward the ferry. It was a long walk, and my legs were sore. But I wasn't in a hurry.

I sat an hour waiting for the next ride to the island, and when I reached the far side of the bay I set off on the same long walk through the trees that I had embarked on two weeks previously. The rain was gone, and the sky was bright. I was passed by a number of locals on golf carts, and a couple even offered me a ride.

I turned them down, my hands jammed into the oversized pocket of a hoodie, wrapped around the Smith.

By the time I crossed the boardwalk and stepped out onto the beach, I was ready for a rest. The seagulls waited for me, clustered in a flock just above the waterline, squawking and fighting over bits of washed-up sea life. But there were no humans around. The beach was as desolate as before, albeit a lot warmer.

It was a gorgeous day. The kind of day postcards are made of. The kind of day I dreamed of sharing with Mia on our honeymoon.

I walked all the way to the waterline and slumped onto the sand, taking the revolver out and cradling it in my hands. The EPD evidence tag was still affixed to the trigger guard, and I tore it off, then ran my thumb across the smooth cylinder.

I thought about all the long days I had carried this gun on my ankle. A faithful friend, something I could count on.

A solution, when my back was against the wall. A way out.

But it didn't feel that way, anymore. Looking at it now, it just felt like a hunk of metal.

I closed my eyes, and I thought of Mia. I still had her photo in my pocket, but for just a moment I wanted to imagine her the way I'd last seen her on the beach, standing behind that impenetrable wall. Only inches away...one press of the trigger.

But I didn't. Instead, I saw her at school, sitting cross-legged on the floor reading a book to her students. I saw her on a trail in the mountains, calling for me to keep up, her face red and sweaty, covered in a big grin. I saw her curled up on the couch, eyes closed, listening to me play "Ashokan Farewell." I saw her damp head pressed against my bare chest in a hot shower.

I *felt* her, like I hadn't felt her since those horrifying moments at the school. I imagined her right beside me, almost in my arms...and, as I did, the memory of those last moments in the school faded, just a little.

I remembered Mia not as she died, but as she lived. And, in an instant, I saw her painting again. The one of the Saint Ellen lighthouse in the thunderstorm, with that whimsical inscription in the top corner.

It's the sunrays in the storm clouds.

I opened my eyes and looked back at the gun. Even in her final moments, back against the wall, Mia hadn't given in to the darkness. She'd fought for those children because she still believed life was beautiful.

If I pressed the trigger now, I could be with her. But it would defile every precious thing she ever believed in. It would be surrendering to the storms, and denying the sun.

I dropped my face into my hands, and for the first time since she died, I sobbed like a child. Not because I saw her bloody on the floor, but because I saw her smiling in the storm. I saw P.J. Sherman laughing with a cigar clamped between his teeth, his boat crashing through the waves. I saw Daniel and Trudy Porter huddled next to their disabled son in a family photograph, grinning at the camera.

All people in a storm. All finding the light.

When I finally looked up, the sun blazed in my eyes, and I felt the knot I had carried in my stomach ever since Mia's death loosen, just a little.

I stood up and walked into the water. It was shallow, and the ocean floor dropped off very slowly. I was a hundred yards out before the surf crashed over my stomach, spraying my face with salt.

Then I reached into my pocket and retrieved the Victorinox. Flipping the metal saw open, I laid the blade against the crane of the revolver and sawed slowly. The surf carried away the little flakes of fallen metal, until at last I twisted the revolver's cylinder and it broke away from the frame—permanently disabling the weapon.

Then I closed the knife and looked into the horizon. I thought of my fiancée and whispered gently over the ocean.

"Goodbye, Mia."

I gripped the Smith like a baseball and hurled it as hard and as far as I could. The gun broke apart in midair before arcing toward the water.

And then it disappeared. Lost in the waves. Carrying as much of the pain as I could let go of with it.

I RETURNED to the ferry with my hands in my pockets, my shoes squishing, water draining off the hoodie. I didn't feel good.

I didn't feel happy.

But I felt okay.

When I reached the pub, I found Marley serving lunch, and I ordered both the burger and the steak—because I was really hungry. Only the burger was listed on the chalkboard menu, but she didn't object, and fifteen minutes later I was chowing down like an old soldier, fresh off the battlefield.

As the lunch crowd dispersed, Marley came to lean on the bar and drink beer with me, but she didn't rush to start a conversation. I appreciated that.

At last I pushed the plate back, and wiped my mouth.

"Why don't you sell me that truck?" I said.

"What truck?" She frowned over the top of her Budweiser.

I jabbed a thumb toward the lot next to the pub.

"Oh, the old GMC? Really?"

I nodded, and swigged beer.

"Why?"

I shrugged. "I need a vehicle. I like old trucks."

"It hasn't run in years."

"I can get it running."

She hesitated a while, swirling her beer. Then she turned for the door without comment, and I followed her. We found the pickup resting right where I'd first seen it, lying on rotted tires, its windshield covered in dust. The graduation tassel still hanging from the rearview mirror.

Marley surveyed it with a subdued smile and swigged more beer.

"It was my uncle's old truck," she said. "He gave it to me when I turned sixteen. A '67 C15, straight-six. Drove it all through high school, and when I came home from deployment. Damn good truck."

"If it's special I can look elsewhere," I said.

She finished the beer, swished it in her mouth for a second, then flicked the bottle into a five-gallon bucket nearby.

"Tell you what. I'll make you a deal."

"Okay."

"One question. Honest answer. Soldier to soldier."

I tipped the bottle back, wondering what she might ask.

Then I decided it didn't matter.

"Okay."

She folded her arms. "True or false. A soldier doesn't stop being a soldier, just because he comes home."

I looked at the truck. Thought about Carrol, and the one shot between his eyes.

Tango down.

"True," I said.

She grunted. Watched me a minute. Then turned for the pub.

"I'll get the keys."

50

I paid Marley five grand for the truck, even though she offered it to me for free. I guessed maybe it was a camaraderie thing, but I had the payout from the Phoenix Police Department, and the truck was worth at least that much. Then I washed it, and bought new tires. Installed a new battery, alternator, spark plugs and distributor, new oil and filters.

Within a couple days it was road ready, still wearing a permanent North Carolina antique vehicle license plate. Marley wrote me a bill of sale, I tossed my bag into the passenger's seat next to the violin, and without looking back, I drove west out of Eastport.

It was Friday. Or maybe Sunday. I had stopped tracking the days and I still hadn't replaced my phone. I was starting to think I never would.

I was starting to think I wouldn't return to Phoenix, either. Not yet, anyway. The memories were too fresh, and I was pretty sure I was done being a cop.

Not because of Mia. But because I wasn't cut out to be a

cop. I was a soldier, inept at the more nuanced forms of investigation.

Too fond of brute force. Too adept at violence of action.

Yes, I was a soldier. And, for a little while, I wanted to be a soldier without a home.

So I turned west, Mia's picture pinned to my dash, her worn leather Bible resting on the seat next to me. And, after driving a while, I turned south. Because I was tired of being cold, and I hadn't visited Georgia since leaving the Army.

With nothing but my thoughts and memories to keep me company, I had nowhere better to be.

ABOUT THE AUTHOR

Logan Ryles was born in small town USA and knew from an early age he wanted to be a writer. After working as a pizza delivery driver, sawmill operator, and banker, he finally embraced the dream and has been writing ever since. With a passion for action-packed and mystery-laced stories, Logan's work has ranged from global-scale political thrillers to small town vigilante hero fiction.

Beyond writing, Logan enjoys saltwater fishing, road trips, sports, and fast cars. He lives with his wife and three fun-loving dogs in Alabama.

Did you enjoy *Point Blank?* Please consider leaving a review on Amazon to help other readers discover the book.

www.loganryles.com

ALSO BY LOGAN RYLES

Mason Sharpe Thriller Series

Point Blank

Take Down

End Game

Fire Team

Flash Point

Storm Surge

Strike Back

Printed in Great Britain
by Amazon